Praise for Personal Statement

"For the striver and slacker in all of us, *Personal Statement* hits deliciously close to the bone with a mordantly hilarious satire of resume-polishing and ambition. For anyone who ever inflated a title, or wished they did. A page-turning delight!" ~Sarah Ellison, *Vanity Fair* Contributing Editor and author of *War* at the *Wall Street Journal*

"*Personal Statement* is a hilarious take on the merciless winner-take-all world of college applications. A wild book." ~Tony d'Souza, author of *Mule*

"Jason Odell Williams' *Personal Statement* is a fast-paced, delightful read. As a parent and a professor, I can say that Mr. Williams' satirically savvy take on the absurdities of the college admissions process is deliciously accurate. And yet his wickedly funny portrayal of four ambitious twenty-somethings is never mean-spirited. Personal Statement should be on the required reading list for all High School guidance counselors, college-bound seniors and their parents!" – Richard Warner, Professor, University of Virginia

"Don't tell the person you hired to take the SATs for you that you are reading *Personal Statement!* This delightful book has a lot of fun with college mania. You will, too." ~ Gregg Easterbrook, author of *The Leading Indicators*

"A fearless thrashing of American ambition in the Millennial age." ~Michelle Miller, author of *The Social Network*

"Hilarious and stunningly accurate. If you were ever a teenager, read this book!"~ Mathew Goldstein, 20, Saint Paul, MN

"Hilarious, authentic, poignant portrayal of pre-college angst and ambition. Williams serves up delicious, right-on characterizations with wit, precision, and sympathy. Intensely contemporary, yet timeless. A must-read for college-bound teens and their parents!" ~ Dr. Judy Rubin, Pediatrician, Maryland

Personal Statement

Jason Odell Williams

In This Together Media

New York

*For my parents, who taught me everything I know
(including everything I learned in high school
and college, because they paid for it)*

Foreword

Back in 1978, the college application process seemed pretty straightforward. I requested paper applications from the schools that interested me (with little or no guidance from any school officials); I took the SAT once with absolutely no preparation; and I dashed off my applications with only modest effort. The endeavor was quick and painless. And it resolved several months later with the arrival of several acceptances, a few rejections, and a simple decision: where did I want to head in the fall?

Today's high school students tell a vastly different story. For some, it is a process that begins almost at birth as parents agonize over preschool waitlists. For others, the pressure ramps up steeply in middle school, as students and their families begin to hear daunting speculation about what colleges are looking for in their flooded applicant pool.

For starters: a report card with only the most difficult classes listed—and unblemished by any grades below an A. Perfect standardized test scores. Playing on a school's varsity sports team. Leadership within the school community. Hours spent volunteering or organizing service projects. A special talent or skill to distinguish each applicant. A sincere, honest account of why the student finds a particular school to be his or her "perfect match". And most important? The personal statement: a finely honed, touching, authentic representation of a student's uniqueness and personality. It's a reassurance to admissions officials that in a student's quest for perfect well roundedness he or she has also developed a singular voice and a knack for pithy self-expression.

It's a tall order, to say the least.

In many American homes, the importance of getting into a top school is drilled into children from such a young age that by the time they are applying to college, every decision in their lives will have been made with college in mind. Enrolling in soccer camp? No, the time is better spent with a math tutor. Interested in poetry? Take Advanced Placement English Literature instead and forego the "less competitive" poetry elective. Content to play third-chair violin? Enroll in extra lessons on Saturdays and maybe the orchestra director will move you to first chair. For too many children, this kind of calculated competition and relentless drive toward "achievement" is woven into the very fabric of their daily lives, in school and out. It's all they know and is the only foothold they have in an overwhelming process.

That is, unless they're lucky, and they stumble upon a magical, life-changing experience that lends itself—perhaps a little too perfectly?—to the college application wildcard: the personal statement.

As a mother of three observing my children and their peers, I see the toll that our cultural obsession with perfection—often in meaningless and manufactured categories—takes on our kids. And I see, increasingly, that even those who receive top grades and test scores and admission at elite colleges are often left unprepared for life after school. More tragically, too many students remain unhappy and anxious, trapped in a schooling system that values "achievement" and "success" more than curiosity, mental health, and engagement.

Spurred by the toxic culture I saw around me, I directed a documentary called *Race to Nowhere* that closely examines our educational system and the impact our collective, narrow vision of school success has on the health and happiness of our children. What I discovered was heartbreaking. Students were taking extreme measures to live up to impossibly high expectations, and they were suffering—in body and mind. I was overwhelmed with stories of students sacrificing sleep or meals to study, or engaging in other self-destructive behavior when they saw no way off the academic treadmill.

Personal Statement captures the insanity of the college application process. An apt and wry commentary, the book's narratives echo the all too real stories I have heard from students across the country, while managing to poke fun at the cutthroat, competitive model of education in which we've become unwilling participants. Through the fictional stories of three high schoolers, we see how each deals with the onslaught of cultural, parental, and societal pressure to achieve admission to a top college—and how each musters a different approach to managing that stress. In the end, the characters' shared quest to volunteer as aid workers in the heart of a coming hurricane is perfect satire: a fictional situation exaggerated just gently enough that it lets us see reality in a new light. As readers, we're forced to ask ourselves: how have we arrived at a cultural moment in which, "How will this look on my college application?" has become a more important question than, "How can I help?" or, "What will keep me safe?" or, "What makes me happy?"

In a society where so many kids and families have accepted busyness as a norm, it's refreshing to find a book that inspires us to think deeply about how we can create a healthier educational culture for our children. And it's invigorating to see such a call to action come in the form of smart humor and playful self-deprecation—a reminder that perhaps it's thinking too seriously and too single-mindedly that set us down our current path of competition in the first place.

Personal Statement is a must-read for parents, educators, counselors, and students. It pushes all of us to rethink the impact of our current educational system on our children. And it urges us to advocate for a new college admissions process. One that replaces the standardization of test taking with the liberty of true learning and inquiry, one that trades padded college resumes for the spirit of aspiration, growth, and new challenge, and one reshaped in light of these honest educational markers.

That kind of transformation would make a statement indeed.

Vicki Abeles with Shelby Abeles
August 1, 2013

Vicki Abeles is a filmmaker, attorney and advocate for children and families. She directed the acclaimed documentary "Race to Nowhere," which challenges common assumptions about how children are best educated and launched a social action campaign dedicated to providing resources and tools to support action connected to the film. Abeles is also the co-author of the *End the Race Companion Book* for parents, educators and students. Her oldest daughter, Shelby Abeles, is currently a student at Wellesley College in Massachusetts. She has two other children, Jamey and Zak, both high school students.

The sea hath bounds, but deep desire hath none.

- Wm. Shakespeare

PROLOGUE

BETTERED EXPECTATION

EMILY KIM

I fucking hate Emily Kim.

Let me clarify. Yes, my name is Emily Kim. But this is not about hating myself. I have no doubts or self-loathing. I love me. I'm awesome.

I hate the *other* Emily Kim. "Stanford-Emily Kim." The bitch who's been making me look bad for almost a decade. The one my parents say I should aspire to be. The one they secretly wish was *their* child. The one whose yellowed photo and article from *The New York Times* is still clipped to our fridge—taunting me whenever I get my morning OJ. The one my mother chides me about at least twice a day.

"She go far in life. And her parents no have pay tuition. She be doctor in no time. Family very proud. You be like her, Emily!"

So even though I'm one of the top students at Fairwich Academy (arguably the best all-girls private school in Connecticut), my parents still push me to do more, be more, achieve more. I think it stems from their inferiority complex about how they got their money. Most of the families around here, aside from being whiter than a paper towel (and about as fun, too), are seriously *old*-money. Their houses have been handed down for generations and their kids come from a long line of people named Chip who sail and play croquet and use "summer" as a verb. My parents are FOB Koreans who made their mark with an insanely successful chain of dry cleaners (Eco-Pure Cleaners—the very first in the state to "go green"). Our house is just as big, our cars are just as fancy, and I pay full tuition like everyone else. But because my parents are immigrants who "run a store" and aren't in one of the more socially acceptable professions (banker, hedge funder, trust funder), we will never be fully accepted into the Fairwich elite. Which is fine by me. Bunch of assholes anyway. But it doesn't stop me from wanting to go where the elite kids will go: to the Ivy League. And it doesn't stop me from wanting to be better than the best: Stanford-Emily Kim.

Eight years ago, Stanford-E.K. became the poster child for how A-list volunteer work could give students virtual celebrity status, and how the Ivies would bludgeon each other for the right to grant enterprising students like her admission. Before Katrina even hit the Gulf Coast, Stanford-E.K., then just a sophomore with a one-month old driver's license, was in her Subaru Outback racing down Interstates 81 and 59. By morning, while the city was still dazed and confused, Stanford-E.K. was at Charity Hospital on Tulane Avenue shining flashlights for surgeons and helping evacuate patients. But she didn't stop there. Two years later, the bane of my existence traveled back to the 9th Ward to build green homes. Someone snapped a pic of her passing a 2 x 4 to Brad Pitt and posted it on Facebook, tagging E.K. The pic went viral and before she even returned home to Connecticut her mom called her cell to report that there were ten voice mails from top schools across the country begging her to attend *their* university. (Notably *not* Harvard, by the way. Take that, E.K.!) She chose Stanford and the rest is history.

But it's not only her annoying fairy tale-like story—one that I swear was written by some covert Hollywood producer her parents hired. It's that no matter what I do, it's never enough. I've been the lead in every musical at Fairwich Academy since freshman year, was studying Linear Algebra and Game Theory at Sarah Lawrence College while in 10th grade, and just recently returned from a highly productive July in Korea where I interned with high-level government officials on issues surrounding the country's notorious dealings in the sex-slave trade. (It's a seriously fucked up situation, by the way. Do *not* get lost in South Korea.)

But even with my amazing successes in and out of school, all my one-dimensional mother can remember is the B that I got in AP English last term. (I'm sorry, but *Tess of the d'Urbervilles* is a horrible book about horrible, boring people, and it's sort of a borderline defense of rape. But I guess Mr. Harper didn't agree with my opinion or my final essay, "Legitimate Rape for Dummies.")

Anyway, that one blemish on an otherwise spotless academic career has me keyed up about the college application process a bit more than usual. And my admittedly unhealthy obsession with

Stanford-E.K. is in full hyperdrive.

"How do we compete with her? How do we compete with Brad Pitt? It's like she's out to ruin my life!"

I say this to my best friend Rani, who sort of shrugs but doesn't roll her eyes. I could kill her for being so patient with me.

We're sitting outside the Pinkberry on Fairwich Avenue, sharing a Mini Original with mango slices, raspberries, and dark chocolate crispies. (Doctors say dark chocolate has healthy heart benefits, okay, so shut up about it.) It's hot and sticky out here, even for August. With Labor Day less than three weeks away, most of Connecticut's elite are still beating the heat at their summer homes on Nantucket or Martha's Vineyard. For most of the rising seniors in our class, that means lazy days tanning and drunken nights hooking up.

Except for girls like Rani and me, girls with our eyes on the prize: Harvard, Yale, National Merit Scholarships, winning the Siemens Competition.

But for me, the honor I covet most, the granddaddy of them all, the Gates Millennium Scholars Program…? That's the only one that seems completely out of my reach.

"God, I would KILL to be black! Or Hispanic. Or Alaskan, even. Ugh!"

Before Rani thinks I'm a total racist, I quickly explain that because of the onslaught of over-achieving Asians in America, great scholarships like the Gates Millennium Scholars Program don't find high-achieving Korean-American students quite as compelling as African American, American Indian/Alaska Native, or Hispanic American students.

"You are SO lucky to have your complexion," I say looking at her golden brown skin, which falls somewhere between russet and sienna. "You could make a long braided ponytail, totally pass for Native American, and walk right into *Dartmouth*. Me…? The only thing anyone ever confuses me for is Chinese. And I'm nowhere *close* to being Chinese. Did you see the Olympics? Those bitches are insane. I'm Korean-American!"

So okay, yeah, I'm a *little* bit racist. But at least I'm up front about it.

I don't mean to sound bitter or upset. I've got it pretty sweet.

But I worked my ass off to get here. And I'm in excellent shape going into our final year of high school. It's just that the bar for girls like me keeps getting raised. A perfect SAT score, 5.0 GPA, and killer extracurriculars are nowhere near enough.

"What we need," I tell Rani, "is a killer personal statement."

The personal statement is what separates the men from the boys, the ladies from the whiny bitches. Nowadays, *everyone* applying to top schools has the credentials on paper. But life experience… frontline, in the trenches, blood-on-your-shirt and sweat-in-your-eye life experience… that's the *only* way to stand out these days. Especially for me. Not only am I competing against thousands of highly qualified candidates. I'm also competing against hundreds of Emily Kims. Not metaphorically. Literally.

It's bad enough to be saddled with one of the world's most common last names. (For every Smith and Johnson there are 25 Kims.) But to compound the problem by *also* having one of the most popular *first* names for Asian-American girls? Who, by the way, are all concert cellists halfway through med school before they can even *drive*! Why couldn't my parents have named me something WASP-y to balance the world's most Asian last name?

"I always thought I was more of a Madison or a… what's WASP-ier than Madison?"

"Morgan," says Rani, unable to hide her contempt. Names are a sore subject for her as well. Her mother is first-generation Indian-American. Her dad's family was on the Mayflower and he's like the *definition* of WASP. When they had their first child, they named her Morgan, so that when the time came for her to go to private nursery school, even with her skin four shades darker than her lily-white toddler classmates, she would fit in.

But four years later, when their next daughter was born, Mrs. Caldwell had a sudden sense of nostalgia for her heritage. She wanted her daughter's name to reflect her multi-cultural background. So they named her "Rani." Four simple letters, yet surprisingly difficult for white people to pronounce. (For the record it is pronounced 'RAH-nee' and sounds exactly like the American boy's name, 'Ronnie.')

"At least everyone knows you're a girl," Rani says. "I sound like some meathead dude who likes Captain America and WrestleMania.

'Hey, Ronnie—wanna go to Comic Con this year?' 'Totally Awesome, man, I'm in.'" Rani says all of this with the flat inflection of a DMV employee. God, I love this girl. She's the only one who gets me. And the only one who shares my passion for academic excellence without being a total "Dr. Who" geek. (Though that *is* a pretty cool show—I just don't have time to watch TV anymore).

Rani finishes off the last chocolate crispy and commiserates with me about the dilemma we face. And that's when I realize we need to think of something huge, something monumentally impressive that will separate our college applications from rest of the pile.

"What we need is a moment like Stanford-Emily Kim's. When that bitch's Facebook pic changed from her birthing those calves in Nigeria to her passing lumber down the line to Brad Pitt? That noise went viral faster than the Chocolate Rain kid."

"I loved that Chocolate Rain kid," Rani says, cracking her first smile of the day.

"We need to find something that will get us that kind of exposure," I say, unwavering. "What we need is another Katrina."

ROBERT CLINTON, III

I. Hate. Martha's. Vineyard.

My family has been coming here since the dawn of time. Not really. But it feels like it. They like to brag to anyone who doesn't know—and plenty of people who've heard the story multiple times—that "the Clintons have been free men since the mid-18th century, long before the Emancipation."

I guess my great-great-great-great-great-great grandparents were such good people that their owners simply *granted* them their freedom. Or granny was humping the white man and he felt guilty. But either way, we're still black and proud and all that jazz. So proud that my parents insist on summering in Oak Bluffs every year, where all of the fancy black families go. I guess it makes them feel good to see so many "brothers and sisters" here living the dream, the embodiment of the African-American success story. But who are they kidding? It's not *that* black. I mean, Oak Bluffs is not Detroit. (It's not even Baltimore.)

The Vineyard isn't all bad though. Most days I hitch a ride down to Gay Head (insert homosexual joke here), where the vibe is more relaxed and you can actually be yourself (in more ways than one, plus the nude beach is spectacular!) But sincerely, it's the only town on this bitch of a rock where the people don't talk with their lower jaw permanently jutting forward. And that includes the black folk.

Yet every year my parents trek to the Vineyard. They even have one of those gag-me-with-a-spoon bumper stickers on their Mercedes GL 550. You know the black and white oval with the letters MV inside? (How pretentious is that?) We drive from Westport in our massive SUV, but park it landside and take the passenger ferry over. My father has a restored 190-SL convertible that we use for "island driving only." (Even *more* pretentious, I know.)

Sometimes I think I was born in the wrong decade. I'm nothing like my parents or my peers. I should have been born in the 80s. I love The Cure and Ronald Reagan, Freddy Mercury and the movie

Wall Street (plus any movie made by John Hughes). I'm basically the black Alex P. Keaton with exquisite taste in clothes and a love of retro music.

Yet here I am. Stuck in this 4,500 square foot summer home, ostensibly working on my college essay, but really flipping through *Details* magazine and daydreaming about my gorgeous roommate Mac (who hugged me goodbye for the first time when we left for summer break; I've been reliving those precious two seconds in my mind ever since) while my parents cavort with other rich Vineyarders at ostentatious cocktail parties, raising money for Haiti or Africa or whatever third-world flavor of the month has been making the rounds on CNN.

I was going to join my parents but bowed out at the last minute, feigning an upset stomach. My father said, "Might be a good time to work on that college essay. Yale doesn't accept *every* legacy, you know."

Yes, Dad, I know, because you've been telling me since fifth grade! And whoever said I *wanted* to go to Yale?! Just because you and mom did. New Haven is the Pittsburgh of Connecticut. Plus, it's only forty minutes from our house in Westport—and fifteen minutes from my stupid high school. So not only would I be forced to spend another four years in basically the same crappy city, I'd have to see *you* every weekend. So, no. Yale. Is *not* happening. Sorry, Dad.

Besides… I've got my sights set higher than that. Well, *farther* would be more accurate. Some place where English isn't the official language and the buildings are older than our ancestors in the cotton fields. And it will happen. Despite your veiled threats to refuse to finance any university *other* than Yale. And Mom's good cop routine isn't working either.

"Don't listen to your father," she said to me last week. We were standing in our enormous gourmet kitchen having a heart-to-heart. (I hate heart-to-hearts.) "You can go to *any* school you want… as long as it's an Ivy. Or Stanford. I don't think he'd have a problem with Stanford."

"What about a school," I offered enthusiastically, "that isn't *technically* in the Ivy League, or here in the Northeast, but *is* highly regarded as one of *the* best universities in the world?"

"…Didn't I say Stanford was okay?"

"It's not in America."

My father heard that and marched in from the study to nip our conversation in the bud. "No, unh-uh. I *refuse* to finance a four-year European vacation so you can study seventeenth-century poetry and *find yourself!* You're not Richard Wright!"

And that was one of the more civilized discussions about my future academic life.

Of course I've researched scholarships abroad—so I wouldn't need money from my parents. There's one to La Sorbonne called the James Baldwin Fellowship—named after the famous expatriate author of *Giovanni's Room* and *Go Tell It on the Mountain*—that offers a full ride plus housing and a stipend to "African-American students who exemplify Mr. Baldwin's spirit and passion for the written word." A seemingly perfect fit for me!

But even with my impeccable grades and my amazing list of awards, clubs, and special skills, plus what's sure to be the most dynamic and powerful personal statement *ever* (the essay portion of the scholarship application is rumored to account for more than *half* of their decision), I'm just a run-of-the-mill applicant. The competition for the Baldwin Fellowship is fierce. I need that *one* extra ingredient that sets me apart. An extraordinary angle that no one else has. Something… epic.

But I can't think of what that might be. And time is running out.

So here I sit, miserable and alone, likely consigned to four more years in New Haven, the *Details* magazine tossed aside, the Weather Channel on in the background for its soothing repetitiveness, and my laptop open with the words "Baldwin Fellowship Essay" at the top of an otherwise blank page, the blinking cursor mocking me with every flash.

And then it happens.

The third-string Asian guy chirps from the flat screen that the National Weather Service has upgraded a storm system 150 miles off the east end of Long Island. In less than an hour it went from a Tropical Storm to a Category 2 Hurricane. He says it's the most powerful system since Andrew and it's building faster than any weather event he's ever seen in that part of the Atlantic. And now it's turning toward New England. Projections indicate it will make landfall near the border of Rhode Island and Connecticut in just over 36 hours. The town most likely to take a direct hit: Cawdor, Connecticut.

In a flash, the idea hits me. I scrawl a note for my parents and tape it to the espresso machine, where I know they'll see it. I grab the GL keys (the car parked *off* the island—I'm not crazy enough to take my dad's vintage convertible), toss my laptop and a few necessities into a backpack, and scramble down Lake Avenue, barely catching the Oak Bluffs to Woods Hole passenger ferry at 6:15 p.m. As the boat chugs across Vineyard Sound, I pull up Google Maps on my iPhone 5 and set a course for Cawdor.

Looking out at the choppy waves spraying their foam on the port side, I can only thank the Muses for the inspired idea since it's really quite uncharacteristic of me. It goes like this: Race to Hurricane Ground Zero before the storm hits; be part of the volunteer rescue effort; write the most impressive essay in the history of the Baldwin Fellowship; win the scholarship abroad; never have to summer with my parents on the Vineyard again.

Rather elegant, dontcha think?

And as Mr. Baldwin himself discovered, Paris is a better place for a young black man with a love of fashion, music, and other men. In America, I'm a joke. In Europe, I'll be an inspiration.

ALEXIS J. GOULD

I hate golf.

I hate the etiquette. I hate how long it takes. I hate the stupid skirts I have to wear.

But I put up with it. I smack a tiny ball around miles of grass for five hours because it's part of my job. It's why I'm here right now, with Governor Charles Watson of Connecticut and his chief of staff, Teddy Hutchins. They invited me to the Wampanoag Country Club (a place I'd normally *despise*—not only for the Native-American man that is their logo, but because I suspect I'm the only person of Jewish descent on the grounds today), and I humbly accepted their invitation. Some people like to have meetings out of the office to lessen the formality. Coffee, lunch, or a quick nine with the governor to discuss joining his team for the next election cycle. He apparently didn't want to raise any eyebrows by meeting me in public. (I also heard he was anxious to get me on the links once he discovered I had a 4.2 handicap.)

So I go with the flow, go where the opportunities are. I'm in the boys' club of politics and I have to play their game. And I play it well.

"Get left," I say nonchalantly after my drive on number nine. My Pro-V1 appears to listen and the ball takes a nice hop off a mound in the fringe and kicks back into the fairway. I'll have about 210 for my second into this par-5.

"Goddamn, A.J.," Teddy says with a cough, as if I literally knocked the wind out of him. "Where'd a little thing like you learn to pound a ball that far?"

"My dad," I say, casually bending down to pick up my tee.

"My dad taught *me* how to play, too," Teddy says, "and I've been 30 yards shorter than you all day!"

"Maybe you should hit from the ladies' tees," Governor Watson suggests wryly.

"Hell, no," says Teddy. "If *she's* hittin' from the tips, *I'm* hittin' from the tips."

"Well then, maybe your dad was just a lousy coach," the governor deadpans, giving me a wink. Then he adds by rote, "Nice drive, Alexis. Excellent footwork."

I nod to him as we hop in our separate carts—the governor and Teddy in one, me in the other, presumably so they can talk about me between shots. (I *am* technically here to talk about a job in the governor's office.) But I don't mind. Gives me time to focus on my game. Because if there's anything I hate more than golf, it's *losing* at golf.

I'm the oldest of four girls. When my youngest sister was born, I was seven; without missing a beat, my dad turned to me in the hospital and said, "Well—looks like *you're* gonna be my golf buddy, kiddo."

My father was an athlete back in the day—a star quarterback and pitcher, one of the few Jews at his high school to letter in both sports—but a torn rotator cuff his senior year forced him to quit and give up any dream (however improbable) of the NFL or the Major League. His freshman year at U Penn, however, his roommate introduced him to golf, where the essentially underhanded motion didn't aggravate his shoulder. He was thrilled to discover a sport he could play without pain. And he didn't realize how much he missed the competition (even if he was mostly competing against himself). So he plunged into the game wholeheartedly, his ambitions to be the next Sandy Koufax replaced by a drive to be the next Corey Pavin, the only Jewish golfer of note. But as quickly as he improved (breaking 80 after only two years!), breaking par proved tragically elusive. Then, during his senior year, just as the game was becoming more and more frustrating (my father told me later that he felt like he was actually getting worse) and he was giving up all hope of ever being happy doing *any*thing, David Benjamin Gould met Lisa Rose Bauman. And in quick succession they got married, had me, and my father went into the family business (a moving company called Gouldie's). He hung up his 'sticks' for several years while he concentrated on being a good husband and providing for his new family.

And he *loved* being a father. Loved showing me off to his friends and saying how proud he was of his little "bubbeleh-angel" (that was me). But he made no bones about also wanting a boy. He and my mother were young, he'd say. They were going to have *lots* of kids. And they did. But after Stephanie, then Robin, then Beth, my mother said *four is enough, oy gevalt*, and that's when my dad transferred all of his pent up father-*son* energy to me. I was going to be the boy he never had.

He even joked about it openly. "This is my daughter, Alex," he'd say, shortening Alexis to Alex (later shortened to A.J., which stuck). "The son I always wanted!" And the men at Shul would laugh and tug my cheek and I'd blush, trying to look sturdy and formidable. I guess my father thought it would lessen the sting if he admitted what he was really thinking. But it didn't. It just made me want to please him even more. Made me want to be something I could never be: a boy.

So I played every sport possible in middle school. Field hockey, basketball, and lacrosse during the school year; golf and tennis over the summer. On Saturdays I took private tennis lessons at the club from a Canadian guy named Thierry who claimed to have been ranked as high as 164th on the ATP tour back in the 90s, though I was never able to confirm it. My father would sometimes watch from the miniature bleachers, sunglasses on, a furtive glance every few minutes toward the driving range across the parking lot where he'd rather be, but most of the time he spent Saturdays with my mom and my sisters.

That's because Sunday was Daddy-A.J. day. We had a standing 3 p.m. tee time at Inverness Valley, one of the best munis in Connecticut. By then all of the old-lady foursomes were long gone, and the course was too hot for anyone else. We'd arrive ninety minutes early like tour pros. I'd spend twenty minutes stretching, thirty on my short game, thirty hitting balls, the final ten back on the putting green working exclusively on five-footers, and then straight to the first tee. And I loved every minute of it. Not because I loved the game so much—though I truly did enjoy it back then—but because it was time alone with my father.

On those Sunday afternoons, my dad never played. He didn't carry my bag, either; that was my job, he said. But he walked the whole way with me. We'd talk about golf, of course, things to work on, options for the upcoming shot (he was the only golf coach I ever had). But we also talked about nothing. And everything. School and current events and movies and books. Even boys. We talked about things on the golf course that we'd never talk about at home or in front of mom. Somehow things said on those expansive swaths of green were permissible there and nowhere else. And from 3 pm until dusk every Sunday in July and August, I had my father all to myself. I didn't have to share him with my sisters or my mom or anyone. It was Daddy-A.J. day. And it was sacred.

So I got good at golf. Very good. At 13, I quit all my other sports. At 15, I won a spot on the boys' varsity team. At 16, I qualified for the U.S. Girls' Junior Amateur. And then it got hard. And not fun. And my dad got hard. And not fun. And Sundays were no longer sacred. Even though I kept playing and kept winning, I learned to resent the game.

I could have gone to Duke (a respectable school, no doubt) on a golf scholarship, but I chose Princeton. Where I qualified for the newly established Kurland Scholarship. (Gouldie's didn't make my family wealthy.) My father couldn't fault my choice, but he also made no effort to hide his disappointment. We talked less and less the next few years—a result of being away from home, of course, but it was also a self-imposed sentence. A break from the intense relationship we'd had throughout my high school years, which were marked by competition, success, and failure.

At Princeton, I threw myself into my studies. After excelling for so long at such a solitary and selfish sport, I wanted to do something meaningful with my life. I wanted to make a difference. So I decided to pursue a career in government.

With a double major in Poli Sci and U.S. History, I graduated Phi Beta Kappa in 2008 and went straight to D.C. where two summer internships on the Hill and my amazing college professor helped me secure a low-level job working for Congresswoman Fiona Clark (D-CT). She taught me that, as a woman in politics, I had to balance being cool and reserved with my usual kneejerk emotional responses. But I also had to make sure that I wasn't being a pushover or a sycophant. In school, good grades and a strong work ethic got me respect. But in the working world—as a *woman*—I came to understand that wasn't enough. "You have to *earn* respect,"

Congresswoman Clark was fond of saying. "They won't automatically give it to you, like they do with the boys." So I had to fight a little harder to be treated as an intellectual equal. In doing so, I quickly made a name for myself as a smart, capable woman who could gossip with the boys and bullshit with the ladies. I had social media savvy, intuition about the younger electorate, I was Jewish, and female. (And kind of attractive, if I do say so myself. Whenever Facebook has "doppelgänger day," I go with Amanda Peet for my profile pic.) After two years in the congresswoman's office, I was a hot commodity. But I (wisely or unwisely) chose to *leave* Washington—and my very serious boyfriend—to be the deputy legislative council for Connecticut State Senator Iva Ellison Eisinger. It wasn't necessarily a step *up*, but at 24, it was part of an impressive resume I was building. (Plus I wanted to be closer to home. I missed seeing my sisters. And—though I'm loathe to admit it—I missed my parents, too.)

So for the past eighteen months, I've been enjoying my time with the state senator. But as anyone in politics will tell you, if you're standing still, you're going backwards. So I quietly put my name out there, and within forty-eight hours, Governor Watson's office was calling for a meeting.

We've played eight holes so far and have yet to discuss anything of substance. I'm biding my time. It's Governor Watson's move to make. And though I won't say relocating to Connecticut was a *calculated* move on my part, I'd be lying if I said being closer to the governor's line of sight wasn't also in the back of my mind when I left D.C.

Because Governor Charles Watson is the new rockstar of the Democratic Party: a man of the people who washes his beat-up Honda himself and still raises money from the one-percent. He's equally at home shucking oysters in the harbor or sailing his 40-foot catamaran *around* the harbor. He's got John Goodman's easygoing approachability wrapped in George Clooney's charm and boyish good looks. People are calling him the lost lovechild of Bill Clinton and J.F.K. Obviously those references aren't lost on me. I've heard the infidelity rumors like everyone else, but I firmly believe all the talk about Governor Watson's wandering eye is exaggerated. Stories strategically planted by the right to squash this star on the rise.

(Seemingly the only way Republicans can denigrate these smart, charismatic, popular candidates is by painting them as immoral womanizers.) But seriously, who cares? In France they don't give a *merde* what their leaders do in the bedroom. Why are we still such Puritans in this country?

They say it has to do with "character," that a leader's morality outside the office naturally translates to his integrity *inside.* But I maintain it's about getting the job done. Tiger Woods is still the best golfer on the planet no matter what deviant sex acts he committed. And I think politics should be no different. It's about getting the win, making lives better, and looking out for the people. If Governor Watson can raise the minimum wage and get the middle class back on track, so what if he's grabbing a little action on the side? That's between him and his wife (who's super hot by the way—no way would anyone cheat on her!) I mean, George W. Bush may have kept his pants zipped, but I'll take Clinton's all-time high economic surplus over Bush's two foreign wars and crippled economy any day.

Charles Watson is going places. And I want to align myself with his star and ride it all the way to the White House. There's been talk about adding the three-term governor's name to the DNC ticket in 2016: if Hillary runs, as her VP; if she doesn't, well then…

"*That's* the word, Chuckie. Or should I say… *Mister* President?"

As we drive down the fairway, I can hear Teddy going on about the increasing talk out of Washington. A few snatches of their conversation drift over our golf carts' puttering engines.

"Knock it off, Teddy… nowhere *near* 2016."

"…prime for it, Chuck… centrist Democrat… bringing Connecticut out of the Factory Dark Ages… mini-Tech boom… All you need now is…."

They finally stop and get out by Teddy's ball in the rough. I park a few yards behind them (as is etiquette) and pretend to be engrossed in my scorecard.

"I'm telling you," Teddy says, pulling a hybrid out of his bag, "everybody hated that little S.O.B. Then 9/11 comes along. Suddenly he's the most beloved mayor in New York City *history*. He made a bid for the *White* House, for Christ's sake! Now I'm not saying you want a terrorist attack on domestic soil. But a… I don't know. A gas crisis.

Or a natural disaster! Hell, look what Hurricane Sandy did for Chris Christie! Now that sack of potatoes is like the G.O.P.'s *golden* child!"

Governor Watson glances over to see if I'm listening. I can't tell if he does or *doesn't* want me to hear, so I keep drawing a "3" over and over on my scorecard with my mini pencil.

"You need something like that," Teddy continues. "Something that sucks for everyone so *you* can come to the rescue. You'll be Bruce Wayne and Batman all rolled into one."

"Bruce Wayne *was* Batman," the governor points out. "They're the same guy."

"You can be friggin' Deputy Dog, Chuck! You have something like 9/11 happen here while you're governor? At the bare *min*imum, you're in the number two spot on that 2016 ticket. Right, A.J.?"

"Mm? I'm sorry, what?"

"It's okay, Alexis," the governor says. "You don't have to pretend like you can't hear Teddy. I think everyone at the *clubhouse* can hear Teddy."

"Hardy-har-har," Teddy guffaws sarcastically as he sets over his ball, takes a few waggles, then promptly hits it fat. His ball lands just sixty yards away, still in the rough.

"Rat farts!" he curses, slamming his club hard into the turf.

The governor smiles wryly at me, almost embarrassed at his chief of staff's poor manners, but I act like it's all standard operating procedure as I climb out of the cart to select my next club. I'm so focused on my irons that I don't notice the governor walking my way until he's standing right next to me.

"What do you think?" he asks.

"He should've laid up with his pitching wedge," I say.

The governor laughs good-naturedly. "No, I mean about 2016. Would you run if you were me?"

And just like that, it begins. This is the job interview. How I respond will not only seal the position for me, it will set the tone for my role going forward.

"You can run, but you won't win. And Hillary won't put you on her ticket, either."

Everything goes quiet. No golf carts puttering up the next fairway. No mowers in the distance. Even the birds seem to have stopped chirping.

Governor Watson blinks at me for a moment, and then smiles. "So. What would you do to *help* me win?"

I don't return the smile, but inside I'm doing cartwheels, backflips, oppa Gangnam style.

§

"It's about the young voters," I say on our way back to the clubhouse. I'm driving my cart, with the governor riding shotgun. (Teddy is now solo, and doesn't seem too pleased about it.)

"Obama figured it out," I say, a touch loudly so I can be heard over the cart noise, "but he had a *massive* ground game. The good news is, social media has made a lot of progress since '08, even since 2012. But to go from zero to sixty and get you known on the national level by early '14—which, let's face it, is when the campaigns begin now—to get you in the people's consciousness *that* quickly, without the luxury of making a convention speech like Obama had in '04... we're gonna have to do something *major*. Winning Connecticut isn't a problem because you're from here; you've put in the hours, people have come to know you over time. But since Hillary's gonna lock up the female vote, you *have* to shore up the youth vote. Getting a healthy piece of the Hispanic vote wouldn't hurt, either. But even that might not be enough. You're gonna need to get lucky, too."

"How can you control luck?" Governor Watson asks as we pull into the cart return area. Two pimply teenagers leap into action, cleaning out the cart and polishing up our clubs.

"You can't," I say. "All you can do is take the first step and hope the staircase appears."

I cringe inside at my fortune-cookie wisdom, but Governor Watson doesn't seem to mind. He nods, eyes off in the distance, seemingly lost in thought, his wheels spinning faster and further into the future, as if he's trying to picture me giving him this kind of advice in his office or on a campaign bus. Or maybe I'm projecting. For all I know he's bored with me and thinking about what he's going to order at the bar inside.

It doesn't seem like he's going to say anything else so I make one last play. "I, um, overheard Mr. Hutchins mentioning 9/11 and Hurricane Sandy? I know it sounds ridiculous, but... he's right. *That's* the kind of thing you need."

Governor Watson takes a deep breath and then slowly lets it out, gazing back at the ninth hole, the fading sunlight lengthening the flagstick's shadow along the green.

Teddy finally pulls up alongside of us, curiously winded since he was driving a cart. Before he can say anything, Governor Watson announces, "She agrees with you. Thinks we need a natural disaster to thrust us on the national stage."

"Smart girl," Teddy replies, catching his breath. "Read this."

He hands his BlackBerry to Governor Watson. After reading it for a few seconds, the governor absently gestures for me to come closer and have a look. It's an email alert from the State Capitol office.

> Major storm system (CAT II/III HURRICANE) headed toward southeastern CT. Landfall predicted in just over 36 hours at noon on Saturday.

Teddy looks at the governor with a shit-eating grin. "Here comes your Chris Christie moment."

Governor Watson nods blankly for a moment then suddenly turns to me. "So Alexis. When can you start?"

"I thought I already did," I say, shocked at my own brazenness.

The governor smiles his million-dollar smile. "Welcome to the team."

RANI CALDWELL

I don't really hate anything.

But I don't love much of anything, either. The only things I even half-enjoy are texting and riding horses. Witness what I'm doing right now: sitting on my bed reading *Horse and Rider* and texting Emily—who I saw less than an hour ago at Pinkberry. (Texting Emily is not that taxing, and can be done while simultaneously writing a thesis paper about Shakespeare; it consists of one-to-three word replies interjected into her monologue, like virtual nodding: *Wow. No way! WTF?! What'd U say? Crazy!*) We'd been texting non-stop (more of her college ranting) since she dropped me off but I haven't heard from her in twenty minutes. The last thing she texted was, "Holy crap! R u watching CNN? This is what we've been waiting for!" I asked her what she was talking about but never heard back, so I let it go. Now I'm lost in an article about the emerging market in calming supplements for nervous horses, daydreaming about my life after high school.

Save the lone horse magazine in my hand, the bed is awash with college brochures. Every day a new one arrives, sometimes an exact copy of one I got a week earlier. I keep them visible in case my mother casually wanders by, attempting to disguise her snooping— which she does all the time, even when I'm *not* around, I'm sure. I thumb through them once in awhile, dog-earing a random page or two, so it at least *looks* like I'm giving the Ivy League serious thought. But it's only out of fear, dreading the inevitable conversation with my parents. I hate confrontation, avoid it like the plague. So I'm holed up in my room doing my two favorite things, hiding it from my mother at all costs.

If I could figure out a way to just ride horses and text for the rest of my life, I'd be a happy girl. No further ambitions, no unfulfilled needs, no drive to take the world by storm the way Emily does.

My family, however, has bigger plans for me. And it doesn't help that I have a preternatural ability to take tests. I'm not bragging—

I'll be the first to admit I'm not the smartest girl at our school. I just understand how to take tests. Especially standardized tests. I got a 235 on the PSAT sophomore year and was a National Merit Scholarship finalist. As a junior, I got a 2300 on the SAT. My parents want me to take it again because they think I can get a perfect score of 2400 (I'd done so on several practice tests in the Kaplan course they insisted I take), but I'm fine with my first score. That plus my GPA should be plenty to get me into a decent school.

My first choice is Sweet Briar College in Virginia. It has the top-ranking women's-only equine studies academic program in the country, and according to Go Equine (the world's largest equine portal site), Sweet Briar's "acclaimed liberal arts education is second only to their equestrian education." In addition to their acclaimed riding program, students can specialize in farm and stable management and riding instruction. Sounds perfect to me. Plus it's in the middle of nowhere. Flying or driving, from Fairwich you're looking at an eight-hour trip door to door. I saw how bad it was for Morgan at Princeton only ninety minutes away, my parents making an excuse to see her at least once a month. If I go to Sweet Briar, my mom won't bug me every weekend, like she would if I went to *her* top choice, Yale. (Less than an *hour* away!)

I haven't told anyone yet, not even Emily, but I'm not applying to Yale. Or Princeton. Or *any* of the Ivy League schools. After twelve years of non-stop academics, lectures, and tests, I can't imagine anything worse than having to do it all over again. For another *four years*! I'd rather be grooming Misty at the barn and texting Em about how hard it is for her at Harvard.

I know it's not the norm for kids like me (good grades, private school, wealthy parents) but I have zero interest in college or scholarships or anything like that. It's weird because excelling at school and crushing the competition is like Emily's entire reason for being. Some people think it's strange that we're best friends. But I've known her since we were six—when she wasn't so tightly wound. Oh, the seeds were planted, for sure. Witness her tenacious resolve to get a female elected to the head of the PTA... when she was eight!

"In conclusion, Principal Cummings," a young Emily lisped, her two front teeth still missing, *"it's 2004, well into the new millennium.*

And you should be embarrassed."

But I love her. She's the only one who gets my sarcasm. And the only one I don't have to *pretend* to about "how hard these tests are." Some of the capital B's at our school aren't so forgiving.

"*I heard she doesn't even study!*"

"*The spine of her U.S. History book isn't even cracked.*"

"*Mr. Harley gave her a 98 on her last blue book. The second highest score was a 77.*"

"*That skank is throwing off the curve!*"

Or something to that effect. That's a mash-up of the greatest hits I heard in the hall freshman year or in the girls locker room before field hockey practice. By tenth grade, I learned to fake it. I'd crack my books and spill coffee on the pages, letting them dry in the sun. Then I'd highlight all the assigned chapters (randomly, while watching "Friday Night Lights") and show up on test day with ink stains on my fingers complaining about another all-nighter cramming.

But Emily didn't care. She never saw me as competition. Because for her, I wasn't. That girl was always naturally smart *and* she worked like a beast. She's had one of the highest GPAs in our class since they started keeping track in seventh grade. Plus we have the same size shoe.

"Damn, Rani—what's an Indian girl doing with such big feet?" she said to me before gym class in sixth grade.

"What's a Korean girl doing with shoes the same size?" I said right back. "I thought you all had to bind your feet in wooden boxes from birth."

Emily cackled that wonderful throaty laugh and I think that's when we actually cemented our lifelong friendship.

But lately, she's gone a little crazy, even for her. Sure, it all started with the *other* Emily Kim, Stanford-E.K., *my* Emily's self-proclaimed nemesis. But it's more than that. As our senior year approaches, she has a drive that's beyond getting into Harvard. It's like she wants to *attack* Harvard. Put it in a pillowcase and beat it against a wall, then cook the bashed-up bits into a pie and eat it. It's vicious and aggressive and it's starting to get on my nerves. But I roll with it. I let her vent and complain like she did today at Pinkberry. In three or four months she'll get that Early Action acceptance letter and this will all be over. And deep down I wonder how much we'll remain in each other's lives after that.

A soft knock on my open door startles me. I deftly shove *Horse and Rider* under some college brochures, careful to leave Yale and Brown on top, and attempt to appear unfazed.

"Hey sweetie," my mother says, standing in the doorway. Although she's been a vehement stay-at-home mom ever since she had kids, I'm always surprised to see her at home in the middle of the workday. She never gave off the "homemaker" vibe. She's too elegant for that, resembling a slightly older Aishwarya Rai (the Miss India and Miss World winner-turned-actress) but with a cutthroat personality.

My parents, Mira Iyengar and Douglas Caldwell, met at Wharton and moved to New York right after graduation in 1986. He landed a job at Drexel Burnham. She was a strategy consultant at Bain. But when she had my sister Morgan at 29, my mother dropped her high-octane career and opted to be a fulltime mother. Instead of making headlines in the *Journal* for advising Fortune 500 companies, she made them by organizing the first ever "nurse-in" on Wall Street. After I was born five years later, my dad cofounded a multi-strategy hedge fund in Fairwich, and our family reluctantly left the 900-square foot Charles Street apartment for a 5,000-square foot colonial in the boonies. My mom quickly made her presence known in the neighborhood by staging a *Titanic*-themed fundraiser for Trevor Green (Morgan's ridiculously overpriced Pre-K–2's program). Why a school swimming in money needed a fundraiser is beyond me, but the event raised nearly $200,000. When I was finally "of age," I was admitted without any sort of interview or entrance exam.

When she's not pressuring me about colleges or homework, my mother is nudging me to follow in her epically charitable footsteps. (Though they don't seem completely "charitable" to me; there's something disingenuous about a bunch of rich ladies throwing fancy parties under the guise of raising money. Or worse, raising *awareness!*) So even though she doesn't fit the stay-at-home mom type, it's all I've ever known, her always being there, helicopter parenting, forever in our business, making our organic lunches, shuttling us to and from school because she doubted Inga the au pair's driving skills. It's hard for me to imagine her as one of the rising strategy consultants at Bain two decades ago. But once in a while (like now), she comes to me with a look on her face that I'm sure she reserved for clients and I can see the hard-nosed businesswoman she once was.

"What're you doing?" she asks.

"Nothing," I say, trying to sound casual, my pulse quickening.

"Any closer to a top choice?"

"Um…. It's tough because they're all so good?" I say, my voice rising at the end like a question.

"School year's about to start," my mom reminds me, stepping into my room, casually lifting things off my desk and inspecting them like a cop. "Then you'll be busy with homework and extracurriculars and pretty soon those applications are going to be due and—"

"I know, mom. I don't want to rush into a decision, that's all."

"It's not like this is sneaking up on you, Rani. Your father and I have been talking to you about college since you were in eighth grade. Everyone at Fairwich seems to have made up their minds. Most choosing early action or early decision. Emily has known her first choice since freshman year."

"Before *that*," I mutter.

"What?"

"Nothing. Mom. Please don't worry about it. I'm fine. Really."

"It's just… when I see you *lying* around reading *horse* magazines—"

"I don't—what?"

"—while all of your friends are so driven and motivated—"

"Mom. I'm never going to be like Emily, okay?" "I don't want you to be like Emily. I'm just saying, a little… get up and go!"

As if on cue, I hear a car skidding into our gravel driveway. "Speak of the devil," I say.

Even though I know who it is (no one else skids into our driveway like that), I hop off my bed and lean across my desk to peek out the window. I see Emily close the door to her Infiniti G convertible, her sweet sixteen reward for having the highest GPA sophomore year (and my ride to school every day, so thankfully she got it before the dreaded "B" in Mr. Harper's class), and walk purposefully toward our front door.

I shrug at my mom like, *I'd reeeally love to chat more about my future, but… Emily's here.* Before I hit the hallway, Emily breezes in the front door downstairs, calling out, "Hello, Caldwells! Anybody home?"

It's always been Emily's way to walk into our house without knocking as if it were the most natural thing in the world, a trait that would ordinarily irk my mother but one she somehow finds winning and charming in Emily—the daughter she *wishes* I were.

"Up here," my mother calls out as if Emily was here to see her. While Emily makes her way up the curving staircase, I lean against the railing and greet her with a casual, "What's up, dude."

"Grab your Hunters and a rain coat," Emily says, all business. "We're driving to Cawdor."

"Um. *What's* in Cawdor?"

"Emily! Hello," my mother gushes.

"Oh, hey, Mira," Emily says, strutting into my room. "Didn't see you there." Emily greets my mom with a hug and a vague kiss on the cheek, another habit my mother finds irksome except in Emily. She's also the only one of my friends allowed to call my parents by their first names. With everyone else it's Mr. Caldwell this, Mrs. Caldwell that. But Emily not only calls my parents Mira and Doug, she's been doing it since she was six.

"So what's this I hear about a road trip?" my mom asks, trying to sound cool.

"Cat 3 hurricane is headed to coastal Connecticut," Emily pronounces like an Aaron Sorkin character. "I figure Ran and I get on the front lines with the pre-storm relief effort. Not only a morally and spiritually nice thing to do, but a final boon to our college applications. Makes for some great essay material, too."

"Just what the Ivies like to see," my mom says, literally nudging me with her elbow.

"Are you serious?" I ask.

"Yes," they say in unison, causing my mother to giggle.

"Seriously, Ran," Emily says. "This is like getting in on the ground floor pre-Sandy. If those Jersey kids could have foreseen what was going to happen in their state and do what *we're* about to do, not only could they have prevented a lot of damage, but right now they'd be packing their bags for Stanford and Columbia."

"Mm-hm," my mother says, nodding like a bobblehead doll.

"So…" I say to my mother, "you're cool with me and Emily driving to some small coastal fishing town where a major hurricane's about to hit? Just the two of us?"

"I think it's a *fab*ulous idea," my mom says, beaming. "It's exactly what your sister did the summer between *her* junior and senior years. And," she stresses, grabbing Emily's arm for emphasis, "I know that Morgan's time at LifeBuilders is what gave her the edge with Princeton Admissions."

Emily nods vigorously, raising her eyebrows at me. "Exactly."

I shake my head and absently check my Facebook page on my phone, to see if anyone liked the photo I posted of me and Emily at Pinkberry. Nothing.

My mother sighs. "Frankly, I'm jealous of you two. Reminds me of *my* high school and college volunteering days. Of course, we had real *causes* back then: the AIDS crisis, feeding Ethiopia, women's rights and the glass ceiling." She looks almost nostalgic, as if she longs for a time when things were *so* bad people had to march in the streets to fix them. "Helping your fellow man—*and woman*—can take various guises. Hurricane Sandy should be a lesson to us all. Grab what you can, girls. These opportunities are few and far between for your generation."

"…Okay?" I say, confused yet resigned, not really wanting to go, not really having a better alternative. Though I tried to convince my parents that working at the stables and riding all summer would be the best use of my time, they weren't buying it. My dad insisted that I find a job "in a real office." When I dragged my heels through April and May and complained that nothing was available, he found a spot for me at his hedge fund organizing files and restocking the supply closet. But even that thrill-a-minute internship ended last week. With three more weeks until school starts and my parents putting the kibosh on long days at the barn, I need *some*thing to do other than help my mom around the house with her never-ending 'project board.' Volunteering for an impending hurricane suddenly sounds like a great idea. "Guess I should grab my stuff."

I dig into my closet, looking for my Hunter rain boots while

Emily and my mom jabber about our upcoming adventure.

"Oh!" my mother exclaims. "You girls should look up Theodore Hutchins. The governor's chief of staff."

"Do you know him?" Emily asks, her radar for inside connections on high alert.

"Dougie and Theo went to Exeter together! But oh, it's not Theo, it's, um... Ted or Teddy. That's it! Teddy. Teddy Hutchins. You should introduce yourself, Rani."

"Yeah, Rani," Emily parrots.

"Not gonna happen," I say, tossing my boots behind me, head still in the closet. I stand and begin searching for the big yellow rain slicker that I never wear.

"What? Why not, sweetie?"

"Because it's totally lame."

"Your father knows him. It wouldn't be lame."

"No way! It's super dorky and I'm not gonna do it."

"I'll take care of it, Mira," Emily says slyly. I give Emily a stinging look but she brushes it off with a carefree shrug, picking up my boots and heading toward the stairs. "Let's go, Ran. Clock's ticking."

I sigh, finally locating the yellow slicker, and trudge toward the door. My mother puts her arm around me and says, "I envy you girls. This really is the time of your life."

"Hooray for me."

My mother hugs us goodbye (offering a seemingly more sincere hug to Emily, I might add) and waves at us from the front porch while Emily opens the passenger door for me and scurries around to the other side.

Standing in the gravel driveway, equidistant from the car and my house, I wonder, *is it too late to change my mind?* Emily slides into the driver's seat and calls out through her open roof, "Come on!"

Against my better judgment, I climb in and we drive off toward the unknown. Before leaving our neighborhood, I turn to Emily and say, "*Where* exactly are we going?"

With an ominous smile creeping across her face, she says, "The eye of the storm, baby."

ACT I
VAULTING AMBITION

ROBERT

With The Cure's *Greatest Hits* and the soundtrack from *A Chorus Line* to keep me company, I make the drive from Woods Hole to Cawdor in record time. By 9 p.m. I'm on the main drag (no pun intended), surrounded by more than a hundred locals helping with the relief effort. *"Oh you'd like to volunteer? Grab a sandbag, young man, and pass it down the line."* They welcome me without hesitation, without judgment. I bet this is what it'll be like in Paris.

Thirty minutes later, I'm on Church Street standing shoulder to shoulder with a large woman named Silvie and her (also large) daughter, Rebecca. We stock gallon jugs of water and boxes of batteries into a van that will deliver them to residents who wait out the storm because they either can't afford to evacuate or plain don't want to.

I slam the van's back doors and pat them twice, like they always do in movies, and I suddenly feel like I *am* in a movie—my own personal Scorsese epic (I'm the star, natch), a steadicam swirling around as I do my best James Dean… though I probably look more like James *Baldwin*. (A good omen for the scholarship.)

As the van drives off, I turn to say good-bye to Silvie and her daughter, but they've already moved down the road and are shoveling kitty litter into garbage bags.

I feel my iPhone 5 vibrate in my back pocket. As I begin to pull it out, I hear the familiar (ironic) ring tone of the DJ Jazzy Jeff & the Fresh Prince classic, "Parents Just Don't Understand." Without looking, I know exactly who it is.

"Hey, mom, did you get my note?" I say without so much as a hello.

"No, darling, what note?" she says, her voice slightly blurred by Sauvignon Blanc.

"Oh. I thought that's why you called."

"No, we just got back from the Visnicks'. Brennan took us out on his yacht…"

"It's not a yacht," I hear my father call out in the background.

"It was a very large boat," my mother says, placating him. "Anyway," she says to me, "where are you? Did you go into town to see a movie or something?"

"Mom. Read the note. It's on the espresso machine."

"What's this note on the espresso machine?" I hear my dad say from the kitchen.

"Oh," my mom chirps. "Your father found it. What's it say, dear?"

There's a pause as my father reads. I step off the busy street and duck down a narrow alley behind a hardware store, away from the noise. I hear some mumbles from my parents and the phone changing hands.

"Boy. Where the hell are you?"

"Hey, Dad. How was the party?"

"Don't get smart. You left the *island*? You're driving around in your mother's car in Woods *Hole*, for crying out loud?"

"Actually... I'm in Cawdor. Volunteering."

"You're *what*?"

"Volunteering," I say a little louder. "For the hurricane. You guys should think about evacuating by the way. The Vineyard may get a glancing blow."

"Don't tell me when to evacuate. And what on earth possessed you to volunteer in some redneck fishing town for a hurricane that hasn't even *hit* yet?"

Luckily, I anticipated this question and have been mentally preparing my answer since I left.

"Anybody can pitch in *after* the storm, dad. And sometimes even *that's* not enough. Look how long it took after Sandy to get things fully restored. But being here from the *beginning*? That kind of forethought and selflessness really stands out on a college application."

Silence on the other end. I can tell he's listening, considering, weighing the pros and cons. I close my eyes, grit my teeth, and say with as much sincerity as I can fake, "Especially Yale."

"Hm," he grunts. And I know I've got him. "Can't say I like you taking the car without permission..."

"I couldn't *call*, you were on a yacht—"

32

"It wasn't a yacht. And let me finish." He sighs with fatherly caution. "I'm not happy that you took the car without permission. But. I'm proud of you for taking initiative. Thinking outside the box. Grabbing the bull by the horns."

"Gather ye rosebuds, win one for the Gipper, insert famous cliché here."

"Okay, wise guy," he says with a smile that I can hear over the phone. "You know what I'm trying to say. And I'm glad to see you've come around on Yale. You have the grades, Robbie." (God I hate it when he calls me Robbie!) "You have the potential. You just need that little extra something. Do this. Volunteer. Be the best one up there. Make a difference. And then… write about it in your college essay. You do that? The fourth generation of Clintons will be attending Yale University, mark my words."

"I will. Thanks, Dad. I gotta go. They need us to fill sandbags."

"Okay. But be *safe*. And check in from time to time. Your mother worries."

"I know."

"And don't stay through the storm. You've got the GL, so… before the rain even *starts*, you drive to safety. Then, when it's all over, you can… go back if you want. Help with the cleanup and what have you. But don't be stupid. You get out while the gettin's good."

"You know, one more cliché and you'll break the all-time record for a five-minute phone call."

"I don't know where you got your sense of humor, but don't ever lose it. It's one of your best features."

"Dad, come on. My *cheek*bones are my best feature."

"Call your mother every couple hours, okay?"

"I will. Love you guys."

"Mm. Be safe." And then he hangs up. I don't know if my dad has *ever* said the words 'I love you' to me. Maybe when I was very young, but I don't remember it. Most sons don't say it to their dads or even their mothers, but I've always said it. To both of them. I love you guys, love you, love you both. And my mom always says it back, without hesitation. But my dad? It seems to make him uncomfortable. That doesn't stop me from saying it, though. Who knows? Maybe he'll come around someday.

I pocket my phone and step back into the controlled chaos, looking for my next assignment. The number of people and slow moving cars making their way to higher, safer ground makes the street look like the lone exit lane out of a rock concert.

Suddenly a voice from behind me says, "Fancy seeing you here."

I turn around, surprised to find my roommate from Choate standing on the sidewalk. He's next to a packed station wagon with what looks like the cast of the Partridge Family inside.

"Hey… Mac," I manage, attempting a breezy, casual manner, trying desperately not to visualize his goodbye hug twelve weeks ago. Man, he looks good.

James MacKenzie has not only been my roommate for the past three years, he's also my only straight white male friend at Choate. (And I've basically had a ridiculous and unrequited crush on him for all three of those years.)

Mac came to Choate on a full scholarship—technically a need-based financial scholarship, but everyone knew he was poached from public school by our ruthless lacrosse coach to help turn our team's losing record around, which Mac did, quickly leading the Wild Boars to two ESA titles and one New England Championship in two years. He was easily going to be All-State, maybe All-American, and get a full-ride at Chapel Hill or Syracuse. But he blew out his knee the day they won their second ESA. The "official story" is that it happened during the game, when he leapt from behind the crease for the winning goal in overtime and was slammed mid-air by two massive Exeter defensemen. He did hurt his knee that day, but the real damage was done three weeks later.

Most of the school had gathered for a monster end-of-the-year-bash at Freddy Parnez's house. He was the lacrosse team's hysterically funny, always up for a good time, 5'5", 200 lb. goalie. They called him "the Jewish Jack Black." And since his parents were loaded and never in town, the Parnez McMansion became our school's de facto party location.

The Saturday after graduation, everyone was at Freddy's, and I witnessed Mac smoking pot with some hot senior girls. They'd been egging him on all night, singing that seriously tacky song "Tonight Tonight" by Hot Chelle Rae. (It was all the rage back in May 2011, with that annoyingly catchy hook: "There's a party on the rooftop, top of the world!") The girls said they'd take off their shirts if Mac actually got on the roof—which he did in record time. Once up there, Mac sang the song back down at the girls like a victory chant, with most of the party standing around the front lawn watching. As Mac got to the "La, la, la, whatever," the three girls who were hooting and hollering (and vying for who would get to sleep with him first, I'm sure) all lifted their shirts at the same time, showing off what even I must admit were six very nice breasts. Mac attempted to stop dead in his tracks to get a clear look but the centrifugal force from his rockin' dance-moves didn't get the memo, and he promptly fell thirty-five feet to the front lawn—tearing his left ACL in the process.

With his lacrosse scholarship dreams essentially dashed to bits, Mac became a little lost puppy. He spent most of our junior year searching for clubs and activities to round out his rather thin resume, because, let's face it: when you think dozens of colleges are creaming their pants at the chance to offer you a full ride to play lacrosse, you sort of don't need much more on the CV.

Standing face to face on Church Street as sweaty volunteers push by us on all sides, I've already got a pretty good idea about what Mac is doing in Cawdor—the same thing I'm doing: looking to give our college applications every possible edge. But I play dumb and ask anyway.

"What are you… doing here?" And looking so fit and glistening, I think, but manage to hold my tongue.

Mac explains in his charming homespun way that he was just driving by with his family, their station wagon crammed with supplies as they made their way to drier ground. Mac is from Stonington, the town directly to the east of Cawdor—and of course not only did I know this, but it was in the back of my mind when I heard where the storm was headed. So much so that on the ride in from Woods Hole, my mind was ever drifting to soft, out-of-focus daydreams about how this event might play out. In all of them Mac showed up kind of like this… with varying degrees of clothing. And his hair was sexier.

Now here he is—in the flesh, as it were—explaining that as his family inched slowly along the evacuation route toward I-95, Mac saw me in the crowd of helpers and yelled for his dad to stop the car.

"It wasn't hard to spot the only black guy wearing seersucker shorts and white bucks," he says, smiling at me.

"I'm that predictable, hunh?" I'm sure my cheeks would look red if they weren't already chocolate brown. Pathetic, yes—I am fully aware that my feelings for Mac are hopeless and absurd. But doesn't every seventeen-year-old have a crush on some highly unobtainable hottie? Mine just happens to also be my roommate. And white. My parents would be mortified. And they're kind of okay with the whole gay thing, relatively speaking. But dating a white lacrosse jock with no money? Not cool in their book. But that's my job, right? To piss off my parents?

While I'm pondering and pining, Mac turns back to the station wagon and grabs his backpack and duffle. After some debate with his family (Mac saying he wants to give back to his community; his mother saying she's concerned for his safety), Mac assures them he'll be fine—he'll help out until just before the storm hits and then get a ride out of town with yours truly.

"Not to worry, Mrs. MacKenzie," I pipe in. "He'll be safe with me."

Mrs. MacKenzie hesitates, staring at me with an expression somewhere between confusion and why-is-this-uppity-black-boy-talking-to-me. Just when it looks like she might say something, she sort of sighs and nods. She hugs her son, whispering loving words in his ear, thinking I can't hear. But since puberty, I've learned how to act like I'm not paying attention and yet secretly eavesdrop on countless conversations. (If you live for gossip, you quickly learn this special skill.)

So as she pulls Mac into a hug, I hear her fiercely whisper in her New England working-class accent, "No goddamn way are you gettin' yourself killed in a hurricane to help out some morons riding out another storm."

Mac pulls out of the hug, and with his effervescent smile he says, "You know, mom, something like this would look amazing on a college essay." (I knew he was here for the same reason I was.) "And this guy?" he says, wrapping a meaty arm around my shoulder. "This guy is eff-ing brilliant. If he's here doing this—it must be a good idea!"

Oh my God! Could he actually like me... as more than a

roommate? Is that why he had his family stop the car? Because he wants to confess his true feelings to me before the hurricane destroys everything we know and love?

I'm getting ahead of myself.

His mom looks over at me and I pretend to kick some sticks on the sidewalk for entertainment. She grabs Mac by the shoulders and says earnestly, "Your knee injury wasn't just a blow to your lacrosse career—it was a real blow to this family. But we believe in you, James. So you volunteer your little butt off and get *another* friggin' scholarship… cuz otherwise, it's straight to your dad's construction company after graduation. Understand?"

Mac looks surprised by his mother's ruthless words of encouragement. But he smiles and hugs her again anyway. Mrs. MacKenzie slips back into the passenger seat and the family drives off (very, very slowly).

Mac turns to me with a big grin, claps his hands together, and says, "All right! Let's get to work!" He flips his messy brown hair out of his eyes with a modest head flick—his signature move—and my pulse quickens. I fear he can hear my crush in every syllable as I tell him I'm glad he's here.

But I press on and lead Mac over to the crowd shoveling kitty litter into makeshift sandbags. As I introduce him to Silvie and Rebecca, I can't help but daydream again—now that he's really here—and fantasize about us running in from the rain as it begins to fall, taking shelter together in a small basement with just a single flashlight, a blanket, and a can of franks and beans. Maybe I wasn't being ridiculous before. Maybe he *likes* me-likes me. And he just told his mom he's here to round out the college essay and follow my lead, but deep down he stopped because he's kind of… into me?

Oh God, I'm doing it again. I'm that guy. The sad gay boy with the hopeless crush on the alpha male. I'm "Posner" from *The History Boys*. (It's a play and a movie—Google it.)

But I silently resolve *not to be that guy*. Yes, Mac is cute, but he's out of my league and it could never work and I'd be an idiot for thinking anything to the contrary. I will not fall for him, pine for him, dream about him, or have any feelings for him other than collegial.

Just then Mac hands me a shovel and smiles at me. My heart melts.

I'm a goner.

EMILY

"Crank it," I tell Rani.

We're flying up 95 with the top down on our way to Cawdor. We've got a six-pack of Red Bull, a jumbo-size cherry Twizzlers, and a dozen new songs downloaded onto my iPhone. I'm so pumped for this road trip.

"This is like literally the best idea I've had in my entire life."

"Yeah. Totally," Rani says, scrolling through my 5G for music. I can't tell if she's being sarcastic or not.

"Are you being sarcastic?" I say, sort of laughing, trying not to sound too bitchy.

"No," she says. "Like my mom said, it's a really good idea. Totally inspired."

I only half-believe her, but press on like I totally do.

"I know, right? Like this is it! This is the edge we need. Getting real life, boots on the ground experience like this? Who else will have this in their personal statements? No one! Stanford-E.K. can suck my vag. I'm going to Harvard, baby."

Rani laughs one of her rare belly laughs, the kind that make you feel awesome because she gives them away so rarely. I feel like I'm on the right path again.

The past few weeks, I admit, I've been acting like Lady M on coke, but it's not my fault. Since I could crawl, I've been taught to have a singular focus. When I was a baby my dad even bought me a pack of onesies with a different Ivy League College for each day of the week! (Technically there were eight in the set, but after Mr. Sinclair—a Harvard alum and one of the regulars at Eco-Pure— saw me wearing the Cornell onesie and joked about it not being "a real Ivy," my father believed him, and immediately tossed that onesie in the garbage.) And my entire seventeen and a half years of living has been leading to one epic event: what college will I get into. Literally every choice I made, every activity, every class, every summer internship has been a step on my road to the Ivies. And nothing was allowed to steal my focus. You think I'm joking? When I was 12, I asked my mom if I could go see the movie Ratatouille with my neighbor and her family.

"You think Ratatouille get you into Harvard?"

It was hard to win many arguments with my mom.

So my life has been scripted. I've stayed on the right path and done everything right. But I realize now it may not be enough. I know I come off as cocky and untouchable, and I was for most of my life… and maybe it's just hormones or something in the air (or that stupid "B" in AP English), but I've had this sinking feeling the last few months. A vulnerable, scared, I-may-not-be-"the-shit"-anymore feeling. And for the first time in my life, I'm worried about my future.

But then this miracle named Hurricane Calliope came along, and my life has a purpose again. I know I'm where I'm supposed to be.

I turn to Rani, who's nodding her head easily to the backbeat. I shout to her over the roaring wind, "This hurricane? Is gonna be epic!"

§

We pull into Cawdor at 9:30 p.m. and my sense of hope and purpose is immediately dashed.

"What's *he* doing here?" I mutter.

"Who?" Rani asks.

But I don't answer. I edge down the crowded, chaotic street to get as close as I can to a small group of volunteers shoveling white dirt into garbage bags. I stop the car and stand up, my head peeking over the windshield, and call out to a guy wearing white bucks and seersucker shorts.

"Hey, bitch, how goes it?"

Robert Clinton turns to see me, his smile ever so slightly morphing into a wince before perking back up and turning forced.

"Hey, girlfriend! This is bananas! You're like the second person I know here. Have you ever met my roommate from Choate? James MacKenzie… Emily Kim."

"Hey—I'm Mac. Nice to meet you." A boyishly handsome lapdog makes his way toward me, wiping a dirty, sweaty palm on his shirt and offering his hand, but I wave him off before he gets too close.

"Yeah. Hey. Likewise."

"Guess this is like the hot spot," Robert says, arching a smug shoulder to his ear.

"I guess," I say, trying to suss him out. "So, like… *what* are you doing here exactly?"

"As if you didn't know. Great minds *do* think alike. Excuse us, doll. We've got a town to save. And I guess you have a college essay to write. Mwah." And he kisses his hand, turning around with more sass than a Real Housewife of Atlanta.

Hot flames of rage course through my body, straight into my knuckles. I pull the car onto the sidewalk, nearly clipping two elderly volunteers, and turn down the next side street. I knock over an empty recycling bin and make a hard left onto a dark residential road. I jam the car into second (I'm *so* glad my parents got me the stick shift) and get as far away from the bedlam on Church Street as possible.

"Whoa," Rani says, bracing her arms against the glove compartment. "Drive much?"

"Ugh! I hate that little dork!" I scream into the night, pounding a fist on the dash.

"Who *was* that guy?"

"If I was gay and black, *he* would be my nemesis, not Stanford-E.K. Uggggh!"

"Can you, like, chill for a sec and stop driving all over the road?"

I slam the brakes so hard, the car stalls out and we lurch forward into our seatbelts. Everything is quiet. The humid air floats in from above and suffocates me even more.

"Why is the whole world out to get me, Ran?"

"Cuz you're too awesome. They want to pull you back down to their level."

I turn and sort of smile at her, but I can feel tears welling up in my eyes.

"You gonna tell me about it or what?" she says.

"It's stupid. He's nobody. Robert something—I barely know him. But you remember that dumb leadership program I went to for our school?"

"That HOBY thing in tenth grade?"

"Right. The Hugh O'Brian Youth Leadership program. Robert was there from *his* school. And on the first day, they put us in small groups of six and asked us to share any stress we felt about being named 'a leader.' Robert and I were the only ones who said our parents were stressing us out. Everyone else loved their dopey parents and said the only pressure they felt was self-imposed—total Miss America/job interview answers. But Robert said he felt daily pressure from his dad, who had been breathing down his neck about getting into Yale since he was 13, so he and I kind of bonded. Plus he loved cheesy 80s pop music—and not ironically."

"He sounds fun," Rani says.

"He *is*... sort of. And if this had been like *any* other day. If we were driving to the Vineyard and ran into him on the ferry, I'd be totally stoked to see him. But now? Seeing him here—doing the same thing I'm trying to do? It's like... how unique am I? He's a gay black version of Stanford-Emily Kim. We're all just Emily Kims. And I'm sick of it."

"...You wanna leave?"

I look at Rani and immediately get what she's trying to do. Asking me if I want to quit, throw in the towel. Hell no. That's not me. That is not who I am. That is not Emily Kim.

"Exactly," I say, turning the car back on.

"Exactly what? Are we leaving?"

"If these guys are doing the same thing—then we just gotta up it a notch."

"Wait. How do you *up* volunteering at a hurricane a notch?

"Very carefully."

"I was afraid you'd say that," Rani says, a slight smile betraying her cynicism.

I step on the gas and drive off. "Next stop," I announce, "the governor's office."

A.J.

"Governor Watson, if I may," an intense meteorologist named Eliza Mason interjects. "Even though their effects on human populations can be devastating, tropical cyclones—or hurricanes, as they're more commonly known—can not only relieve the drought conditions we've been plagued with this past summer, but they also carry heat energy away from the tropics, making them an important part of the global atmospheric circulation mechanism, maintaining equilibrium in the Earth's troposphere. As a result, storms like are actually a good thing."

The dozen or so "weather experts" begin to talk at once, debating the relevance of Eliza's statement, fighting for stage time and the governor's attention. I have no idea what any of them are saying. Considering where I was 24 hours ago, I still can't believe I'm even in this room—the governor's office in the State Capitol in downtown Hartford. My head is spinning faster than the hurricane bearing down on the Constitution State. I'm too overwhelmed to focus on the meat of their arguments: barometric this, climatological that. So I sit quietly in the corner, trying not to draw too much attention to myself.

"Ladies and gentlemen," Governor Watson finally says, quieting the chaos, "I appreciate your advice and wisdom, but what can we do right this second to help people? That's what I need to know."

The team quickly launches into explanations of wind speed and forecast projections, showing off PowerPoint presentations on their iPads about past hurricanes, disaster relief, and emergency planning. I can't follow it all—and I can't believe the speed at which everyone here talks, thinks, and moves.

FEMA has already communicated that they'll "be at the governor's disposal should the need arise." On the ride back from Wampanoag (in a limo!), I even witnessed a phone call between Governor Watson and President Obama. The White House wanted to reassure the governor that the safety of our state was a top priority, and that the governor should feel free to call on the White House at anytime. At least that's what I gleaned from the bits I could make out, distracted as I was by Teddy sitting across from me, pointing at Governor Watson, mouthing the words "the Democratic Chris Christie" and making the 'rock and roll' gesture throughout the entire three-minute conversation. I'm not sure why the governor puts up with Teddy-the-overgrown-child, but I think it has something to do with them being best friends since college and the governor preferring to surround himself with people he trusts rather than the smartest or most qualified candidates. I think the governor is aware of this Achilles' heel, and my being here may be a step toward rectifying that.

At least that's what goes through my mind when I'm feeling confident and worthy and like I truly belong here. But that confidence wavers every five minutes.

"And that's why," Eliza says, pointing at a satellite photo of New England, "storms like this one are so rare in this part of the country."

"Okay. But shouldn't we just… drive out there," the governor suggests, "and see what's what?"

No one seems to like this idea. Especially Teddy.

"Bad idea, Chucky."

"Why?"

"Because." And for a second it seems like that will be the beginning and end of Teddy's argument. But then he adds, "I mean… did 'W' go to New Orleans *before* the hurricane? Hell no! You do not put elected officials in the path of a storm. 'Wait and See' is the government's stance. FEMA has promised to be at the ready should it come to that, but we don't take any *actual* measures now. We simply go on TV, warn everyone in the area—*strongly*, like Christie did—advise them to evacuate and take precautions, wait till it's passed, and *then* we visit the devastated area, looking like war heroes walking over a smoking battlefield."

The minions nod and concur, but Governor Watson seems unsatisfied with Teddy's answer. I look around the room to see who will speak next when I suddenly notice all eyes (including the governor's) are on me.

"Alexis," he says, seemingly intent on being the only one to call me that. "You've got the freshest eyes here. What do you suggest?"

"Um… I think you can do both?" I say, sort of like a question.

Governor Watson seems intrigued. The minions seem pissed.

"Go on," the governor says.

"Well," I begin, not completely sure where I'm going with this. "You have to go downstairs and do the press conference, obviously. Answer the looming questions, reassure people at home that their governor is on top of things, ask them to take precautions, as they said. But tomorrow? You could head out to the battlefield. See first hand how the storm prep is going. Cawdor's only an hour drive from here, it could be a day trip. Or even an overnight, and you could evacuate Saturday morning. That way… you do the safe thing *and* the brave thing. And maybe get some free TV time doing it. People like to see elected officials getting dirty with the regular folk. Especially *young* people."

The room is quiet for a moment. The governor seems impressed. He looks over his shoulder, gives Teddy a satisfied nod, and then smacks his hand on the table. "Let's do it!"

Teddy immediately barks orders and everyone scatters, looking busy and important. Someone thrusts a newly pressed suit, shirt and tie into the governor's arms and he disappears into a hidden bathroom I had no idea existed. Within thirty seconds, the room is empty and I'm sitting alone. Did the governor of Connecticut just take my advice? Am I officially a policy advisor? What the hell is going on?

I can hear some of the other staffers down the hall chattering away on their phones, and I wonder if *I* should be calling someone. Or emailing or texting or doing *something*. Am I supposed to be a self-starter, or do I wait for instructions? Just as I'm eyeing the liquor tray on the bookshelf, Teddy and the (newly changed) governor sweep back into the room, followed by a swarm of new assistants and handlers I haven't seen until now.

"Okay, now, be cool down there, Chucky," Teddy says like a boxing coach before a prizefight. "Be the governor-in-chief. And when the shit hits the fan in…" He checks his Tag Heuer. "Thirty-seven hours—we'll be there to clean things up. Nothing unites people like a natural disaster."

Governor Watson nods. I stare at him hard, hoping he'll look at me, reassure me that what I said was okay and that he's happy I'm here. But he doesn't even glance my way. He takes several index cards with notes on them from an assistant and the whole gaggle walks out together, headed for the Nathan Hale statue in the lobby where an "impromptu" press conference is being staged. I have no idea if I'm supposed to stay up here or watch from downstairs. After a moment's hesitation, I scamper behind them, pulling up the rear as we all make our way down the grand staircase.

"Now be prepared," Teddy warns the governor. "In addition to the questions we went over already, there's bound to be some hotshot-upstart-asshole down there, gonna question our motives as impure, claim we're doing this all for political gain somehow."

Teddy stops suddenly on the stairs, forcing the governor and all of us behind him to stop too in an almost comical train-car pile-up kind of way. Teddy stares down the governor and says, "You gotta be *ready* for that shit. Ready to pounce."

And now I see why Teddy's here. He's the "motivator." The hard-ass realist who keeps the governor focused on staying on message and connecting with the press… and the people. He may not have a firm grasp on policy or numbers, but he knows what people need to hear. I'd hire him, too.

"Come back aggressive," Teddy asserts. "This can*not* look like a political 'win' for you. It *can* be. And in the end it *will* be. But it can't *look* like that. So when they say: 'Governor, some are suggesting you're attempting to turn this into your own 9/11 or Hurricane Sandy and make a bid for the White House in 2016…' Come *right* in. Don't even let them ask the *question*. You hear 'White House' and '2016' you come right back with…"

§

"I have no idea about that, nor am I the least bit concerned or interested," says Governor Watson. "I've got a job to do here in Connecticut that's much bigger than politics, and I couldn't care less about any of that stuff. I've got 3.5 million people in this state, more than half of them in the path of this storm. It could mean hundreds of thousands without power. Devastation along the shore. Flooding, fires, loss of life, you name it. So if you think right now I give a damn about presidential politics, then you don't know me. Next question, please."

Not bad. I even believed him myself—and I was there when Teddy basically fed that response verbatim to the governor.

As the reporters thrust their hands up and shout Governor Watson's name, Teddy steps in behind him at the podium and whispers in his ear. God, I wish I knew what he was saying. It's always assumed that the guy is whispering something like "only two more questions" or "don't forget to mention X, Y, and Z." But having spent just a few hours in the presence of Teddy Hutchins, I think he said something more like, *"And that. Is how you throw down the gauntlet. Hillary better watch her little pant-suited ass in 2016."*

Whatever Teddy told him, the Governor just nods soberly and then says into the bank of microphones, "Okay, just a few more, then we need to wrap this up. Yeah—Susannah."

"Governor Watson, have you been in contact with the White House to request Federal Disaster Relief funding?"

"Well, let me preface that by saying, blah blah blah blah blah…"

I zone out and scan the crowd. They all look so sad and lonely, these reporters called to a press conference at 10 p.m., two days before a hurricane. So detached and dispassionate, as if they lost their lust for being reporters long ago. Or maybe they lost it when they realized they'd be stuck covering Hartford for the rest of their lives, their dreams of New York or D.C. long since crushed.

Only one reporter in the room seems to have a spark in her eye. A young Asian woman near the back. She's wearing a plain black slipover tennis knit kind of thing. A touch too sexy for the Hartford press corps, but maybe she was at an event or out with her boyfriend when she got the call. Regardless of what she's wearing, there's a hunger and enthusiasm in her eyes. She's hanging on every word, clocking everything around her. She can't be more than 22, 23. Definitely younger than I am. God I hope *I* haven't lost that spark yet. I hope I never lose it.

And just like that, I realize that the governor needs to call on her. She's here for a specific reason, not because some fifty-year-old editor forced a mundane assignment on her. She has an agenda. Whatever she asks could be the game-changer we need to take this hurricane to the next level and get the governor that much needed *national* coverage.

As inconspicuously as I can, I motion at Teddy to get his attention. He finally makes eye contact and shrugs, *What?* I point to my phone and send him a text.

> Gov needs to call on young Asian reporter - back row, black dress.

> Why?

> Cuz she's the only one in here under 30. She'll ask an unexpected question.

> So?

> The hurricane was the luck. I think she's the miracle.

> Thanks, Oprah.

I stare at him, pleading with my eyes. He shakes me off like a petulant pitcher ignoring his catcher's signs. I point at my phone again. Teddy rolls his eyes but obliges and looks down at his BlackBerry.

> He hired me for a reason. Trust me!

Teddy glares at me, and then begrudgingly steps to the governor, whispering in his ear. The governor seems surprised and exchanges a few words with Teddy, who mouths my name and gestures toward me with his head. Governor Watson turns my way; I stand tall and try to look as confident and experienced as possible. With a look of vague suspicion he steps back to the mic and says, "Yes—uh, in the last row... No, no, with the, uh—in the black. Yes, you, miss."

I take a deep breath and hold it. Here we go...

"Thank you, Governor," the girl says, exuding professionalism and intelligence. "Emily Kim, rising senior at Fairwich Academy and head blogger at Cons-ti-TEEN-tion-dot-com with a two-part question. I'm hearing a lot of talk stressing the severity of the storm and the need for residents to take the appropriate precautions and evacuate in an orderly manner. But what are the state's plans for *after* the storm? In that vein, whatever task force you have advising you, I'd suggest it is severely lacking in one key demographic, one we all know can make or break an election—witness the past two national cycles. Of course I'm talking about the *youth* vote. So my second question to you is: are you doing anything to get the young people of Connecticut involved and connected to this relief effort?"

"Uhhh..."

Oh God, don't blow it. She's handing you the miracle on a silver platter!

"Might I suggest, Governor, to better keep up with our times— social media and all—that two high school students be appointed to your task force? They can more efficiently keep the public informed and safe via Facebook and Twitter. And, not to put down my peers, but we all know how apathetic and selfish today's teenagers have become. I think our generation should be made more accountable for the problems facing us, facing the country, facing the world. And to help set an example, I think you, sir, should look to some highly qualified and motivated high school students to propose a solution to the flooding and devastation that may result from Hurricane Calliope."

Boom. There it is.

I text in a flurry (typos and autocorrect be damned!) and hit send.

"Well, Miss... uh..."

"Kim. Emily Kim."

"Well, Miss Kim—I think you make some… excellent points. And today's youth should be more involved… in government and politics, especially at the, uh, the… local level. Because the children are the future. We've got to, uh… teach them well. And let them. You know. Lead the way. And, uh… Excuse me, one second."

Mercifully, Teddy grabs the governor by the arm (before he quotes the entire Whitney Houston song) and shows him my text.

> Have a contest. All caters 18 or yogurt. Bast idea for how to deal w after effects of strom will be implements and fury place twine gets a commendation from gobs office plus 20k for college.

I re-read the sent text and wince at all the typos. "Caters" instead of "CT'ers," "18 or yogurt" instead of "18 or younger," "Fury place twine" instead of "first place team"? But I realize the gist of the message is clear when I notice a hint of a smile from the governor. The light back in his eyes, he grabs the microphone with a renewed sense of purpose.

"Miss Kim," he begins, clearing his throat and with it, all traces of doubt, "I absolutely *love* your idea. I mean, look: I'm so fired up about it, I almost broke into *song!*" The members of the press laugh, breaking the awkward tension, thank God. "But," he continues, "I think we can take that idea a step further. Instead of just *selecting* someone, we'll have a *contest*—for any resident of Connecticut eighteen years or younger. We want to hear—*I* want to hear—from today's youth. I want your best ideas for how to deal with the aftereffects of this hurricane. So I'm proposing that each person, or *team*, present a demonstration of their relief effort plan at… 8 a.m. Saturday morning. Before the storm hits at noon. Candidates will come down here to my office. I'll listen to all of the proposals. The winning idea will be implemented and the first-place team will receive a commendation from my office along with a $20,000 award toward college."

The press applauds (is that even normal for one of these things?), and I glance at Teddy who nods appreciatively back at me. I turn back to the crowd of press and catch the eye of the young Asian girl who started it all. She looks less than pleased. She looks downright pissed. What the hell is her problem?

"So," the governor says, quieting the crowd, "I'm issuing a call to arms for Connecticut's young people. A call to action." And then he looks right into one of the TV cameras, pausing for dramatic effect. "Will *you* answer that call?"

Nice.

"All right, thank you. Thank you everyone, no more questions. We'll see you all tomorrow." And he's off, disappearing up the stairs while the press shout follow-up questions, all of which he ignores.

By the time I fight my way through the crowd and back to the governor's office, the team is buzzing. Standing in the doorway I can see Teddy talking logistics with some IT guys, figuring out a link they can add to the official "Governor of Connecticut" website where kids can get information. Everyone else is on a phone or a laptop. Except the governor. He's standing directly across the room looking at me. Well, looking *toward* me. His eyes are cast in my general direction but sort of directed at the floor so I can't tell if he's mid-thought, pondering something serious to say to me, or just daydreaming while his eyes happen to be looking at my feet. Before I can decide, he breaks into the slow clap.

And everyone stops what they're doing to look up. Look up at the governor, who is now looking directly at me. And they all join in. Two dozen people I hardly know are applauding me. I'm totally embarrassed and flushed and nervous. And proud. The governor gives me a (kind of dorky but totally sincere) thumbs-up. Then he says, "Ladies and gentlemen, Miss Alexis Gould." More applause. Some hoots and hollers.

"Okay, folks," he says after a bit. "We haven't won anything yet. Back to work."

A few people nearby pat me on the back and shake my hand. The governor—whose praise I crave most, not just because he's the governor and my boss but also because he reminds me of my dad—

has already moved on to other business and is fully engrossed.

Teddy edges his way toward me, offering a congratulatory hand. "Nice work, A.J. Welcome to the show."

RANI

"What the *fuck*?!"

Emily is walking five paces ahead of me, storming back to her car like a woman possessed. She literally has not stopped pissing and moaning since we left the governor's press conference.

"What the fuck what the fuck what the FUCK?!"

I hate when she's like this. And it's been getting worse the last three months.

"He hijacked my idea, Rani. Fucking hijacked it! On national television!"

"I think there were only local stations in there," I say, but she doesn't seem to hear me.

"So instead of being *appointed* to the task force, like I wanted—I mean, HELL-OO?! It was *my* friggin' idea in the first place, he never would have thought of something like this on his *own*. So shouldn't the person who *came up with the idea* be the one allowed on the task force? Yes! Of course! That would be the *logical* thing the to do. The morally *correct* thing to do. But now—*now* I have to compete with an entire *state* of over-sexed half-wits dying for their fifteen minutes. Uggghh! There is no justice in the world!"

"Yeah," I say. "It's a bummer."

Emily finally stops walking in the middle of the empty street and turns to face me. "You know what this means, right?"

"We can go home?"

"We're gonna have to work *ten* times as hard to win those spots."

"Aw, man. Seriously?"

"Otherwise," she says, grabbing me by the shoulders and looking me dead in the eye, "no killer personal statement—and no Harvard! Are you with me?"

I let out a long sigh. I want to tell her, *No, Emily—I'm NOT with you. This is the stupidest idea since the 'flying tank.' I was barely with you when we left my house for Cawdor, and I was even LESS with you when you decided to crash the governor's press conference to somehow get us appointed to their task force. How ludicrous is that idea? It's pointless, unnecessary, and a total waste of time. We're seventeen years old. It's still August. We should be on a beach drinking flat beer and making out with dumb boys who smell like ChapStick and s'mores.*

But I don't say any of that. Because she's my best friend. And also because when she gets like this… I'm kind of afraid of her.

"Of course," I say. "Totally with you."

Emily hugs me super tight, with more desperation than affection, and then she's off again, five paces ahead, beelining to her car, chattering all the way about how to strategize and brainstorm. I immediately regret staying.

§

The entire ride back to Cawdor, Emily doesn't stop talking. She talks about where we should stay: "I have my mom's Hampton Inn Rewards Card. We should stay at a Hampton Inn—we passed one on our way up to Hartford." She talks about using social media to our advantage: "Not only integrate it into our plan for the governor but also tweet and update what we're doing live… like document it and maybe cite the tweets and status updates in our personal statements!" She talks about her*self* ad nauseam: "I feel like there's a big fat target on my back, ya know, like everyone either wants a *piece* of me or wants to take me *down*. I guess that's the way all visionaries and trailblazers feel. I should read the Steve Jobs biography." I listen in and out (mostly out), secretly wishing I could go back home and lay on my bed reading *Horse and Rider*.

Then I realize: I *can* go home.

It'll be so easy. After we settle in at the hotel, I can wait until Emily is in the shower (she *always* showers before bed, it's part of her O.C.D. about being super clean all the time). Then I can sneak out to the train station and catch the Northeast Regional back to Stamford. It's the perfect plan. The only "rub" will be dealing with Emily at school for the next nine months before we go off to college. But it seems a small price to pay for my freedom at this precise moment.

We make the fifty-five mile drive back to Cawdor in under an hour and get a room on the "top floor" of the Hampton Inn— which is the second floor. We drag our overnight bags up the stairs (no elevator) and walk along the outdoor balcony/hallway. Emily slides our key in the door and heads straight for the bathroom, still yammering.

"Oh my God, we should enlist some *celebrities* to tweet about the hurricane prep and recovery effort! But, like, *young* celebrities. Emma Stone and Andrew Garfield. Ooo, what about Chloe Sevigny… isn't she *from* Connecticut? And John Mayer is from Fairfield. Oh this is perfect! Can you Google those guys and try to find their, like, agent or manager info? I'm sure they'd totally be into helping out a good cause like this. Eek! Exciting!"

And she's off, closing the bathroom door behind her and turning on the shower. I give her a few minutes to make sure she's not going to rush back out with another brilliant idea. When she starts singing John Mayer's "All We Ever Do Is Say Goodbye," I grab my stuff and head out the door.

And it's exhilarating. The night air seems fresher. The sounds crisper. My feet step in time with my pounding heart. My head is buzzing. I can hardly contain my excitement as I walk to the station. I bang off a quick text to my mom, who has been pestering me for updates every hour since we left.

> Coming home on next train.
> Will call if I need ride from station.

Then I realize there may not be another train until morning. Emily will figure out where I went and come find me and badger me with her oh-so-convincing-ways, forcing me to stay with her. I pick up my pace. For the last block and a half, I'm in a dead sprint. I bang through the doors of the tiny station house, breathless, and look up at the old-fashioned announcement board. A southbound train is scheduled to arrive in four minutes, departing for Stamford (only a ten-minute cab ride from home). I should be back in my own bed before 2 a.m. It couldn't have worked out better if I'd planned it.

My phone buzzes with a text. I freeze with fear, terrified that it's Emily wondering where the hell I am. Thankfully, it's just my mom.

> Why are you coming home so soon?

Long story. Will explain in person..

I hit send, slip the phone in my shorts pocket, and sit on a wooden bench, still catching my breath. Looking around for the first time, I'm surprised to find that I'm not the only one in the station. There are three other people—a family of some kind that I guess to be a brother, sister, and their grandmother. He looks like he's around my age. The girl looks to be 11 or 12, and the woman is in her seventies and uses a walker.

"Excuse me," I say to the group, but sort of direct my attention to the boy. "Is this the right place for the Amtrak train to Stamford?"

"I think so," he says. "There's only one more train tonight, the 11:17 to New York. I think it'll stop in Stamford, too, but you should check with the guy at the counter…" He points to the empty ticket counter. "If there *was* a guy at the counter. Uh…" He smiles and sort of laughs as he digs for his phone. "Hold on—I can pull it up it two seconds."

"Oh, no—it's cool. I'm like ninety percent sure it stops there. I was just double checking."

"Right on. So you've only got like a ten percent chance that you'll end up in Canada."

"Which would be cool because I love ice fishing and riding moose."

"Do people ride moose? I'd think the moose wouldn't really dig that."

"No—they hate it. But I ride them anyway. Show 'em who's boss."

He smiles and laughs again, and I feel like I'm living someone else's life. Who *am* I right now? Witty, charming, dynamic? Starting and leading a conversation with a total stranger? I have *no* idea what's gotten into me. Maybe it's the freedom of being out from under Emily's thumb, out from under my parents' thumbs. Whatever it is, this guy seems to like it and he's definitely easy on the eyes. Messy curly brown hair. Strong nose and chin. Blue eyes and a slightly crooked smile. Like a younger Seth Meyers from SNL. If he's funny too I may just ask him to marry me on the spot. I know my dad would love it. I think his biggest fear when he had two girls was that we'd bring home a boy he wouldn't know how to talk to. If I brought home an Indian boy (even one born in America like me), Dad wouldn't know what to say to him. And even though my father gave thousands of dollars to *both* Obama campaigns, I don't think there would a quicker way to give him a heart attack than to tell him I was dating a black guy.

My mom is even more of an enigma. Even though she married a white guy, she's been on this Indian kick for the last two decades. It started when she named me and has gotten deeper and more absurd ever since, culminating with the Bollywood-themed fundraiser she organized for my school this past April. Ever since her *Titanic* fundraiser was such a huge success, she's been reluctantly topping herself each year. This time she had a group of "Bollywood Funk" instructors from the city headline the evening's festivities. During the interactive performance my mom turned to me, mid-Backward Bhangra Pivot Step, and said, "Why don't you marry a Tamil Brahmin, Rani? You'd make the most exquisite babies. And Indian men are far more refined than Americans, your father included."

Aside from the open dig at my father, I found the notion extremely offensive. Why do parents think we can *control* who we like? Why would I block out an entire race of potential mates just so my parents can be more comfortable at Thanksgiving?

All of this races though my mind in an instant—but apparently not instantaneously enough, because the boy at the train station is looking at me expectantly.

"I'm sorry—I totally spaced out for a second. What did you say?"

"I said, my name's Tyler." He stands and crosses over to me from the bench he was sitting on so we can hear each other better. "What's yours?" "Oh," I say dumbly. "Rani. Rani Caldwell."

"Good to meet you Rani. You from Stamford?"

"Close. Fairwich."

He leans in and drops his voice, presumably so grandma and sis can't hear. "I figured you weren't from around here."

"Why—because I'm Indian?"

"Uh. No. Because I would have noticed a pretty girl like you before."

"Oh... Did I mention I have racist Tourette's? It's very rare but it makes me say stupid things to cute white boys."

"Lucky me." And he smiles his charming crooked smile and I get goose bumps all up and down my left arm. Oh man, is he cute. I should sit across the aisle from him on the train. Or maybe right next to him? His sister will sit with his grandmother and I can sit with him. It's almost too perfect.

"So," I say, trying the keep the conversation going. "Where are you headed?"

"Oh, I'm not going anywhere. I'm just getting my little sister and grandmother on the train. Out of the storm's path. My parents are in New York already—so they'll ride out the hurricane with them."

"You're not going?"

"Nah—I'm gonna stick around. My grandmother's lived here her whole life, so… I'll board up her windows, get the house storm-ready. Then see if there's anything else I can do to help out in town. Seems kind of selfish to just run for higher ground if I'm young and able-bodied, know what I mean?"

"Yeah… Totally."

"What about you? What's in Stamford-slash-Fairwich for you at one in the morning?"

"Um… my parents?"

"Okay…"

"Yeah. I came up to help out with the hurricane—volunteer and stuff?"

"Oh, that's awesome! Good for you."

"Yeah… it was."

"So you did your part, now you're headed home. That's cool."

"It is. Isn't it?"

He turns toward the track. An approaching headlight reflects in the window.

"Guess that's your train," he says.

"Guess so…"

"Well it was nice to meet you… Rani." He holds out his hand and I shake it. It's soft and strong and feels like hot cocoa by a warm fire, like picking apples upstate, like a carriage ride through Central Park.

"Yeah… um. Actually. I think—yeah, I'm probably gonna stick

around... another day or so?"

"Really?" he says with a hopeful smile.

"Yeah, my friend was also gonna stay maybe. So I could stick around. I'm sure there's more to do, right? Able-bodied teenagers and all?"

"Right on. Lemme, uh... lemme get these guys on the train and... I can give you a ride back to town?"

"Oh no, it's fine—I can walk."

"No, no. It's no trouble. Just give me two minutes."

"Okay. Cool, thanks," I say, trying to contain my excitement. He grabs the two small bags by his bench and escorts his sister and grandmother out to the platform. The grandmother smiles at me and holds my gaze so long that I feel like she's trying to tell me something with her wise old eyes. *Yes, my dear, this was meant to be. All the stars are aligning so you could meet your future husband. Go forth and procreate.* Either that or she's in the early stages of dementia and thinks I'm Princess Anastasia. I smile and nod and watch them exit through the old-fashioned doors.

What the hell am I doing? Sticking around a possibly deadly natural disaster for a *guy*? This is the craziest thing I've ever done in my life. And the *second* craziest was walking out of the hotel room while Emily was in the shower. Either I'm completely insane and making a series of rash decisions based on hunger, hormones, and a lack of sleep... or maybe I'm finally growing up. Maybe I'm finally living my life for me. Doing things that I want to do, without checking with my parents or teachers or Emily. And that's why it's so scary and exhilarating. And it's why I *have* to do this. Why I have to stay in Cawdor and volunteer. Not just for Tyler. This is the first time in my life that I've done something without thinking about it—without thinking about consequences or college or other people's feelings. The first time I've done something just for me.

My phone buzzes.

> What time does your train arrive?
> Daddy says he'll come get you.

I peck back as fast as I can.

> **False Alarm. Staying here.
> Will call in AM. xo.**

The train sounds its horn. I look up to see Tyler waving at the slowly moving cars as they begin to pull away. Once the train is out of sight, he heads back inside, smiling shyly at me. My phone buzzes again.

> **Are you sure? What's going on sweetie?
> Everything ok?**

I discreetly read the text and then slip the phone in my back pocket.

"Everything okay?" Tyler asks.

"Yep. Good to go."

§

Friday, August 16, 7:55 am

There are literally hundreds of volunteers all up and down Church Street.

"What'd I tell you?" Emily says as we stand on the second-floor balcony outside our hotel room. "Oversexed half-wits all looking for their fifteen minutes."

Emily and I watch as a small army of teenagers makes its way toward the town center—here not because the spirit of compassion and helping their fellow man kicked in overnight, but because they're all gunning for the governor's top prize. And who could blame them? I mean it's not like *we* arrived with completely altruistic intentions.

But Emily is still pissed about it.

"Hijacked, Rani. Completely hijacked."

Emily closes the hotel room door in a huff and I follow her toward the stairwell. She has no idea about my impromptu escape-

and-return last night.

Just past 11:30, when Tyler dropped me at the Hampton Inn, we exchanged our info (with a cell phone "bump"—vaguely erotic, subliminally sexual) and he promised to find me in the morning. I would have stayed and talked longer with him, our silhouettes the only things moving in the quiet hotel parking lot, but my phone kept buzzing with texts from my mom, plus I was anxious to get inside and deal with the wrath of Emily. Luckily, when I crept back into the room she was still in the shower, singing. Two minutes later and the jig might have been up about my little train station adventure. I sat on the edge of the bed and texted my mom a more complete explanation—a lie about the people here saying they had more than enough volunteers and were sending some of us home for safety, then miraculously finding other jobs that needed to be attended to and begging us to stay. I can't believe she bought it! It was a terrible lie, made possible only by the lateness of the hour causing that perfect storm in my mother of tired-plus-white-wine-drunk, a state I've taken advantage of throughout high school. It's just as well I didn't have to explain myself to Emily, too, who was neither tired nor drunk. I hadn't even planned out a lie for her. More of this new unthinking Rani, just going with the flow.

In the hazy morning light, Emily and I walk across the hotel parking lot and wade into the mass of bodies marching west. We don't ask questions, just follow the mob.

Though obscured by a mass of clouds, the sun (not even up for two hours) is already raising the temperature in town. I can tell it's going to be a hot one. There isn't breath of wind. The trees are still, the flags by the post office are completely limp. Is this what they call the calm before the storm?

The crowd assembles around a statue in Duffy Square. It reminds me of the statue that the bullies are decapitating in the opening credits of *The Simpsons*. In fact, the whole area reminds me of that fictional Springfield with its small "everytown" kind of appeal, the only difference being Cawdor's proximity to water and the smell of fish and saltwater in the air.

As we face the empty stone steps of the library, the buzz around us is that the governor will be speaking soon—along with "a special guest." Some are guessing that it's a local celebrity or athlete. Others predict that "we" are the special guest, the same way "we" were the *Time* magazine Person of the Year in 2006. I silently note the irony that one of the most coddled and selfish generations ever is here "to volunteer" while simultaneously assuming "they" are the story—that "they" are the most important part of this equation, not the fact that a major hurricane is bearing down on the East Coast yet again, and, according to every weather forecast, this town will take a direct hit.

As I look around the crowd of 16- to 18-year-olds—the kid that Emily knows from HOBY and his Abercrombie & Fitch-like partner, a large group of crunchy kids (six guys and four girls) wearing Birkenstocks and "Occupy Life" T-shirts, some sort of Amish-looking brother and sister team that have not stopped praying since we arrived—I can't help but think that perhaps all of our parents were *too* loving and supportive. We never wanted for anything. We were supported and encouraged and enriched and taken care of every step of the way. None of us had a chance to build up healthy insecurities or neuroses. Just ego and an insane drive to be the best.

Emily gives me a slight jab in the ribs with her elbow and a head nod toward the odd brother-sister duo.

"If that's our competition," she whispers slyly, "we got this in the bag."

I give a nod and a half-smile back, but I'm secretly horrified. Emily truly sees everyone as a rival. The whole world is an Olympic event and she must win the gold or face shame from the coaches in her homeland.

Emily points to a craft services table behind us. "I need coffee. You want something?"

"I'm good," I say.

While Emily ducks under the temporary tent, perusing the muffins, bagels, and fruit, I scan the crowd for Tyler. He must be here somewhere. I'm instantly upset with myself for being so anxious to find him. I've got butterflies. I'm adjusting and readjusting my hair every five seconds. I'm discreetly touching my butt, hoping it looks okay in these jeans I haven't washed in a week. After several furtive minutes I finally spot him near the front by the library steps. He's with a bunch of theatre-hipster types wearing knit beanies (in

August!) and hip European sneakers. I watch him, hoping he'll notice me, willing him to find me in the crowd. Then, for no apparent reason other than perhaps my mystical mind-powers, Tyler turns and locks eyes with me. It's too arresting to look away. I'm sure I'm blushing, but I try not to betray my nerves. I give a little wave and a smile. Tyler does an ironic salute-twirling-gesture with two fingers a la Conan O'Brien. It's hopelessly dorky and cute. He gently jerks his head as if to say, Come on over, meet my friends, and without thinking (as seems to be my MO of late) I start toward him, but I'm thwarted by Emily, who's suddenly mid-bitch, thrusting a cranberry muffin that I didn't ask for into my hands.

"So I was just grabbing some breakfast stuff for us," a more-than-usually irritated Emily says, "and sort of offered up the plate to some people around me—like totally polite—like, 'do you want to grab one first,' you know. Totally in the spirit of camaraderie and good will and all this volunteer crap. Not forcing anything on anyone, right? And you know what that queer little farmer girl just said to me? She asked if I would 'kindly remove the processed toxins' from her face because she doesn't eat anything that has more than five ingredients! She and her creepy twin brother are homeschooled locavores—so like everything they eat has to come from their own garden. I was like, whatever, Little House on the Prairie. A muffin from Starbucks is not going to kill you." Emily takes a big swig of her coffee and launches right back in. "Like, what was she even doing by the craft service table if she can't eat anything in there?"

"I don't know. They can probably eat fruit. Or water."

"Jesus, Rani. Whose side are you on?"

"No one's. I'm just saying—"

"Whatever. I'm over it."

Emily gulps her coffee again and before things can get too tense, the crowd breaks into polite applause. I glance up to see the governor making his way to the podium. I look at Tyler, who I guess was watching the exchange between Emily and I. He gives a bemused shrug and then holds up his phone and points to it. I look down at my phone and see a new text.

> Looks like someone got up on the wrong side of the bitch this morning ;-) …and that emoticon was ironic, in case u didn't know.

I look back at him but he's already turned around, facing the governor.

"What's that?" Emily asks, looking at my phone, nosy as ever.

"Nothing," I say, offering no further explanation.

"…Ugh. I wish this hurricane would just get here already so we can win that scholarship. Mother Nature is sooo slooow."

Times like this make me really question our friendship. Before I can think too much about it, Governor Watson addresses the crowd.

"Good morning, everyone. On my way here, driving through this great state of ours, I was reminded of an old joke: You know what they say about Connecticut? It's just like Massachusetts, only the Kennedys don't own it yet!" A lot of people laugh, including the kids who don't seem to know who the Kennedys are, and the governor smiles at his well-played opener. "But seriously," he continues as the laughs quiet down, "it truly warms my heart to see so many Nutmeggers here volunteering their time and energy. It says so much about our great state and the spirit of the people who call it home. And speaking of people who call this place home… I want to introduce a special guest. One of Connecticut's finest. Someone who hails from this very town. A man who's gone from amateur theatre at our community center to gracing the stages of Broadway and entertaining us on television in the long-running series, John Proctor, Homicide. You know him, you love him, here he is. Richard. Gains!"

And, seriously… the crowd goes wild. They started hooting and hollering as soon as the governor said the name of the TV show (which I've seen maybe two minutes of in passing during the six seasons it was on… eight years ago!) But I guess he's kind of a big deal. And maybe there's a sense of pride in having a famous actor from your home state, but I really don't get it. How does being born in the same part of the country connect you to someone else? It's as arbitrary as liking someone because they wear the same brand of socks.

But the crowd cheers mindlessly anyway as Richard Gains shakes the governor's hand—all manly and filled with meaning and whispered jokes and heads tossed back, laughing. It all looks so calculated. I wonder if Emily's jaded personality is rubbing off on me. Or maybe I'm just cranky about being here in the first place and not getting enough sleep last night. No matter how tight you close those hotel blackout shades, there's always a sliver of light that creeps in and seems to land right on your face at dawn.

As Richard Gains takes his place behind the podium, I can sort of see his appeal. Piercing blue eyes behind thin wire-framed glasses. Salt-and-pepper hair tousled just so. A smile that makes you wish he were your cool uncle getting you backstage at intimate unplugged rock concerts.

"Thanks, everyone, for that warm welcome," says Richard Gains. "And thank you, Governor Watson. It's a testament to you that the people of Connecticut are so inspired to be here this morning. And I just want to say—looking out at all of these faces—this diverse, and might I add, very attractive group of citizens…" As the requisite laughter erupts on cue, I think: oh, he's good. "I look out at you all, my fellow Nutmeggers. And it restores my faith. My faith in humanity. My faith in America. And it makes me proud not only to be from the great state of Connecticut. But to be a person from the great state of MANKIND."

Oh, he's *really* good. I even get goose bumps up and down my arms. You gotta hand it to him: The guy gives "great speech."

"So in that same spirit of generosity and human kindness," Richard Gains continues over the cheering crowd, "I'd like to offer up The Tao of Peace, my not-so-little B&B that I recently opened with my fiancée. But not just to *any*one. I want to extend free room and board to the *kids* here today. The high school kids here not only to volunteer their time, but to come up with a *solution* to the problem. And I'd like to extend that *first* invitation… to the young lady from the press conference last night. Miss Emily Kim! Emily, where are you?"

I turn to Emily, who looks genuinely surprised and embarrassed. She raises her eyebrows at me and mouths the words, *what the fuck.* So she's clearly still Emily. But also different. Her usual sharpness fades. Her typically aggressive eyes are opened wider and even tear up a little. Her shoulders have dropped ever so slightly. And her butt—still fierce and in shape—is just a little less clenched. It's like she was waiting for this moment her entire life: a little recognition, a little validation. (God knows her parents aren't great at offering encouragement.) And when she got it from this crowd of strangers, her body relaxed. And mine did too. Maybe this little excursion will be worth it after all.

The crowd slowly turns like concentric dominoes to face Emily. They applaud louder and some kids even pat her on the back. Then the crowd instinctively parts, allowing her an unobstructed path to Richard Gains. Emily looks at me one last time and kind of shrugs. I smile and clap the loudest, whistling as best as I can.

Emily reaches the front and Richard Gains gives her one of those Oprah greetings, where they grab hands and sort of wiggle them up and down, staring into each other's souls. It's awkward and creepy and smacks of that Scientology thing where you suck the energy from other people. But Emily seems to enjoy it. Then Richard Gains holds up Emily's right arm like she just won a prizefight. He gestures to her with his other free hand and the crowd erupts again.

"This is why we're here," he intones into the mic. "One of you. One of our own! A high school student had the guts to say: We. Should be doing. More! And the governor responded. With a call to arms. And here we are. With hope. And enthusiasm. And joy. So let's get to work! Thank you, thank you all."

Richard Gains pulls Emily toward him and does that thing where you have to talk loudly into someone's ear because of the crowd noise, like when they go to commercial break on a talk show. Emily smiles and laughs, throwing her head back, just like Richard Gains did earlier. She's perfect in the spotlight, exactly where she wants to be.

Then I see Tyler. He's waving both arms over his head, gesturing for me to come to him. I fight my way through the crowd. When I'm within shouting distance, Tyler shouts, "How cool is that guy?!"

I nod my head and walk the last few feet to Tyler.

"Man!" he says. "Aren't you blown away? That was like watching Bill Clinton or something. Totally inspiring. And your friend is all chummy with him now? You gotta get her to introduce me."

"Uh, sure. I'll try."

When I walk up the library steps toward Emily, two Secret Service-looking guys immediately accost me.

"It's okay," Emily shouts toward them. "She's with me."

The security guys are dubious, but they allow me through.

"And, uh, I'm with her," Tyler adds, quietly riding my coattails.

"Holy shitballs, Em," I gush. "That was so cool!"

"I know, right?" she gushes back, beaming. The last time I saw her this genuinely happy, we'd just won the middle school talent show in seventh grade with our version of "The Sweet Escape" by Gwen Stefani. (Totally lame, but Emily still loves to watch the DVD of our performance.)

Tyler taps my shoulder and nods his head toward Richard Gains. "Oh right," I say, "Em—you think you could, like, introduce us to your new famous friend?"

"Totally. Hey, um… Mr. Gains?"

He turns around with his charming smile. "Please, call me Richard. Or 'Dick' after you get to know me a little better."

Emily sort of laughs, then puts a hand on my shoulder and says, "I wanted you to meet my best friend, and my partner in this competition, Rani Caldwell."

"Hi," I say, waving like a dork, not confident enough to shake his hand. "It's a real pleasure to meet you, sir."

"Likewise, Rani."

"And this is… um?" Emily says looking quizzically at Tyler. Before I can say anything, Tyler takes the reins, extending a hand to Richard Gains and shaking firmly.

"Tyler Voss. Great to meet you, Mr. Gains. And can I just say—I saw you play Richard III at BAM two years ago…"

"Ah. Another tricky Dick. And oodles of fun."

"Yes, well—it *totally* blew me away. Like… *breath*taking!"

"Are you an actor yourself?"

"…Is it that obvious?"

"In a good way. I'll tell you a funny story about how the posture for that role came to me…" Richard Gains puts a manly arm around Tyler as the boys talk shop. Emily asks me who Tyler is and I tell her

I'll explain later. She shrugs it off, gazing out over the crowd, and asks me what we should do first. Before I can answer, she lists some options, but I split my attention, trying to overhear Tyler and the TV star. It's tough to make it out over Emily's enthusiastic plans and the crowd noise, but I catch bits and pieces.

"...my soon-to-be-wife-number-three is abroad," Richard Gains tells Tyler, "shooting a swimsuit calendar... what I wouldn't give to be in your shoes... the quality of tail has gone up *exponentially* since I was in high school..."

I lose them as the crowd noise ramps up and Emily gets close to my ear, talking about how we "must, must, *must* use social media in our presentation." I see Tyler shake hands goodbye with Richard Gains, who then heads off with the governor and his team: a fleet of boring middle-aged white dudes in grey and navy blue suits, plus one lone girl, in her twenties, who seems too cool for that crowd. Must be someone's daughter.

Tyler turns to me like a kid who just met Santa Claus. "Ho. Ly. Shit!"

"I know," I say, noncommittal.

"That dude is epic! D'you know he's in talks for the starring role in the next Spielberg movie? After the success of *Lincoln*, he said Spielberg wants to do another American history type film. Some William Jennings Bryant biopic?"

"William Jennings Bryan," I correct. "No 't.'"

"Right. Bryan. Who *is* that—like a founding father or some VP back in Lincoln's day?"

"Sort of," I say. "He was a politician around the turn of the century. Scopes Monkey Trial?"

"Yeah, he said something about monkeys. Maybe it'll be like *Abraham Lincoln: Vampire Hunter*—like a mash-up of old-timey history and cool shit exploding. I mean, you gotta figure with Gains and Spielberg, it can't just be like a History Channel doc. It's gotta be like *Planet of the Apes in the Old West* or something."

"One can dream," I say, but Tyler doesn't register my sarcasm. He doesn't seem to register what I say at *all*.

"Whoo! I'm so friggin stoked! Let's go kick some hurricane ass!"

As Emily, Tyler and I leave Duffy Square, I can't help but think: *maybe he's not the man of my dreams after all.*

ACT II

SOUND AND FURY

ROBERT

"Ugh," I say to Mac, "I'm so bloated after gorging on those stupid Duffy Square muffins." I'm hoping to elicit a sympathetic response or a backhanded compliment about what great shape I'm in, but he just nods absently.

Hurricane Calliope is set to make landfall in twenty-seven hours. Mac and I make our way from the governor's remarks—with surprise guest Richard Gains (boring)—down to Church Street, where the mass exodus seems to be migrating.

"And seriously," I continue, "do the people of Cawdor not know that the name 'Duffy Square' is totally ripped off the one in New York? I bet there are some 'friends of Dorothy' in this town who named it as an homage to the Great White Way."

"Friends of Dorothy?" Mac asks.

"Aren't you sweet." And then I whisper, "It means gay."

"Oh… Cool."

I glance at Mac to see if there's a flicker of fear in his eyes or some other indication that he may still have one foot in the closet… but nothing. He's as un-self-conscious as they come. A lovably naïve (and gorgeous) boy who I'm cursed to be in love with until I the day I die. Or graduate, whichever comes first.

We arrive at Church Street, a narrow two-block stretch that has, you guessed it, a church at the end. But the cobblestoned road has been transformed into a kind of street fair or a Christmas bazaar, with dozens of little stations lining the entire road. Each station has painted signs around it, tables spread with clipboards, cups filled with pens, and organizers fanning out from behind the booths, wooing potential volunteers: *Come join our pack, we're doing the most good—and having the most fun while doing it!*

I have no idea how these people got this together so quickly, but it's pretty impressive. Or maybe it's sad. Why do they have so much free time? Are they all out-of-work crackpots clinging to the first thing in months to give them a reason to get out of bed? I try not to think about it as I look around at the booth options: There's

"Sandbag Prep" (self explanatory), "When the Levee *Doesn't* Break" (re-enforcing the levees upriver), "Water Water Everywhere" (getting clean drinking water and other essential supplies to the shelters and people in low-income areas that can't evacuate... which obviously wouldn't fit on the sign), "This Old House" (boarding up windows on houses, commercial stores, and public buildings), "Pets Are People Too" (helping people and their pets evacuate), and an intriguing one called "The Low Spark of High Heeled Boys," which disappointingly turns out to be a groovy reference to some 1970s band called Traffic. Those volunteers are going to help direct traffic along the evacuation routes (shoot me now).

Mac turns to me, bright-eyed and bushy-tailed. "They all look so great. Where should we start?"

"Um. Which one do *you* like?"

"I'm kinda thinking the one with levees or the one where we board up windows. My dad's in construction, so I'm pretty good with my hands."

I bet you are. But I don't say that. Instead I scrunch up my forehead and give a curious, "Hm. I was leaning more toward the one with the pets?"

"We can do both! Start off with the houses and then take a breather with the pets. Sound good, partner?"

"...Sounds great... partner." But I'm secretly dreading the manual labor. The only screwdriver I know how to use comes with freshly squeezed OJ and Ketel One. But the upside of boarding up windows is getting to see Mac in action. Sweaty. Out of breath. Muscles bulging... Hm. Maintaining my focus might be a *skosh* more difficult than I thought. I need to keep my eye on the prize: winning that scholarship, writing a kickass personal statement, securing admission to La Sorbonne. Then it'll be, *Bonjour, la Seine. You're looking très beau in the moonlight.*

Waiting on line at the "This Old House" booth, I eavesdrop on some of the other groups around us. To our left, not really in any line, just kind of taking up space in the street, a Buddhist/drum circle/Pilates instructor-looking guy is talking animatedly to his friends about what I assume is their most excellent proposal.

"Dudes, I got it. We call it RELIEF JAM." (The others chime

in on cue: *right on; epic, bra; killer idea, Rors.*) "It'll be a benefit concert," the seeming leader of the group continues. "Ya know. For the victims."

A few more mumble words of agreement but an attractive biracial girl with green eyes and dreads asks, "Isn't that exactly what they did after Sandy? The 12.12.12 concert?"

The leader freezes, temporarily stymied. But then a small light bulb goes off behind his slightly stoned eyes and he presses on. "Totally. One hundred percent. This... is an *homage.* To all those great benefit concerts that came before us. But what makes ours unique is... this concert will not only raise *money* for the victims of the storm... it will also raise *aware*ness. To prevent future disasters like this one."

Again, most of the group nods and mumbles its approval. But this time a guy with a wispy blond beard puts down his devil sticks and balks. "Wait, Rory—I don't mean to kill the buzz, but... how can you *prevent* future hurricanes?"

Rory quickly loses his easygoing vibe, and lashes out. "By flippin' reducing your carbon footprint, Josh! And ending global warming! That's how! Like, just take two seconds to *think* before you slam someone's vision, bra!"

This group will be zero competition. Even if they manage to not be stoned the entire time, infighting will surely tear them apart. Based on my experience with the HOBY Leadership program, groups larger than three don't tend to work in these situations. (Have you *seen* Vegas Week on "American Idol?" The smaller groups *always* do better!) And these eventual-granola farmers number almost a dozen. But maybe a little gas on the flames will help crush this team for good and send them back to the Ultimate Frisbee Tournament from whence they came.

"Hey, guys," I butt in. "Pretty big group. Are you all on one team, or...?"

"Yeah," Rory says proudly. "We're the *Grateful Ten.*"

"The Grateful Ten. Okay. So you're like... also a band?"

"No, we're not a band! Jeez! Why does everyone think we're a band?"

"Sorry, it... sounds like a tribute band or something," I offer, but

Rory isn't amused.

"Tribute bands are the lowest form of entertainment. We're a co-op. A group of like-minded students from the local public school trying to make a positive impact on our community, our country, and our planet."

"Right on," I say (trying not to ooze too much sarcasm) and turn back to the This Old House booth, confident that dissension within the Grateful Ten is nigh.

"Ya know, Rors," I hear one of the uber-crunchy girls say, "it's *that* kind of attitude that makes people not want to be part of our group."

"Good!" Rory says indignantly. "We can't take newbies anyway. It'd ruin our numbers and force us to change our name."

"Unless we kick someone out," the dreadlock girl adds.

"What's *that* supposed to mean? Like seriously, do you even want to *be* in this group? Gah!"

Before I can overhear the imminent demise of the Grateful Ten, the team in front of us finishes up, making Mac and I first in line at our booth.

"Hey," a peppy Anna Kendrick-type chirps at us. "I'm Lauren Hodges. What's your name?"

"James MacKenzie. And this is Robert Clinton, III."

I have no idea why we're giving such formal introductions, but I roll with it and give a polite nod.

"You guys wanna board up some windows with us? It's *super* fun!"

"I'm *super* excited," I say ironically.

"Me too!" Mac says, without the slightest bit of irony. "This is awesome!"

When he high fives Lauren, I know I'm in for a fabulous day.

§

"Robert, hand me that box of nails, would ya?" Mac hasn't stopped smiling since we started working two hours ago. We're in a decaying neighborhood across from a sad little strip mall that looks as if no one has shopped there since before anyone had heard of Kim

Kardashian. (Oh, how I wish we *still* hadn't heard of her!) We've been going from house to house boarding up windows, though I honestly think half these homes are unoccupied or abandoned. But who am I to question the wisdom of a booth organized by over-zealous teenage volunteers?

Instead of handing Mac the box of nails, I sit down on the porch steps and say, "We've been working pretty hard, Mac. Maybe we could take a little break?"

"Good idea," he says. "A rested worker is a productive worker."

When did he turn into Kenneth from *30 Rock*? It doesn't matter. I'm just happy he stopped pounding away on those nails. We've hardly talked at all this morning except about the task at hand. I was hoping for more gossip or insight into his backstory. But so far it's just been, "Can you hand me that hammer" or "Does this board look straight?"

I grab two cold bottles of water out of a nearby cooler and hand one to Mac. "Maybe," I suggest, "we can talk about our proposal for the governor."

"Yeah. Totally!" He grabs a seat on the stair above me, holding the perspiring water against his forehead and neck. "What were you thinking?"

"Well, I kind of thought with *my* engineering skills and aesthetic design sense, along with *your* nuts and bolts knowledge from working at your dad's construction company—we could design a mockup of, like, low-income sustainable green housing? Sort of piggybacking on what Brad Pitt is doing in NOLA. From rooftop solar panels, to energy efficient appliances, the houses could replace storm-ravaged coastal homes or take the place of already dilapidated homes in the area. I mean, just witness these creaking eyesores from the 1940s, right?" I pinch a bit of peeling paint off one of the crumbling porch columns as evidence. "We'd not only make stronger, longer lasting structures that can literally weather the next storm, but homes that have a smaller impact on the environment and give their owners a sense of pride and importance. We could make something practical that's *also* an architectural breakthrough."

"Whoa," Mac says, a little awestruck. "Sounds like you've been thinking about this for a while."

"A little," I say modestly. "But just, you know, while we were working here this morning. The idea kind of… came to me. Do you like it?"

"*Like* it? It's friggin' awesome! We're totally gonna win. Man! I knew it was a good call getting out of the car!"

I lock eyes with Mac, who sort of betrays his naiveté for a moment. As I suspected, his motives for volunteering were not completely selfless. But I don't let him know that I'm 'wise to his game.' I just pretend like I didn't hear that part.

"Cool. Glad you like it. Maybe we can sketch out some designs or…"

"Slackin' on the job as usual, eh, Trip?"

I turn to see Emily Kim clacking down the sidewalk toward us. She's wearing that 'power shirt' with the aggressive collar she wore like every single day at HOBY. (Did she have it dry cleaned at the hotel every night?) It's her version of Tiger's red shirt on Championship Sunday. (And yes I know that Tiger Woods wears red on Sunday! I haven't been living under a rock the past seventeen years. Besides, as an African-American man, no matter what your political leanings, sport preferences, or taste in music, you are required to know the basics about Barack Obama, Tiger Woods, and Jay-Z. It's like the Trinity for black boys growing up in America.)

"Hey, E.K. What's the haps?" She hates being called E.K. almost as much as I hate being called Trip (as in 'Triple,' as in Robert Clinton the *third*).

"You know," Emily says, "saving lives, making a difference. A day in the life."

"Tell me about it," I say wiping my brow dramatically. "This is like our fifth house of the day. We must have boarded up fifty windows by now."

"Nice," Emily says looking around aimlessly. "Rani and I boarded up about seventy-five. So we're gonna bounce. Our services will be much more valuable at the levees, anyway. That's where the *real* work needs to be done."

"You sure it's not because your little hands are too delicate for this work?"

"No, but thanks for your concern."

"Wow," Mac says, impressed. "You guys are going to the levees? Let us know how it goes!"

Emily turns to Mac, almost offended that he dared speak to her without being spoken to. "Um. Why?" she says flatly.

"Oh, uh, I don't know..." Mac fumbles, thrown by Emily's directness. "I just... hope it goes okay, ya know. Like, whatever needs to get done, uh... gets done? So there's no flood or anything tomorrow?"

"Yeah, sure, we'll keep you posted. See ya 'round, boys."

"Yeah—back at the B&B."

Emily stops. "What do you mean?"

"Well," I say coyly, "Mac flagged Robert Gains down after his remarks this morning and he's personally invited us to stay at his B&B, too. I know there's a limited amount of space, but Mr. Gains assured us we'd have one of the 'best rooms at the inn.'"

"Fantastic," Emily spits out, barely hiding her contempt. "See you there."

As she clacks away, the Indian girl who's with her gives us a half-smile/half-wave, a gesture that's equal parts courtesy and apology for her rude-ass friend.

Once the coast is clear, Mac asks, "Who is that scary Japanese chick?"

"First of all, she's Korean-American. If you ever call her Japanese or Chinese or... Taiwanese, she'll rip your freaking head off. Second of all. That. Is Emily Kim. My natural-born 'frienemy.'"

I go on to tell Mac all about my time at HOBY—the four-day leadership program for promising sophomores around the country—and how Emily and I were placed in the same six-person mini-group and bonded about our tyrannical parents who made us the overachievers we are today. By the water cooler on a ten-minute break, she confessed that she hated her mom for being so hard on her but felt sorry for the losers in her school (and our mini-group) who had no direction or focus. We became instant friends. We both loved The Cure and fashion and bitching about stupid people. By the third day, however, our friendship turned competitive when we learned that just *one* student was going to be selected to give a speech on the final day. It wasn't a real award or prize or anything. Just an honor.

And something extra to put on the college application. But Emily and I still wanted it badly. And though we remained friendly for the rest of the weekend, there was an unspoken distrust. A fear that the other was one step ahead, one step closer to the success we both craved. And we coveted something neither of us had, yet viciously suspected the other was hiding: a leg up, an "in."

But a girl from Yeshiva K'tana of Waterbury, a school with a grand total of EIGHT students in the tenth grade, this little *maideleh* Gabby Freidman (complete with a glass eye), was selected to give the closing student remarks. And we were all *"really happy for her."*

"Since then," I tell Mac, "Emily and I run into each other here and there. And it started out friendly—at least *surface*-friendly. But near the end of junior year, like right after we got our first SAT scores, Emily stopped trying to even hide her contempt. Now she just straight-up loathes me. Hence, my natural-born frienemy. And I'm sure it's killing her—*killing* her—that I'm here. I totally saw the look on her face when she spotted us last night. That, *I thought I was the only one who'd think to volunteer for the hurricane relief effort* face. Well, newsflash, E.K. You got some compet-ish. And you. Are goin' down!"

I get kind of swept away during the last part of my rant. When I look down at Mac he seems frightened and impressed at the same time. Might not be a bad thing.

"Cool," he says. I can't tell if he's really laid back, really stupid, or some kind of evil genius using us all to his advantage. "Better get back to work before the rain starts. Weather-dot-com says we might get showers as early as this afternoon."

"Psh!"

The mocking voice comes from behind the tall hedges in the side yard. Mac and I turn to see a skinny Latino boy with thick rim glasses emerge from around the corner. He's wearing an "OBEY" T-shirt with pegged jeans and suspenders, along with an iPad that's tied into some contraption around his neck allowing him to be hands-free. So while he's typing with one hand, he's finishing off a 5-hour ENERGY shot with the other. "Weather-dot-com," he says authoritatively, "is the MySpace of meteorology. It's for grandmas and morons."

"So it's *not* going to start raining this afternoon?" Mac asks innocently.

"It's barely going to rain *tomorrow* when said 'hurricane' reportedly makes landfall."

"Wait," I interrupt. "Are you saying there's not even gonna be a hurricane?"

"Not here. Lady C's gonna miss to the east by over a hundred miles. Hardly hit land at *all.* I mean, don't even take into account the indicators I'm picking up—or the European models that say the high pressure coming in from Canada might push her offline—or the *Clipper* model which says she'll get shoved out to *sea.* The only storms that do any *real* damage have *real* names. Names people actually *go* by. Andrew, Katrina, Sandy. Those babies packed a punch. But who the frack is named Calliope? Sounds like a saggy Greek stripper. Unh-unh. No one goes by that name anymore. Means this storm will be DOA."

"We're not gonna get hit at all?" Mac asks.

"Enh, we'll get some wind, *maybe* some rain. But more like a wimpy thunderstorm. Nowhere near the Cat 3 they're predicting."

"But all the forecast models—"

"Are wrong. Those things are so outdated, we're lucky to know when *sun*rise is gonna be each day. The way to predict the weather isn't about *guessing.* It's about *knowing.*" He gestures to the iPad strapped around his neck. "Exhibit A."

"What, like social media—with Twitter and Facebook?" I ask.

"Sure," the mini-hipster replies smugly, "if I want to know what's up in 2007. I'm talkin' about Reddit, Banjo, Forecast, Path, and Sonar. Cutting edge apps that my generation actually *uses.* And with this kind of reach, I can track every weather event in the world. From real people, in real time. I know when it's raining in North Carolina or hailing on Long Island. Or 89 and sunny in Cawdor, C-T," he says gesturing to our very un-ominous weather.

"Can't meteorologists do that too?" I offer.

"They have at *least* a one-minute delay, if not ninety seconds, because of all the radio frequency interference—not to mention the solar interference the geostationary satellites encounter daily. But I know second-by-second what's going on because hundreds of people are constantly tweeting and updating their Facebook statuses. I'm not relying on one signal. I've got multiple confirmations simul*tan*eously. I've been the most accurate weather forecaster in this part of the state for the last twenty-one months. And I'm only fifteen. All right, Gordo, on my way."

"What? Who's Gordo?" I ask.

"Sorry," the kid says. "I was talk-texting with my glasses."

"No way!" Mac stands, excited. "Are those Google Glasses?"

"Just a prototype," the kid says casually. "Got a buddy who worked with Sergey out on the left coast." He lifts off the glasses for Mac, who accepts them gingerly, like he's holding a bird with a clipped wing.

"What are Google glasses?" I ask, already afraid of the answer.

"Augmented reality eyewear," Mac gushes, inspecting them closely. "Do these have the virtual retinal display?"

"Yeah—takes a while to get used to. And they're still working out the kinks. But in five years, those babies'll be more popular than cell phones."

"These are totally badass," Mac says.

"I know." The kid takes the glasses, blows a bit of unseen dust off a lens, and delicately puts them back on.

"I'm James MacKenzie, by the way. People call me Mac. And this is my friend Robert."

Not that it means anything, but I note that when introducing me this time, Mac called me *his friend*.

"Gentlemen," the new guy says, formally shaking our hands. "Duncan Rodriguez. Amateur weather enthusiast and Twitter sensation."

"Really. A *sensation*?" I ask, dubious.

"I've got over 200,000 followers."

"Whoa! Two-hundred *thousand*?" Mac blurts. "That's impressive."

"It's ample," Duncan says, looking around for more interesting people to brag to. "I'm certainly on my way."

"So... you want to be a famous weatherman or something?" I ask.

"Nah. I just want to be *famous*. I don't care what *for*. Tracking weather was something that happened kind of by accident. I consider myself a renaissance man of the twenty-first century. A techno-philosopher. Part Timothy Leary, part Neo from the *Matrix* trilogy, and part Javier Bardem—not so much who he is as a *person*, but more his onscreen persona and general badass-ness. I'm like a curator of inspiration, ya know. Gave a TedX talk last month down in Costa Rica about counterculture technology. I post stream-of-conscious video blogs about the ever-changing landscape of scientific advancement. No long-term game plan. I do what I feel like, ya know, let it take me where it takes me. Long as it gets me famous." His iPhone 6 buzzes and chirps. Duncan takes a peek at the screen. "Uhp. My shit's blowing up on the Inter-webs. Gotta bolt. Later haters."

And quickly as he appeared, he's gone. After a moment, Mac busts out laughing. "Who was *that*?"

I watch Duncan walking away, a phone to his ear in one hand while he types on the iPad around his neck with the other. "That," I say to Mac, "is the next generation."

EMILY

"I can't *believe* that stupid Robert."

Rani and I are just outside of town at the Lennox River levee. We're taking turns filling sandbags (I shovel, she holds the bag open; she shovels, I hold the bag open). I was kind of hoping to drive the machinery, but apparently you need a special license to operate this kind of equipment, so we're relegated to the real grunt work.

A dozen volunteers are here at our "station." After we load each twenty-five pound bag with sand, we stack it on a big pile. Then a guy on a mini-bulldozer looking thing (someone called it a "skid steer" but that sounds made up... and gross) comes by every fifteen minutes and moves a bunch of our bags further upriver to reinforce the levee. Rani and I have been here for two hours, since lunch, and have only finished a dozen bags. This is harder than I thought. But I don't let on that it's getting to me. I keep talking about stupid things to distract me from the backaches and the blisters and the heat.

"How'd that little snot talk his way into Richard's B&B? Once again, *my* thing... becomes *everyone's* thing. I'm so sick of it."

"Let's take a break," Rani suggests, and I readily agree. I drop my shovel where I'm standing and we move into the shade by a big Gatorade cooler filled with ice water, where we gulp mightily on the godly nectar of H_2O. After three triangle paper cups each, Rani says, "We should probably have a plan for tomorrow morning's presentation, right?"

"Oh!" I say, trying to catch my breath after drinking so fast. "I can't believe I didn't tell you yet. I've totally got the best idea ever. It came to me last night in the shower. A 'Loan Your Guesthouse' social networking site."

"Sounds promising," Rani says. "What is it, exactly?"

"So—remember that thing I was showing you on the drive up, about how after Hurricane Sandy, Facebook got rid of the middleman and made giving directly to needy families so much easier? Like someone would post, 'My sister-in-law in Red Hook needs food and baby clothes for her nine month old,' and then dozens of people would share that status until someone in the area with food and baby clothes to give saw it and replied, 'I can do that!' then drove the supplies right to the person in need?"

"It's okay to breathe once in a while when you talk," Rani says, patting my arm.

"I know. I'm just super excited about this. Okay. So our idea would piggyback on that concept. People with guesthouses in non-flooded areas can log onto a secure website—which we'll create, like, a beta version of for tomorrow, maybe, if we have time—and they can post the details: location of their guesthouse, number of bedrooms, bathrooms, whether or not meals with their family will be provided, whatever. Then those locations are matched to families in need of temporary housing. And this doesn't have to end with Calliope. We can develop a free app version for the charity-minded Connecticuter-on-the-go, and any family in need can be linked up to families with spare bedrooms, spare clothes, or extra furniture. Instead of just giving randomly to Goodwill or the Red Cross, you're helping out your fellow neighbors and residents of the Nutmeg State. Whaddaya think?"

"I like it. What's it called? The site."

"I don't know. I thought Loan Your Guesthouse-dot-com."

"Mm. We need something flashier," Rani says, standing up and pacing. This is what I hoped would happen, that Rani's long-dormant creative and competitive juices would start flowing. Together we'll be unstoppable. "Something with pop culture appeal that still stands on its own and represents what we're offering."

"Crash On My Couch-dot-com?" I suggest.

"No," Rani says, "not quite. Let's think: We've got rich people with an extra room… who want to give of themselves. Want to give back. Want someone to benefit from what they have. And feel good about helping others. So what do they have to give?"

"A guesthouse?"

"Right. They have a spare bed, a spare room. An empty room. For people in need."

"That's good."

"It's close. Uh… Oh, I got it. *Friday Night Lights*!"

"That name's already taken, Ran."

"No, like what Coach Taylor says. 'Clear eyes, full hearts...?' But we change it... *Empty Rooms, Full Hearts.* Boom!"

"Holy shitballs, you're a friggin' genius."

"Enh. Beginners luck."

"No, I'm serious, Rani. That was like some Don Draper Jedi-mind shit. You should go into advertising or marketing or something."

"...Maybe."

Rani takes another sip of water and sits, lost in thought again. Any competitive instincts that almost woke up seem to have left the building. She's been different this whole trip. More reserved and distant. I can't quite put my finger on what's changed. But I'm not one to sit around and hypothesize. I like to get down to it.

"You okay?" I ask, easing in.

"Yeah," she says. "Kinda tired. Shoveling dirt is no joke."

"Right? But, I don't know. You seem more than just... tired."

"What do you mean?"

"I don't know. Like, kind of... distant. Like you don't want to be here?"

"I want to be here."

"Really?"

"Of course. We're best friends."

"Yeah, but... you shouldn't be doing this for *me*. Cuz you're my *friend*. You should be doing this because you *want* to. Because you want to help out or... write a killer essay or meet new people or... meet new *guys*."

"Whoa. Meet new *guys*? What does *that* mean?"

"Exactly what it sounds like. Who was that guy that geeked out on Richard Gains earlier? He seemed to know *you* pretty well."

"Not at all. We *just* met."

"When?"

"Excuse me?"

"*When* did you meet him? I've been with you like every second of this trip. And that was the first time I laid eyes on him."

"What is this, the friggin' Inquisition?"

"I'm just trying to figure out the deal with this guy that's suddenly in your life. Or maybe you've known him for a long time. A secret boyfriend or something—"

"That's the most ridiculous thing I've ever—"

"It would make more sense than what I used to think."

"Which is…?"

"That maybe you're a lesbian."

Rani sort of chokes on air and can't even speak. But I press on, unsure where this tirade is coming from. Lack of sleep and raging hormones, maybe? (I got my stupid period last night—it's why I bolted into the shower once we got to our room.) But no matter what my motivation or emotional reasoning behind this line of questioning, I blindly press on anyway.

"Think about it, Ran. You never really liked *any* of the guys from Saint G's."

"Because Saint Geoffrey's is nothing but tools and douchebags."

"Granted. But you could at least hook up with a tool once in a while. Or use one of the DB's as, like, arm candy for the spring formal. But nothing. The closest thing was that double date with me and the Grover twins last summer."

"Exactly. Who would want to date any of those guys from that dorky school when their idea of dinner and a movie was the Crusty Knot's all-you-can-eat-pizza bar and *Thor*?!"

"You're not answering my questions."

"That's because I don't know what they *are*."

"*When* did you meet that guy and *are* you a lesbian?!"

"Is *who* a lesbian?"

I turn to see the governor's chief of staff, Teddy Hutchins, about twenty yards away near the side of the road, two black stretch town cars silently idling behind him. He's waving as he walks toward us along the muddy path marked by loose hay.

"I'm just kidding," he says once he's closer. "Wondering if you ladies wouldn't mind posing for a photograph with the governor."

"Uh, yeah, sure," I say, with a little shrug toward Rani. She nods at Mr. Hutchins who says, "Great!" and then turns and waves back toward the road. The governor, a photographer, and three other people hop out of the town cars. Teddy takes a few steps back toward the road to meet them halfway, and I pull Rani close. "That's Teddy Hutchins. You gotta introduce yourself."

"I'm not telling him who my dad is."

"Why *not*?"

"I told you yesterday. It's dorky and lame."

"What's the point of doing *any* of this if not to make connections and get ahead?"

"Shh."

Governor Watson and his mini-entourage are here. The photographer asks Rani and me to hold a shovel and a sandbag while he instructs the governor to circle behind us and stand in the middle. This is so surreal.

"Thank you, girls, for all your hard work," the governor says to us, offering his hand. "Charles Watson."

"Emily Kim," I say, giving him a firm handshake. "We sort of spoke the other night."

"Oh yes—the young lady who made all this happen," he says, breaking into a very charming smile. "Teddy, did you know this was the young lady from the press conference?"

"Right, of course," Mr. Hutchins says. "Exactly what we were thinking too."

Is he serious? He had no *idea* who I was when he first came over. Whatever. A photo with the governor of Connecticut isn't exactly Brad-Pitt-in-NOLA territory, but it'll look good in a college application. (And it will totally drive the Fairwich Academy girls bananas when I post it on Facebook!)

"Forgive me," the governor says offering a hand to Rani. "Very nice meeting you, too, young lady."

"Thank you, Governor. Rani Caldwell." She gives Teddy Hutchins a furtive glance, perhaps hoping he'll recognize her last name, but he's talking intensely to the photographer and I'm sure he doesn't hear her at all. I look at her and mouth the words, *tell them who your father is,* but Rani shakes me off.

"Okay everyone eyes on me here we go please," the photographer shouts rapidly without a breath. "In three two one perfect. One more annnnd… Got it very nice moving on thank you girls."

And before we know it, Hutchins and his crew are walking back to their cars. But the governor sort of hovers, not wanting to be completely rude. "So. How's everything going? You ladies enjoying yourselves?"

"Oh, yeah, it's great," I lie. "Loads of fun."

"Well," he says, nodding at nothing, "we're looking forward to hearing your proposal tomorrow. I'm sure it'll be fantastic." He gives me a reassuring/condescending pat on the shoulder and turns to go.

"Thank you, sir," I say as they all make their way back to the road. But the only female in the entourage stops (a sort of younger and shorter Amanda Peet). And she's totally staring at Rani. Just when it gets awkward, I turn to Rani and ask, without moving my lips, "Um. Why is that hot girl staring at you?"

"Maybe she thinks I'm a lesbian," Rani mutters.

"Well, we're about to find out, here she comes."

Mini-Peet says a quick word to Mr. Hutchins and then trots over to us.

"Hey," she says, her voice a little raspy, "sorry, this might be totally out of left field—and now as I'm running it in my head, maybe a touch racist, but—are you by any chance related to *Morgan* Caldwell?"

"Yeah," Rani says, surprised, "that's my sister."

The girl looks relieved, "Okay, cool. So I'm not racial profiling, I swear. I was Morgan's RA. At Princeton? And you look *so* much like her and then when you said your last name, I thought…"

"Not a lot of brown girls named Caldwell?" I finish.

Mini-Peet isn't sure if I'm being funny or not, but once Rani laughs, she does too.

"Right, right," she says to me. "Good one. *Any*way. I'm A.J. A.J. Gould. I should get back, but please say 'hi' to Morgan for me when you see her, okay?"

"Might be a while," Rani says. "She's in South Africa on her Fulbright."

"Oh, wow," A.J. gushes. "Good for her! I knew she'd do well no matter *what* she ended up doing. Always so smart and driven."

Rani doesn't respond, just jabs at the dirt absently with her shovel.

"And by the way," A.J. says, unfazed, touching my arm in a slightly too familiar way, "I *loved* what you said at the press conference last night. Exactly what the governor needed—a good swift kick in the pants." She laughs a throaty laugh and I smile awkwardly. "Okay.

Thanks, you guys. Hope to see you later."

She hustles back to the governor's car as quickly as the muddy path will allow while Rani and I stand there, befuddled.

"So… *that* happened."

"Let's win this thing," Rani declares.

"What?"

"Fuck Morgan and her overachieving Fulbright ass. I'm just as driven as she is. And smarter, too."

"Yeah, you are," I say, stoking the fire. "*Way* smarter."

"And you were right. I *was* sort of distracted and… not really into this and phoning it in. But now I'm ready. You and me? We're gonna crush this hurricane."

That's the Rani I know and love. But I don't say that because it would be super weird. Instead I say, "Damn right, we're gonna crush it." We smile and look at the dirt pile behind us, not really wanting to get back to work.

"And hey," I say, trying to clear the air, "sorry for being so chafey and saying you might be a lesbian." I instantly realize that was equally weird, but Rani lets it slide.

"Yeah, that was unexpected."

"I know… I'm *tired*. And that *lunch* was super lame."

"*Ser*iously lame, I mean I know we're here voluntarily but can't they spring for some decent eats?"

"Totally." We're both laughing as we get back to work, things quickly returning to normal. Rani holds open a sand bag and I grab the shovel. After five digs in silence, though, I can't help myself.

"But seriously—how do you know that guy?"

"Ugh! Can we not talk about him? Please?"

"Yeah, sure, whatever."

Clearly I've touched a nerve, so I let it go. For now.

§

We work for another twenty minutes, hardly talking except about the task at hand. And I actually like it! It's soothing and therapeutic in a strange way. Nothing but the immediate and achievable goal of getting dirt in a bag. Beautiful in its simplicity. Elegant in its purpose. No extraneous thoughts. Just the sounds of metal into dirt and dirt into a bag. The sky has mercifully stayed overcast and the breeze begins to pick up (a sign of the impending storm, I suppose), breaking the sweltering heat and making the manual labor almost fun—when it's rudely interrupted.

"You know," a boy says over my shoulder, "if you lean the bags against each other, they can act as anchors and you can fill four at a time."

Of course. It's that impossibly blonde farmer kid and his "maybe sister/maybe girlfriend/maybe both" telling us how best to dig dirt. And the girl (who looks like a mouse holding in a fart) has a smug-ass grin on her face, as if they've just shared the key to eternal happiness.

"We like doing it this way," I say, already irked. "It's nice to work as a team."

"Oh, we agree, sister" the girl says. "We mean no disrespect. We were just trying to increase your productivity."

"Uh-hunh," I say, convinced they're up to something. No one offers free advice to fellow competitors without an ulterior motive.

"Forgive our rudeness," the boy says. "We are Elijah and Prayer Jones. From Seyton up in Windham County."

I'm momentarily speechless. The boy (who I'm really seeing for the first time) smells like fresh-cut grass, and looks like Zac Efron with piercing green eyes.

"Hey," Rani says, coming to my rescue. "Rani Caldwell. And this is Emily Kim."

"*The* Emily Kim?" the girl asks. "From Stanford?"

"Ew," I blurt out. "No, that girl's like in her *twenties*. Do I look that old to you?"

"Forgive us once again," says Elijah. "I'm sure my sister was just excited. Emily Kim is a name spoken with much reverence on our farm. What she did after Hurricane Katrina was… an inspiration to us all."

"Yeah, whatever," I say, jabbing the shovel hard into the pile of dirt. I'm totally over his dreamy eyes and back to despising him as much as the girl. I mean, *Prayer?* Seriously, what kind of a name is that?

"So," Rani says, attempting to smooth things over, "are you guys working on the levees too?"

"Oh, no, sister," Prayer replies with an equal mix of disdain and earnestness. (And okay, for real now, what is with them calling us '*sister*?' Is this the 1600s? Are we all Pilgrims?) "We are simply observing the proceedings. And going where the Lord guides us."

"I think, Prayer," her brother offers, "that they are asking if we are here for the governor's scholarship. And no, we are not. We are simply here to help our fellow man. However the Lord sees fit."

"You're not here for the competition?" I ask.

"No," Elijah says, his eyes as serene as Fiji's coastal waters. "My sister had a vision of a terrible storm and said we must travel to Cawdor right away."

"Wow," I deadpan. "A vision of a storm. Was she watching the Weather Channel at the time?"

"We don't have a television," Prayer adds, rather snidely.

"Is that a fact?"

"Yes," Elijah says. "And after her vision, Prayer was certain the Lord wanted us to come here. To help prevent a disaster."

"And how do you plan on doing that?"

"We're not at liberty to say," Prayer answers. "But our Savior will tell us when the time is right."

"Is that code for: you have no plan?"

"I'm not sure we follow you?" Elijah asks innocently.

Rani steps in, "Well, I think it's great you're both here helping out. Every pair of hands counts."

"Thank you, sisters," Prayer says with a smirk. "Now if you'll excuse us, we have some matters that need attending to."

"It was a pleasure meeting you both," Elijah says, but he's mostly looking at me. "We hope to see you again soon."

Then the Jones twins amble off toward the main road and begin to *walk* back toward town.

"Is this a joke?" Rani says. "What's with all the strange encounters today?"

"Those two were creepy," I say, watching them leisurely stroll along the single-lane highway. "And totally full of shit."

"Creepy, yes. Full of shit, though? Really?"

"Not here for the scholarship? Come on. Total BS."

"*We* weren't here for the scholarship."

"We *invented* the scholarship! It wouldn't exist without us."

"That guy Robert was here before the contest."

"I mean everyone that came *after* us! Why else would they be here?"

"To help their fellow man?"

"Oh, please. Those farmer geeks are up to something—trying to get credit for volunteering when they're *really* back on their farm knitting their own jeans and chicken-whispering."

"What?" Rani says laughing.

"I heard some of the other kids talking at lunch. They say the boy, Elijah? He's like known around this part of the state for his mystical livestock healing powers. They call him the chicken whisperer."

"*That* has urban legend written all over it."

"Come on. They're totally hiding something!"

"They're just flakey. A little *off* or whatever. Like *almost* Amish."

"Almost Amish? That's not a *thing!*"

"I know it's not a *thing*, Emily. I just mean—they seem nice enough. Just kind of… dorky."

"Mm. I'm gonna find out what they're up to."

"Why are you obsessing about them?"

"I'm not *obsessing*."

"Then why do you care so much about them? There are hundreds of other kids here competing for that scholarship."

"Don't you want to win?"

"Yeah, of course."

"So. Keep your friends close and your enemies closer."

"…Maybe you just *like* him?"

"What? Ew. Gross. No way! Bleh."

"The lady doth protest too much, methinks."

"Thanks, Hamlet. But I don't like him."

"Gertrude said that line."

"Whatever! I'm not protesting too much, Rani. I just think he's *weird*. They're *both* weird. And I'm gonna figure out what their secret plan is so we can stop *it*, crush *them*, and *win* that scholarship ourselves."

"…Whatever you say," Rani smiles, I think not quite believing me.

I'd keep arguing but I don't want to "protest too much." And come on, seriously? How could I 'like' Farmer Ted or... whatever his name is? See? I've already forgotten his *name!* Plus—I'm Emily-fucking-Kim. I've achieved Olympic-level skills as the crew team's coxswain and finished my first sprint triathlon last year in 1 hour, 23 minutes. Farmer Geek back there makes his own *soap*! I mean, what a total loser! There is no way I would ever be caught dead in the same *room* with that guy if I could help it.

But I don't say anything more to Rani. I play it cool. We shovel dirt into bags like good little volunteers. Then Rani slides a few bags next to each other, pouring a bit of sand into the bottom of each. She opens all four bags so the corners touch each other. I shovel once, and the dirt magically goes into all four at the same time—just like the Amish boy wonder said. Rani looks up at me, grinning with her eyes.

"Pretty smart for a farmer," she says.

"Shut up."

A. J.

"News 4 did a snap poll this morning," Teddy announces in the car. "We've got a seventy-three percent approval rating—the highest since you were *elected*."

"Imagine how high it will be once the storm hits," the governor says flatly with a wry glance toward me.

"Exactly!" Teddy exclaims. "Calliope's on schedule to make landfall at noon tomorrow. That's less than twenty hours, and the prognosis is still Category 3 with severe wind and flood damage to low-lying coastal areas, Cawdor being right at the center of that, so your numbers are bound to..." Governor Watson turns to Teddy and gives him a scathing look. "Oh. You were being sarcastic."

"I knew you'd get there eventually," the governor mutters.

Teddy sort of huffs through his nose and flips through his phone log looking for the next number to call. The governor sips on a bottle of water while I tap my fingers on my knees like a nervous kid who's been called to the principal's office. We're driving to the various volunteer stations for more photo ops like the one we just got with Morgan's sister, Rani, and Emily Kim. For some reason, I was selected to ride in the car with Teddy and the governor while the others ride in the follow-car. I assume it's because this whole contest thing was (sort of) my idea, but I haven't been asked to do anything specific. No one sat me down and said, "This is your job, this is what's expected of you, this is your first project, these are the deadlines you need to hit." I'm in uncharted waters. And I feel like the job interview is still happening. Like maybe the next few days are my tryout.

Sitting across from the governor and his chief of staff in a stretch town car, I attempt to act cool and give the appearance of relaxed casual: the personification of broken-in jeans. But inside my stomach is churning and my heart is racing like I just ran a 5K.

Since the photo with Rani and Emily, the governor has hit the bottled water station, found a few kids boarding up windows, and made a long stop at the pet rescue area. (Teddy was positive the governor and a puppy would make the front page tomorrow.) But no matter where we stop, it's all basically the same: We get out, talk to a few key people, shake hands with some teenage volunteers, the governor smiles for some photos while holding a shovel or a hammer or a puppy, and then we hop back in the car and drive off to the next station. In the back seat, Teddy and the governor are rolling phone calls. While the governor talks on one phone, Teddy makes a call on the other. From what I can piece together, the calls are from various news organizations looking for sound bites and FEMA reps assuring the governor they have a plan in place and are ready to move once the storm rolls through. The second Governor Watson finishes one call, Teddy hands him the other phone, whispering the caller's name. It's all very calculated and political. And obviously working the way Teddy intended, because he seems even more giddy than usual.

The governor, however, seems increasingly grumpy. And it's starting to irk Teddy, who, during a brief lull between rolling calls, mutters, "I don't see what's so wrong with capitalizing on the cards you're dealt."

"We're not *capitalizing*," Governor Watson bites. "We're taking *advantage*."

"To-may-to, to-mah-to."

"It smacks of insincerity."

"*Politics* is insincere. That's the game, Chuck. Whoever can sound and seem the most sincere *wins*. I mean, back me up on this, A.J.—isn't that *why* we're holding this contest?"

I open my mouth to respond, but the governor jumps in. "Why can't we just *be* sincere? Do something because it's the *right thing to do*. Does it always have to have some sort of *upside* politically?"

"Yes! It does!"

The governor waves him off and looks out at the passing scenery. Teddy shakes his head, gives me a "don't worry, he's fine" look, and then buries himself in his BlackBerry. I turn to gaze out the same window as the governor and see for the first time how beautiful it is here, even in the middle of August, with temperatures climbing into the 90s and humidity at nearly a hundred percent. The character on the residents' faces. The weathered houses that look like a Norman Rockwell painting.

As if he can read my mind, Governor Watson says, "I love this place."

It seems like he wants someone to respond, but Teddy either didn't hear, is too engrossed in his email, or is choosing to ignore him. After a moment, I offer a timid, "Oh, yeah?"

"Mm," Governor Watson affirms, eyes still on the passing trees and houses. "This whole area. New London County. Porter Sound. My great-uncle lived here. His entire life before he died three years ago. Worked on a lobster boat, so he always smelled like fish." He grins at the memory. "No matter how much he bathed or washed in lemon juice. It's like it was… in his blood."

"Right," I say with a soft smile.

"He busted his ass, over fifty years. Never complained. Loved his job, his life, his family. But most of all… he loved this place. Connecticut. His home state. His hometown. The friends and neighbors he met here. And loved here." He points out the window at some people helping a family load their belongings into a pickup. "I want to help them, Alexis. The people that live here. I want to make sure they're safe and have clean water and their homes are protected and the levees stay strong and that we prevent as much damage as possible before the storm, and then clean up and fix whatever we can't control. *That's* what I want to do. That's *all* I want to do."

Wow. That's the Governor Watson I remember voting for. His passion and desire to help are so real and sincere. No wonder he's the next great hope for the Democratic Party. I look across at Teddy, whose eyes are watering like he's about to cry. He turns to the governor. "Jesus, Chuck. I wish you'd said this sooner."

"I know," Governor Watson sighs. "But it's not too late to change what we're—"

"No, I mean—I wish I'd had that for your *speech* earlier today. *Dammit!* That shit was beautiful. And talk about sin*cere*. Why wasn't I re*cord*ing that?! A.J., did you get any of that? Oh, oh! Say it again. There's a… voice recording thingy in here somewhere…"

"God, were you even *listening* to a word I said?"

"Yes!" Teddy replies, digging into his various bags. "All of them. And they were brilliant. It's *exactly* what you need to say at the 4 o'clock press conference."

The Governor sighs at me and then lifts his head slightly to call out to the driver. "Can you stop the car, please?"

"What…" Teddy lifts his face up out of his bag. "Oh, come on, Chucky…"

"Hank. Can you pull over?"

"Now, sir?" Hank asks.

"Yes, please. Thank you."

"Hey, what're you doin'?" Teddy pleads. "Don't be like this."

"Anywhere along here is fine," Governor Watson tells Hank, who eases onto the shoulder. The governor hops out before the car comes to a full stop. Doesn't even close the door behind him, either, just starts walking back toward our last stop. The follow-car pulls over in front of us, stopping about forty yards north. Teddy looks at me, momentarily hopeless.

"When's he gonna learn having a conscience in this line of work is counterproductive?"

He scoots out after the governor. I stay put, keeping the door open so I can hear, and turn to the driver. "Does this happen a lot?"

"Couple times a week," Hank says, already bored, reading a newspaper. "Gov thinks he's selling out. Hutch talks him off the ledge. He'll be fine after he gets some food in him." Hank flips the page and starts looking at a Sudoku puzzle, which is already half-penciled in. I turn toward the back windshield to watch the ledge-talking.

"This is normal, Chucky," I hear Teddy say. The two men are standing in the unmowed grass along the side of the road. "Totally normal."

"What—hating my chief of staff?"

"You're just stressed." The governor turns away as if he doesn't want to hear anymore. "You know what you need to do," Teddy continues. "Need to blow off some *steam.*"

The governor shakes his head. "I don't know. Maybe."

"Come on. You know *any* kind of change freaks people out. Up until now, you've been coasting on charm and broad appeal—"

"I thought you were trying to make me feel *better.*"

"And that works fine," Teddy presses on, "at the local level, even the state level. But this is a big honkin' country, Chuck. And in case you haven't noticed, it's pretty divided. Lot of red out there that hates anyone or anything from the Northeast."

"So I'm just supposed to pander, is that it?" The governor walks back to the town car and slides his butt up on the trunk to sit down, his back to me now.

And for some reason, I take that as a cue to add my two cents.

"Excuse me, Governor," I say, stepping out of the car and standing by the trunk, "but if I may... I think you should forget about big picture national election stuff right now. Focusing on how to help the residents of Connecticut during a natural disaster *is* the right thing to do. You've mobilized over a *thousand* people in this part of the state, more than a hundred of them eighteen years old and younger. What they're doing is amazing!"

But Governor Watson won't even look at me. Just casts his eyes to the tree line across the road. Teddy seems stymied as well, but I ignore them and continue to make my pitch.

"I think if you just stay on this path for the next day or two, keep *doing* the right thing? The word will get out among the voters that you need—the young voters, Hispanic voters, women. They *don't* want you to pander. They just want to trust that you'll always do what's best for the people. *All* of the people. Including them. And *that's* how you win votes."

A lone eighteen-wheeler roars by, momentarily blowing the men's ties and my hair into our faces. Then the road is quiet again. The governor looks at Teddy and sighs. I may be imagining things, but I could swear Governor Watson gives the slightest signal with his hand and eyes. Teddy gives a subtle nod and then steps toward me, a gentle yet condescending arm around my shoulder.

"A.J. Why don't you, uh... sit tight a few more minutes. We'll be with you shortly."

I glance at the governor as Teddy escorts me back to the car. Again, he refuses to look at me.

I take my spot in the back seat, the one facing the trunk, as Teddy leans in the open door. "Don't sweat it, A.J. Takes a while to earn his trust—'specially when he's in a *mood*." Teddy double checks to make sure the governor can't hear us, and then says quietly, "He likes to act like he's 'above the fray,' But he's not. *Believe* me, he's not."

I watch Teddy carefully, trying to understand what he means. "Is there something about the governor you think I should know?"

"Hmm?" Teddy looks at me and then glances away. "Oh, no, no. Chuck's a good man. Father of two kids in college, loving husband of twenty-five years. He's the *ideal* candidate. He just likes to, you know... *remind* us that he's the one in charge. That he's 'the decider.' It's why he won't really listen to anyone else's opinion. Nothing personal, ya know. It's partly for himself and partly for show. So I let him have his outbursts. But he needs to understand: We're here to help him get reelected."

"Of course."

Teddy's eyes are shifty and he seems self-conscious for the first time since I've met him. He coughs and clears his throat. "All right then. Give me a couple minutes with him, 'kay?"

I nod and he shuts the door. I can't hear them, but I can see them talking and gesticulating.

Not above the fray? What did Teddy mean by that? Maybe Governor Watson isn't as squeaky clean as he appears, but so what? I mean... no one can be the perfect candidate. Can they?

RANI

"I'll have a double burger, medium well, no cheese, no mayo, no onions and hold the bun. Sweet potato fries instead of regular fries and a side of steamed kale."

The heavyset waitress, her nametag that reads "HEY, I'M PEARL" slowly rising and falling with each breath, just blinks at Emily.

"We don't have sweet potato fries *or…* what was that other thing you said?"

"Kale?" Emily asks incredulously.

"I don't know what that is, but we don't got it."

"What kind of greens do you have as a side?"

Pearl thinks for a moment and then suggests enthusiastically, "I could put extra *lettuce* on your burger?"

Emily sighs and hands the menu back. "That'll be fine. And a Diet Coke with lemon."

Pearl the waitress scribbles on her pad and then looks at me.

"Oh. Uh. Grilled cheese on wheat toast, please, and the tomato soup."

She seems relieved by my order, takes my menu quickly, and waddles off to the kitchen before I can change my mind.

Emily and I are the only two people in this small diner, which is a few blocks from the town center. She insisted we ditch the last hour of volunteer work to "get some *real* food." If we'd stuck around the levees till sunset at 7:45, we'd have been forced to go with the group for bad pizza or eat more of the lame offerings from lunch, which consisted mostly of PB&J's on white bread.

"Thanks for coming here," Emily says, fiddling with the sweetener packets. "My stomach just can't digest bleached flour anymore."

I nod and gaze out the window. The sun is going down over the treetops and it looks almost peaceful outside. Other than the blisters on my hands and the throbbing ache in my shoulders from lifting sandbags all day, it feels almost like I'm back home, hanging out with Emily at a crappy diner instead of our usual Pinkberry. I sort of wish we *were* back home, but I don't confess that to Emily.

We're ostensibly here not only to eat but to talk about our *Empty Rooms, Full Hearts* plan—iron out the details for the presentations tomorrow morning.

"You realize our acronym is ERFH," Emily says. "Sounds like a cartoon character getting hit in the nuts. *Erfh!*"

"Okay," I say smiling. "So we add some letters. Like Soho or Tribeca. Make it… EMROFUHS."

Emily laughs. "That's too close to MOFOS."

I laugh too and tell her not to stress about the acronym. "We can't choose our own nickname. The public chooses it for us. And maybe they'll just shorten it to, like, 'Empty Rooms' or something."

Emily ponders this for a moment. "Hm. That doesn't completely suck…" She puts down the sweetener packets and says, all business, "Okay. I've got my cousin in San Francisco. He's a computer genius at a Mac store out there? He's working on a web design for us. Not an actual working website yet, just like templates for the landing pages that we can present in a slide show tomorrow."

"Cool," I say, absently sliding the ketchup bottle back and forth between my hands.

"And I got a woman in my dad's office—her brother is an agent at William Morris. She's tracking down the contact info for those celebs we mentioned. Chloe Sevigny and John Mayer? I think they'd totally do, like, a PSA for us or give us a blurb for the banner. Drive traffic to the site."

"Nice."

"I really think we have a shot at winning this, Ran. That photo thing with the governor was no accident. I'm sure they're only doing that with potential winners, dontcha think?"

"Mos def," I deadpan.

Emily pauses and sizes me up. I look back at her but quickly avert my eyes.

"Don't you want to win?" she asks.

"Of course. Ten grand each would be pretty sweet, right?"

"It's not just the money," she says. "We'll have won a state-sponsored scholarship. The only one of its kind. We can write our own ticket after that!"

"Groovy."

"Okay," she says, banging her hands on the tabletop, making the silverware clatter. "*What* is your deal?"

"Nothing. I have no deal."

"If you wanna go home, go. I can do this by myself."

I don't respond. Just stare at the napkin I'm ripping to shreds for no reason. I feel like I'm being chastised by my dad.

"This could be really big for us, Rani. We could be *known* for something. Like the way Stanford-E.K. is 'the girl with Brad Pitt on Facebook.' We could be 'the Calliope girls.' A picture of us and the governor right before we rescued the town of Cawdor. We can do something no other high school kid could *ever* do!"

"But so what?" I say, still looking at my napkin art.

"So *what?*"

"Yeah. I mean… that girl after the photo today? Talking about Morgan and how awesome and driven she is? Yeah, it got me fired up to win. Like, show up my sister or prove something to myself. But the more I think about, the more *pointless* it all seems."

"Whatever," Emily says, playing with her phone. "You're just 'hangry.'"

"No. This is exactly what happened to Morgan: busted her ass at Fairwich, then Princeton, and now she's on her stupid Fulbright in Cape Town studying the British Raj or Taj or whatever. And you know what? Aside from Morgan and the pervy academics who are hot for anything Asian or exotic, no one cares!"

"Where is that stupid waitress with our food?" Emily turns toward the kitchen, but I grab her arm and look her in the eye.

"Hey—I'm serious. What's the endgame? Let's say we win the contest. *You* get into Harvard. I go… wherever. Then we're in college with a bunch of other overachievers who won National Spelling Bees and science grants from Exxon and invented a gluten-free kind of paste so dumb kids that eat paste won't *also* have an allergic attack. And it's like—okay, now we're back to square one. Trying to beat *those* guys out for a summer internship and then a job and then a contract and then a spouse and then a spot on the PTA, a spot on the board, and finally we get a building or a road named after us and then we die and all that's left is a stupid street sign that says 'Rani

Caldwell Way' but no one cares because it's really West 52nd street and that's what it will always be and what's the stupid point of *any* of this?!"

Pearl is suddenly standing by our table with my soup and Emily's Diet Coke.

"I can come back," she mumbles.

"No, it's fine," Emily says, eyes fixed on me. We stare at each other in silence as Pearl lays out our stuff and scoots back to the kitchen.

"Sounds like you're having an existential crisis," Emily says. "Or a nervous breakdown."

"I'm sorry, I just... I've been getting it non-stop from everyone about college. Morgan texts me from South Africa like every week: *Hey sis. Would love to B able to go to Princeton reunions with U! Hint hint!* Then that stupid girl today with the governor, talking about how awesome Morgan is! And my dumb parents are just as relentless. '*Where are you going, what are your top choices, Morgan knew her top choice since freshman year!*'" I'm doing a bad impression that sounds less like my mom and more like Cartman from *South Park*.

"I knew when I was ten," Emily adds.

"I know! So they expect me to be exactly like you and my sister, but when I try to tell them I'm *not*, they don't listen. It's like—they don't want me to get into a good school because it's what's best for *me*. It's so they can *brag* to their friends that their kid got into an Ivy. Like last weekend. I was at Equinox and this super ripped MILF on the bike next to me knew, like, everyone in the gym. And anyone that walked by, instead of saying 'hello' to them, she just said 'Yale'—like a flat declaration. And the other person would immediately get it and high-five the woman. And not a cool 'good-for-you' high five, a really douche-y aggro high five."

"What the hell for?" Emily asks, sipping her Diet Coke.

I stir the not-very-appetizing-looking soup, trying to cool it off. "Apparently her daughter just got in—off the friggin' *waitlist* by the way—and this über-mom was holding court like she just won the Super Bowl. So then her squeaky little daughter, her face all pinched and annoying, came in and tells the story to everyone *again*—how she was bummed to miss so many Pilates classes this summer because she couldn't *sleep* until she heard from Yale."

"Barf," Emily says.

"Exactly!" And I immediately breathe easier. Because Emily gets it. She knows that kind of crap isn't cool. This is why she's my best friend. "It's like—is that really what it's all about?" I say, slightly calmer. "Get into Yale so your mom can high-five some loser at the gym?"

I sip the soup. It tastes like warm watery ketchup. I immediately put down my spoon.

"Well. She was proud of her daughter—nothing wrong with *that*."

"Of course not. But she was *advertising* it. Flaunting it. It wasn't pride; it was ego. Self-satisfied, disgusting, smug ego."

Emily laughs, and I start to finally ease up and see the humor in it, too.

"I wanted to take my little sweat-drenched towel and shove it in her face!" I blurt out and Emily laughs harder, almost choking on her drink. Once she regains her composure, I look at her sincerely and say, "Look, if anyone's doing it for the right reasons, it's you. You've known what you wanted since you were *six*. That's awesome. But… I don't *know* what I want. Why can't my parents be *happy* that I'm giving it so much thought? Why can't they just respect that maybe I don't want to decide the rest of my life over one summer when I'm seventeen?"

"Parents think they know what's best for us. That's all."

"No. They just want to high-five their crappy friends like that stupid mom. It's all parents want. To humble-brag about their kids and feel superior. Sorry if I don't want to be a part of that equation."

Just as Pearl brings my grilled cheese and Emily's burger, Emily's phones buzzes on the table top. Pearl looks at Emily's phone like it's magic.

Emily reads for a moment and then says, "It's a group text from the volunteer center. The governor wants to talk to everyone at 8 o'clock in Duffy Square again."

"Tonight?" I ask.

"Looks like it."

Pearl, seemingly impressed that we "know" the governor, says with large toothy smile, "Can I… get you ladies anything else?"

Emily looks at her burger for the first time, then at my greasy sandwich. "Nope. We're good."

Pearl smiles and trudges off.

"Let's get outta here," Emily declares.

"Yeah," I say. "This food kind of blows."

Emily pulls out a $20, slides it under her Diet Coke, and heads for the door. I hesitate then pull out a $5 for a tip (just in case) and slide it under her $20.

Stepping into the humid evening air, walking the five blocks back to town, Emily tells me not to worry so much about my parents. "It's their job to pressure you. The more they annoy you, the more they love you."

"Yeah?" I say. "Then they must love me a *lot*."

ROBERT

"And we can put solar paneling here, as well as on the roof."

I'm showing Mac my green housing design. We just finished our volunteer assignments—utilizing every ounce of daylight we could—and are hanging with some of the other teenage Samaritans in Duffy Square where the governor and Richard Gains spoke exactly twelve hours ago (and, according to the group text we got, are due to make another announcement any minute). A long day, for sure. Tiring yet invigorating. In fact, the whole experience has been a contradiction of sorts, filled with genuine acts of human kindness and the most selfish, competitive, vindictive behavior I've ever seen. Imagine Mother Teresa competing on *Big Brother 14*, and you'll have a pretty good picture of the atmosphere around here.

But Mac and I are a good team—we keep our heads down, do solid work, don't make waves. After several hours boarding up windows and getting houses in the red zone hurricane-ready (the red zone is what they're calling the area most likely to be impacted by the storm), we moved on to 'Pets Are People Too.' We met dozens of families (mostly old ladies) needing assistance evacuating their cats and dogs and one prickly cockatoo that did not want to budge. But it was totally fun and sweet and exactly what I was hoping for from this experience. To help people in need... and feel better about myself in the process. I think my personal statement will be a total slam-dunk over the goal line. (FYI, I don't care about sports.)

"And this section right here," I show Mac, "will be made entirely from recycled wood and metals recovered from the devastated neighborhoods."

"Nice," Mac says grabbing my sketch to get a closer look. He leans to his right to catch the light from the streetlamp as the last moments of twilight finally fade away. The renderings are crude, since I only have a pencil and loose-leaf paper, but the raw ingredients are there. And Mac seems impressed. "These are awesome, man."

"Thanks," I say, trying not to sound too excited.

"My only question is... I know from my dad's construction company what this stuff will cost, and even if some of it's built with recycled materials it's still gonna be expensive as hell. I'm not sure the governor will go for it."

"But it's not just about *initial* cost," I insist. "It's about longevity. Over time the houses will pay for themselves by not needing as many repairs, plus the cost of heating and cooling them will go down, and—"

"That saves the home*owner* money. But not the home *builder*— which in this case is the state. I think Governor Watson's looking for plans that help get people back on their feet but are also economically sound."

"When did you get so smart?" I ask, sort of flirting.

"You must be rubbing off on me," he says. And I swear he's flirting back. Again! Oh my God, what do I do, what do I say next?

"Excuse me, please! Coming through? *Gah!*" It's Rory from the Grateful Ten, perfectly breaking the mood. I barely have time to nod at him before he shoves his way by, sulking about something.

"What's his problem?" I ask Josh, the guy Rory chastised earlier.

Josh strokes his wispy blond beard that can't seem to fully commit and gives a classic stoner grin. "Ah, just Rory being Rory. It was a tough day out there, getting clean water delivered. And in the afternoon, most of us got stuck with traffic detail on Route 1. It was hot as balls out there, bra. Plus, we just got word that Phish is passing on Relief Jam, so…"

"Whoa," Mac says. "You guys were trying to get Phish? I thought they broke up."

"They did in '04. But they started touring again in '09. Just here and there. Very selective venues. But we thought since Vermont isn't super far from here—and it's a good cause and all—we might convince them to headline. But. They say they're committed on the West Coast. Rory thinks they're afraid to get caught in the storm, even though he repeatedly told their manager the concert would be *after* the hurricane passed, but… What are you gonna do?"

I sort of nod, assuming the question is rhetorical.

"So with Phish a bust," Josh continues, "it's looking pretty grim. So far we've just got Widespread and SCI—each committing with a 'soft maybe.'"

"CSI?" I ask ignorantly. "Is that a band?"

"Nah, bra," Josh says, giving me a silly shove. "SCI. The String Cheese Incident? They're freakin' jammin', man. After Phish and Widespread Panic, they're like the best live band out there. If we can get those guys, I think the Guv will totally dig our plan. How 'bout you two, how's it going?"

"Oh, it's great," Mac says enthusiastically. "We've got this sweet plan for green housing—"

"But it's not really feasible," I interrupt. "Not as ideal or complete as Relief Jam anyway."

I give Mac a raised eyebrow that I hope sufficiently conveys my subtext (*don't tell anyone about our plan!*), though I don't know why I'm being covert in front of Josh. He only seems to catch about thirty percent of what's going on around him. Mac shrugs at me, confused by my eyebrow communication, so I sort of nod at Josh, indicating that's the end of the conversation.

"So, maybe we'll catch you later?" I reach out to shake Josh's hand to really put an end to this exchange. Josh undercuts it, forcing me into a 'bro shake'—the underhanded clasp plus half-hug with the other arm. (I hate how everyone assumes that just because I'm black, I prefer the 'bro shake' to the traditional handshake. Because I don't!) When Josh pulls me into the hug phase, my other arm gets caught between us. It's super awkward and weird. Mac turns around to avoid giggling in my face. Once Josh is out of earshot, Mac busts out laughing.

"Dude, that was hilarious! You looked like a robot hugging an alien. I wish I'd snapped a pic on Instagram."

"Hey, uh… don't tell people about our idea, okay."

"I didn't," Mac says, still smiling.

"You *almost* did. Before I cut you off and saved the day."

"Hey, take it easy."

"I think you're taking this *too* easy."

"Whoa. Chillax, man."

"Ew. What? No. Don't tell me to 'chillax.' Is my name *Brody*? Is this a teen dramedy on the CW?"

"Okay—my bad."

"And I'm serious, Mac. You gotta keep it close to the vest. Didn't you ever see *The Godfather*? 'Never let anyone outside the family know what you're thinking.'"

"…So I'm family now?"

"What? Oh—I don't know. Sort of. Yeah. Why not?"

"…Cool." He nods and slaps me on the shoulder. "Point taken. Lips sealed."

"…Thank you."

My heart is beating a million miles an hour. I don't know if it's the adrenaline rush after getting upset at Mac or because he seems to be flirting with me—again! I can't get a read on his signals at all. Ugh! Straight boys are maddening.

"Hello, hello? Can everyone hear me?" I look up and see someone standing on the library steps, holding a bullhorn microphone. It's Governor Watson, presumably ready to address the troops one last time. A light flaps on, illuminating the governor and now I see a few TV cameras filming the proceedings. Mac and I sort of smile/nod at each other, then turn to watch the speech.

"Okay," the governor says happily. "I wanted to thank everyone for their courageous and selfless efforts today. I'm told the levee has been expertly reinforced, adding three feet of additional height on both sides for over half a mile. And it looks like more than ninety percent of the residents in the direct line of the storm have been safely evacuated—so give yourselves a round of applause."

While applauding, I see Emily Kim standing a few feet away. She sees me too, and we nod like gladiators about to square off. Behind her, I catch a glimpse of two kids who look seriously out of place. Totally Rumspringa or *Big Love*. The girl's blonde hair practically reflects the surrounding light. And the boy looks like Jesus without the beard: serene and wise and full of hope.

There's something different about them. A quiet confidence. As if they *know* they're going to win because they're guided by some higher power. I get a sudden chill along my arms and a shiver inches up my spine. But I shake it off and turn toward the governor again. No way could those weirdoes win.

"And now, Richard Gains has a special announcement. Richard."

Richard Gains steps up and takes the bullhorn. "Thanks, Chuck. Good evening, my fellow Nutmeggers!" The crowd sort of apes back a 'hello.' "I've had the great fortune to get to know many of you today, filling sandbags side by side or hammering plywood over windows. And to thank you for pitching in with such enthusiasm, I want to invite you all back to The Tao of Peace, my little B&B up on Porter Road. Nothing fancy. Some pizzas, burgers and dogs. Maybe some local lobster and clams. And for those of you over twenty-one… some adult beverages! And, uh, if the governor's not looking—maybe for those of you *under* twenty-one, too, 'cause we all know you're already drinking, right?"

The crowd cheers wildly. The governor steps in, pushes the bullhorn down, and whispers intensely at Richard, who gives a shit-eating grin and protests lightly. Governor Watson takes the bullhorn microphone and says, "Uh, all kidding aside… there will be *no* underage drinking. Sorry, folks."

The crowd 'awws' and 'boos.' The governor smiles good-naturedly but shakes his head 'no' as he hands the bullhorn back to Richard Gains.

"Boo. Come on, Chucky, don't be a party pooper," Richard Gains goads the governor, who shrugs but will not budge.

"Well," Richard Gains continues, "*I* think you all deserve a cold beer on a hot summer night—especially after the great job you did today. But if the governor says no… I guess we should respect that."

Governor Watson shouts "thank you" and waves to the crowd apologetically as he gives a worried look to the TV cameras.

"But it'll still be lots of fun," Richard Gains says into the mic. "So even if you aren't staying at the B&B tonight, please come on by. The backyard is spacious and the pool is spectacular. And we'll have sodas and juice and stuff for you young'uns. See you all soon!"

Everyone applauds again, but less enthusiastically this time. While Richard Gains and the governor laugh and shake hands and the TV crews' lights snap off, I see a younger woman (in her 20s, I'd guess) looking very serious among the entourage of staffers. She keeps trying to get the governor's attention but he keeps ignoring her. Finally she grabs the governor's chief of staff and speaks very intensely to him. The chief of staff nods and then whispers in Governor Watson's ear. The governor shakes his head 'no' and walks off while his staff scrambles to keep up. The chief of staff sort of shrugs apologetically at the girl and makes the 'we'll call you' gesture.

The girl stands for a moment, an actress alone on stage after the curtain call. I feel an instant kinship and have the urge to go talk to her. But before I can do anything, she steels herself with a breath and heads off (notably, not going the same direction as the governor and his staff).

"Now what?" Mac asks.

"No idea." I turn behind me to see what the other kids are doing. Among the teenagers dispersing, I see boys and girls jockeying for position, trying to stake early claims on their hook-up of choice. But mostly I see teams sizing up the competition, whispering about their plans and spreading rumors about others. And then it hits me: the insanity of it all. My dad has been harping on me for years about getting into Yale, bragging about how he and Grandfather were accepted so easily. "And those were the days *before* affirmative action," he always reminds me.

But I think it's infinitely harder to get into college now. I mean, they never had to deal with *this*. There are over a hundred high school kids here and every last one of them, myself included, is *after* something. Not one is in Cawdor out of the goodness of his or her heart. These are highly motivated, successful students (like Emily Kim) with perfect SAT scores and 5s on their AP exams—exams in esoteric subjects like Mandarin, Macroeconomics, and Comparative Government & Politics. These kids are the leads in their school plays, speak three languages, play nine instruments and still, *still,* they come here looking for a leg up—that extra edge that will guarantee a top-tier acceptance letter in the spring. When did it get to be so crazy?

Just then, that 15-year-old hipster, Duncan Rodriguez, saunters by and says, "Gonna be a lot more heartbreak than triumph after all is said and done."

"What?" I ask.

"Well," Duncan says, pulling off his Google glasses and polishing the lenses with his skinny black tie, "not only are most of these sex-starved teens gonna go home with nothing more to hook up with than their hand, they all think being here is like some golden Wonka Bar ticket, like it's gonna seal the deal with their top choice school. But there's no way you can *all* get in to your top choices."

"Why not?" asks Mac innocently.

"Cuz," Duncan says, putting on his glasses again. "Numbers don't add up. Harvard had an acceptance rate last year of 5.9 percent—the lowest rate in the history of the school. That means out of the 34K and change applications, just north of *two* thousand were accepted. There's like a hundred or so rising seniors here, yeah? And I bet thirty or forty of them have Harvard as their top choice, right?"

"I know Emily does," I blurt out without meaning to.

"There ya go. So that means of the, let's say... thirty-five that are applying to Harvard, only two will get in. *Two!* That's thirty-three disappointed sets of parents back home. And still, all of these posers are positively salivating at the prospect of another Katrina or Sandy hitting their home state and the opportunities they think will come with that—chance to pad the resume, give weight to their personal statements, add gravitas to their entrance interview. '*Oh you were there when Hurricane Calliope hit... what was that like for you?*' It's the new blood sport, gentlemen. Competitive volunteering."

Holy crap, he's right. This isn't just volunteering. It's *competitive* volunteering. And Emily Kim is the poster child. Of course, I'm not completely without fault. I'm here looking to suck out any and all opportunities from the impending natural disaster as well, but at least... Well. At least nothing. I don't feel bad about it. I actually feel vindicated to hear it articulated so clearly. (Jesus. Maybe I'm worse than Emily.)

"So," I say nonchalantly. "Let the games begin."

"Touché," Duncan says. "More power to you. But I'm tellin' ya, boys, the shelf life for this kinda thing is another six months. A year, tops. It's like that whole backlash to the backlash curve."

"What's that?" Mac asks.

"You know," Duncan says, "that thing in *New York* magazine where they chart a new book or movie or actor that's getting a lot of press. It starts down here with the *pre*-buzz." He demonstrates by beginning to trace a bell curve in the air with his hand. "Then it rises with the buzz, up some more with the rave reviews, topping out at the saturation point up here. Then the inevitable decline where it's overhyped, bottoming out at the backlash, then getting a mini bump back up with a backlash to the backlash. Boom."

"Never heard of it," Mac says.

"Whatever." Duncan is looking around, clearly feeling like he's already spent too much valuable face time with us. "I'm just saying this ultra-competitive college entrance stuff is about to hit its apex. In three years, when it's my turn, it'll be declining fast toward its nadir. So I'm staying ahead of the curve, skipping the whole secondary education jam completely. By the time I graduate high school, I'll have generated enough national name recognition to raise a hundred mil in VC, start my own sneaker line, or come up with the next big thing our 2013 minds can't even *fathom*! You guys are the last of a dying breed. The kids that bust their asses for killer grades and an Ivy league degree, a degree that's increasingly meaningless in terms of landing a profitable job? Ancient history. With sites like Coursera and the whole digitalization of higher education? Anyone in the world with a freakin' Internet connection can take Harvard and Stanford-level classes for *free*. So even if it's really about learning stuff—which it's not—why would anyone drop all that coin for something they can with*out* going into crippling debt? College is the new print media. And the university system as we know it is going, going, *gone*. I mean, Peter freakin' *Thiel* paid twenty kids 100K each *NOT* to go to college!"

"Yeah, and I heard they were all floundering," I interject. "The first twenty-four and now the new crop of twenty. No major income or progress or innovations from any of them."

"Like forty-four kids is a big enough sample," Duncan scoffs. "You know how many people graduate from college each year? How many of *them* came up with something innovative because of that killer Intro to Psych lecture from Miami University—in *Ohio*!"

"Well—"

"Face it," Duncan says, cutting me off. "It's a global economy now. And Harvard means nothing to the guys running China and India. Need to learn a skill? Get it on the job or figure it out online. Otherwise, the only currency of value is fame, brand recognition, and a massive social media profile. Anything else? Might as well be the Stone Age."

"Are you serious?" I ask.

"Bout which part?"

"All of it. Not going to college, it's a thing of the past. Are you serious?"

"Did the cast of *The Jersey Shore* go to college? Or Kim Kardashian? No way. She graduated high school, leaked a sex tape, got a million Twitter followers, now she's worth over forty million and rising."

"Sixteen million," says Mac.

"No, Huckleberry. I know my numbers. She's worth forty million dollars."

"Oh, I'm sure you're right about her net worth. I just mean Twitter followers. Kim Kardashian has over sixteen million of them."

"See what I mean?" Duncan says, pointing at Mac but looking at me. "It's not about higher education. It's about *brand recognition*. And this here," he gestures around Duffy Square and the town of Cawdor in general. "All *this*? Just kids spinning their wheels, trying to feel important. It won't *do* anything for you long term."

"How about make me feel like a better person?" I ask.

"Whatever floats your boat. But I don't need four years of sonnets and art history to end up owing some bank $200K and living with my parents again cuz the only job I'm qualified for is working at The Gap. Sorry, fellas. Not worth my time."

As Duncan starts off, I call out to him, "Guess you're not going to the party then."

"Oh, I'm going to the party," Duncan says, turning to us but continuing to walk away backwards. "Free booze and grub, plus decision-impaired ladies? Never pass up that combo. See ya there?"

I stare at Duncan, unsure if he means what he says or if it's all an act. Or maybe it started as an act and now he believes his own hype. Finally I just nod and say, "Yeah. See ya there."

Duncan nods back. "Ciao, boys." He turns on his heels and catches up with the crowd down the street. I see him slap the back of a few guys and launch into another monologue.

And then I realize: some of what he says has merit, but mostly he's just starved for attention. He's the youngest one here and probably feels totally out of place. He's lonely, a little sad, and kind of full of shit.

"Wow," Mac sighs.

"Tell me about it."

We watch the crowd of teenagers move as one down the road.

They're joking and smiling and being kids. I wonder how much of what Duncan said is true and how much is him justifying his own choices. Would I have the guts to *not* go to college? Is that really courageous—or even *smart*? I wonder what Duncan's parents are like. Did they send him to one of those Reggio Emilia schools where the kids lead the curriculum and finger painting is considered as important as reading and math? He looks like one of those kids whose parents still go to rock concerts and let their kids call them by their first names and screen important documentaries and pretentious foreign films while their children drink lattes and set their own bedtimes. Is that really what the generation behind me is like? What the hell is this world coming to?

"Should we head over to the party?" Mac finally asks.

"Yeah, but..."

"What?"

"...I got a bad feeling about this."

Duncan Rodriguez
@DRod3000
Counter-culture techno-philosopher.
Amateur weather enthusiast. Idea-DJ.

4,375	8,682	214.3K
TWEETS	FOLLOWING	FOLLOWERS

Tweets

Duncan Rodriguez @DRod3000   8/16/13 8:45 PM
Off to hurricane-volunteer fiesta @TaoOfPeace. Nothing says altruism like throwing yourself a party.
#ThingsThatMakeYouGoHmm

Duncan Rodriguez @DRod3000   8/16/13 8:53 PM
Lanterns, pig spit, glowing orbs floating in pool... Did I just step into Gatsby's playground? #TooRichForCawdor

Duncan Rodriguez @DRod3000   8/16/13 9:01 PM
Richard Gains reliving Tony acceptance speech with a gaggle of not-so-adoring fans. #OldCelebsMakeMeSad

Duncan Rodriguez @DRod3000   8/16/13 9:09 PM
Rumor circling that weird farmer twins got 50 neighbors to help construct a dam of some kind for Gov's contest.
#HeyGod,IsThatCheating?

115

Duncan Rodriguez @DRod3000   8/16/13 9:32 PM
Tonight's drink of choice: Calliope Cool-Aid. Grain alcohol + punch mix. Glad Gov & his team opted NOT to make appearance. **#ThisCouldGetUgly**

Duncan Rodriguez @DRod3000 RETWEETED   8/16/13 9:58 PM
Sammy Diaz @AshtonSucks Hey @DRod3000 - What's the over/under on number of kids puking by midnight?

Duncan Rodriguez @DRod3000   8/16/13 10:03 PM
@AshtonSucks Well if it's any indication, it's only 10pm and I've already seen 3 pukes. **#NerdsKnowHowToParty**

Duncan Rodriguez @DRod3000   8/16/13 10:22 PM
Naked fat guy in oversized foam cowboy hat just ran by on his way to the pool. **#StuffICanNeverUn-see**

Duncan Rodriguez @DRod3000   8/16/13 10:23 PM
Switching from beer to Calliope Cool-Aid. **#LetsGetThisPartyStarted**!

Duncan Rodriguez @DRod3000   8/16/13 10:35 PM
Hot 18 yr old totally flirting with me. **#ThisPartyRocks**

Duncan Rodriguez @DRod3000   8/16/13 10:38 PM
Hot 18 yr old just left with some total DB wearing a trucker hat. **#ThisPartyBlows**

Duncan Rodriguez @DRod3000   8/16/13 10:44 PM
Many sexy girls are jumping in the pool and begging me to jointhem. **#99ProblemsButThisAintOne**

Duncan Rodriguez @DRod3000   8/16/13 10:58 PM

Did anyone ever see that movie Project X? This party is cRaZiEr! #ThankGodForAlcohol

Duncan Rodriguez @DRod3000   8/16/13 11:11 PM

11:11! Make a wish CT! Mine is for World Peace. And everlasting fame and fortune. But also world peace. #YouKnowYouWantItToo

Duncan Rodriguez @DRod3000   8/16/13 11:32 PM

Two girls and a guy are making out. I'm aroused and confused. #TriangleKissingIsAwkward

Duncan Rodriguez @DRod3000   8/16/13 11:40 PM

Saw two dudes kissing by smoldering pig spit. #WhyIsEveryoneHookingUpButMe?

Duncan Rodriguez @DRod3000   8/16/13 11:49 PM

Am I the only one on Twitter tonight? Where are all my followers? #Hellooooo?

Duncan Rodriguez @DRod3000   8/17/13 12:23 AM

Everyone is either passed out or MAKING out. Why am I still here? #SecretlyLonely #JustPlayin'I'mAwesome! #LaterHaters

A.J.

To: <Charles.Watson@ct.gov>
Cc: <Theodore.Hutchins@ct.gov>
Subject: Concerns

Dear Governor Watson,

I wanted to call your attention to a few things that are causing me concern. First of all, the gathering at The Tao of Peace at this very moment is a horrifying display of teenagers run amok. I know it's not technically something that you endorsed or are responsible for, but I thought you should know that Richard Gains (who is nowhere to be found) is completely ignoring your stated request that there be no underage drinking. Clearly, kids will be kids, and we all had our share of beers and wine coolers in high school. But the level of reckless abandon with which these volunteers are behaving goes beyond anything I've ever seen. You should be prepared to address this with the press tomorrow, should word get out about the gathering.

But beyond that, my major concern is how we left things this evening. After the announcement in Duffy Square, I assumed we'd all hunker down at a diner or in a hotel room to strategize for storm-day, but I felt that any suggestion I made toward that end was met with resistance. If I've done something wrong in the past twenty-four hours to upset you or cause you to have reservations about having me on "your team," I hope you'll address your concerns to me directly, and not shut me out of your decision-making process. I took a big risk leaving Washington, and an even bigger one leaving the state senator's office for you. But it's because I believe in you, sir. I believe in what you stand for and I believe you're capable of taking this country in the right direction. But I also believe that I can help you win on the national level. I cannot do that, however, if I'm shut out of meetings and shot down when I present ideas.

I look forward to hearing the presentations tomorrow and discussing this with you further in person.

Have a good night,
A.J.

§

After countless revisions, I stare at my email for twenty minutes before finally hovering the pointer over the little garbage can icon in the bottom right corner. The words "discard draft" appear and, after another minute of pondering, I click on the garbage can and trash my email to the governor without sending it.

I'm probably overreacting. To the party, to him "dismissing" my ideas. I'm sure he just has a lot on his mind with the hurricane and the contest and all of the talk about 2016. I'm the last thing he needs to be concerned about. He's a good man with good values. He probably wanted to go get some sleep and recharge the batteries before tomorrow. It's going to be a long day. I'm just being silly. Thank God I didn't send that email. Everything will be all right in the morning. Except for the hurricane, of course. There is still that. I need to turn off my brain and get some sleep myself.

I shut off the lights in my quiet room across from The Tao of Peace. Things have settled down quite a bit in the last hour. I was reading about unlocking the youth vote when I heard the sounds across the street go from "backyard barbecue" to "insane frat party." I tried earplugs, but high-pitched squeals of laughter and thumping bass kept coming through anyway. I glared at the party through my window like an old man glares at kids on his lawn, but large hedges around The Tao Of Peace obstructed any real view of what was happening. So, like a good curmudgeon, I put on my shoes and went to check it out.

I'm no prude or goodie-goodie nerd. Some beer pong or a glass of wine for the underage kids would have been totally reasonable to me. But when I saw Morgan's little sister cuddled up with a boy on a lounge chair, I was taken aback. And when I saw a large naked kid in a cowboy hat passed out on the lawn while two boys made out on the bench next to him, I was appalled. Then I saw Emily Kim practically attacking some boy with her mouth while another girl threw up in the pool, and I was done. Richard Gains was MIA, and the backyard looked like a bomb had exploded red plastic cups and hot dog buns.

I stormed back to my room in a white-hot rage, drafted that email, revised the email, slowly calmed down, and ultimately did nothing. I must have arrived at the height of the party's "epic-ness" because a few minutes after I got back to my room, the music was turned off, and the loud laughter dwindled to a few conversations, which dwindled to silence as everyone finally went to bed.

The party was annoying, which is why I started channeling my rage into that email. But what really got me angry was the way Governor Watson dismissed me so handily earlier today. Yes, I'm new and I'm young and he doesn't really know or trust me yet. But I thought I was brought on board specifically *because* I'm younger. I thought that was an *asset,* Governor!

No. I'm not doing this. I'm not going to play out wishful conversations in my head or debate myself and drive myself insane with what I should have said, should have done, what others think of me. It gets me nowhere. I need to relax. About everything.

I climb into bed, turn on my side, and close my eyes. I take a few deep breaths and calculate that if I fall asleep in the next few minutes, I'll get about five hours. More than enough. Everything with the governor will be fine. I'm just projecting. Letting my own insecurities get the best of me.

But every time I try to will my brain to accept that rational thought, my gut says something else is going on. Something bigger than the governor not trusting me or not liking me.

It feels like he's hiding something.

ACT III

STRANGE BEDFELLOWS

EMILY

Where. The hell. Am I?

I wake slowly. Open one eye. My left one. My right one is pressed hard against the mattress. Or maybe it's the sofa. Either way I can tell I'm drooling all over it. My left eye moves, trying to take in my surroundings, but I'm not getting enough information. Red plastic cups. A random seat cushion. Manicured bushes? Um. *What?* Why are there *bushes* in my room? And why is it so effing *bright* in here? Did Rani leave the curtains open?

I try to raise my body. Zero movement. I'm sure I'm giving my arms and legs the signals from my brain that would ordinarily elicit motion. But nothing happens.

"Jesus Christ, Rani," I moan. "How much did I drink last night?"

"…Who's Rani?"

I sit up with a jolt and look around the room, the foggy world edging into focus: paper plates… a smoldering fire… a pool! Oh God. It's coming back to me. I'm not in our *room* at the B&B. I'm *outside* the B&B!

I pick myself up off the bed, my dress that I slept in relentlessly clinging to me, only to realize I wasn't sleeping on a bed. It's one of those fancy outdoor loungers with a privacy canopy. I try to stand, my legs not fully cooperating, the hazy sun (already burning hot on the horizon) forcing me to squint and shield my eyes with my hand. WTF *happened* last night?

Wait. Didn't someone just *say* something to me? I do a quick 360-scan of the pool area and backyard. Empty. Quiet. Just a few birds chirping in the trees. Nobody else around. Maybe I'm hearing things. Or I'm still drunk. Or dreaming. I rub my eyes with my hands and then release them. When the stars in my eyelids fade away, I notice a boy's oxford folded neatly by a pair of saddle shoes on the lawn.

Oh God.

Last night comes back in a flash: Rani ditching me for that weird theatre dude who went crazy for Richard Gains; some Star Trek geek giving me a wildly alcoholic drink called Calliope Punch; eating a hot dog against my better judgment; eating two more because the first one was so freakin' good; downing more punch; peeing in the bushes because the line inside was too long; the three hot dogs in my stomach not seeming so awesome anymore; deciding another glass of punch was exactly what I needed to feel better; cornering Farmer Ted and telling him off; planting a massive *kiss* on him; stumbling back toward the B&B; throwing up on the grass; Farm boy getting me water and a cool towel, trying to coax me up to my room; me refusing, saying I'd be better off outside in nature, under the stars; cleaning my face over the edge of the pool; staring at my rippling warped reflection on the water; wondering who I am and what I'm doing with my life; curling into a ball on the lounger; the boy sitting next to me, stroking the hair out of my face; feeling secure and taken care of; moving to kiss him again and then... and then... Oh God! I can't remember anything after that!

A body slowly sits up from the ground. Even though I'm completely dressed, I instinctively duck behind another lounger to cover myself. So *he* was the voice in my head just now: Farmer Ted. Or—dammit! What's his *name*?

"Hey," he says to me, eyes still sleepy, dirty blonde hair tousled but sexy. He's wearing one of those sleeveless undershirts that I thought only Ryan Gosling could get away with, but this kid is pulling it off nicely. Man, those farmers got it figured out! Wait. He said something. And I'm just staring blankly at him, weirdly half-crouching behind outdoor furniture. Say something back, you idiot!

"Hey."

Brilliant, Emily. A perfect SAT score and *that's* the best you can come up with?!

"So, uh..." the boy begins. But I don't let him finish.

"Yeah, I gotta go." As I look around, hoping, *praying* no one else is witnessing this debacle, I notice the now-defunct pig spit a mere three feet from where I was sleeping all night. Great. I'm going to smell like a pork chop all day.

"...What?" the boy asks, still in a haze.

"Go. Me. Now." I run a hand through my hair, try to make it less rat-nesty, but there's really no point. I'm sure I look disgusting. Whatever. No time to waste on appearances. "I mean. This was fun. I think? But... Where are my shoes?"

"...What?" he repeats.

"Shoes. My shoes. Where are my shoes?"

He points to a chaise lounge where one J-Lo wedge sits by itself, like it's ready to get a tan. Where's the other one? Damn it, where's my other shoe!? Oh there it is—under a table strewn with red plastic cups and beer cans. I cradle both shoes and plop down on the grass, trying to strap on the left one.

"Are you okay?" he asks.

"Me? Yeah. Great. Always. Just gotta. You know. Get ready. Presentation day. You do too, right? Damn it!"

My shoes are not cooperating. Screw it, I'll carry them. It's only twenty yards across the flagstone to the B&B, I'll be fine. I stand up, head pounding, smooth out my dress, wipe the grass and dirt off my butt, turn to the Amish Wonder and say, "So. Again. Fun. Thank you. Good times. But. Yeah. I'll uh... see ya."

"Wait!" he calls out. I could just keep walking. But something tells me not to be my usual curt self, so I turn to hear him out.

"You know nothing happened last night, right?"

I blink at him. "What do you mean?"

"I mean you kissed me. Twice. But that was all."

"...Really?"

"Yeah," he says with a shy smile. "Then literally one second later you passed out on this lounger." He pats it in case there was some confusion as to which lounger I gracefully blacked out on.

"Right, I... knew that."

"Really? Because you're acting awkward and embarrassed but you shouldn't be."

I stare at him. He's unlike any boy I've ever met. I think that's a good thing.

"So we just... kissed?"

"If you can even call it that," he says with a light chuckle. "You were, uh, kind of yelling at me? And calling me 'Papa Yoder' a lot. Then just sort of... kissed me."

"That's kind of my thing," I say in a rare moment of transparency.

"Your thing?" he asks.

"I yell at boys and then kiss them. It seems to work."

"Yeah, because you're pretty hard to ignore."

I can't tell if he's insulting me or complimenting me. But he does look cute sitting on the grass behind the lounger.

"Anyway," he says, "after that first kiss, you stumbled around and got sick and I tried to help you inside but you just wanted to stay here. Then you kissed me that second time."

"*After* I puked?"

"Yeah, but you mostly missed," he says pointing to his cheek, "so... it wasn't gross or anything, it was completely fine. And then you, uh... fell asleep. So I stayed here. With you. To make sure you didn't get sick again or anything."

I nod and size him up. "You're a lot cooler without your sister around."

"...I get that a lot."

"Do you wanna... go inside?" I ask. "Maybe grab something to eat."

"Absolutely," he says. "I'm starving." As he starts to rise, it's clear that he's just in his undershirt and boxer shorts.

"Whoa, whoa, hang on!" I say turning away. "If nothing happened, why are you in your underwear?"

"Because," he says innocently, "I can't sleep in my pants. It's uncomfortable."

"Oh," I say, still not facing him. "Right. Well. Okay then. I guess you can... have breakfast with me. If you want."

"Thanks, Emily," he says and I'm mortified because I still don't remember *his* name. To cover, I decide to help him with his clothes.

"Here, let me help," I say, tossing him his button-down which he catches it with one hand. As I toss him his pants, some pages fall out of the back pocket and scatter across the lounger. I pick up the papers, about to hand them over as well, when I notice that they're plans of some kind: sketches and designs.

"What are these?"

"Oh, that's our plan," he says yawning. "For the governor."

I scan them quickly, flipping from page to page. "I thought you weren't part of the competition."

"We weren't originally," he says buttoning his shirt. "But Prayer said she mentioned our idea to Governor Watson and he convinced her that we *should* make a presentation, so..."

Looking at the schematics I mumble, "You're building a device... that will divert the river away from town?"

"Yeah," he shrugs. "It's pretty decent."

Pretty *decent*, I think. It's *epic*! Life-changing. The kind of plan that gets you on the national news! But I have no words for him. I'm too flabbergasted. Stunned. Standing there in my wrinkled dress in the early morning light, feet cold on the wet grass, hundreds of thoughts racing through my head, most notably: *Holy shit. We've been playing on the edges of this volunteer thing while the Jones twins are smack dab in the middle of it. They're playing GOD!*

I step gingerly to him (his pants mercifully zipped up) and hand him his pages. Then I slap him hard across the face. The sound and force of it surprise us both. I cover my mouth with my hands, shocked at my own brutality. Without thinking, I climb on top of him, forcing him back down to the ground, and kiss him passionately. Then I come to my senses and push myself away from him. I see a large red handprint starting to develop on his left cheek.

"Sorry," I blurt out. "Sorry. Um. I'll go inside. Now. Then you. But wait a few minutes. Okay? *Don't* follow me."

Still reeling from the discovery of his almost biblical plan, I turn on my heels and storm toward the B&B, back to the room I should have slept in with Rani, thinking that I should be freaking out even more and breaking every piece of pool furniture I can find. But it doesn't matter. I'm gone—away from him, away from his plan.

I race across the moist-with-dew flagstone and up the four little steps to the back patio. Once inside the drawing room, I stop. Breathe. Think. No. My head hurts too much to think. So I keep moving. Quietly through the large common area and up the stairs. I'll find Rani. Tell her what the hell those freakish twins are up to. Probably have to confess *how* I found out about it. Oh my God oh my God oh my God. This is not happening. Not today. The most important day of my pre-college career and I went and did something as stupid as this! I've kissed three boys in my entire life.

Why would I choose last night of all nights to be my fourth? Am I self-sabotaging? Is my conscience trying to tell me something? And how the hell can our dinky guesthouse idea compete with Moses and his literal parting of the sea? Especially since instead of following up on those celebrity leads and my cousin's website templates for our presentation, I came here last night, got drunk and kissed someone I just *met*! What is wrong with me? I try to put it all out of my mind as I come to the second floor landing, turn right and—

"Ahh!"

"Ahh!"

I run head on into that hunky roommate of Robert's. Mark or Max or whatever. We silently size each other up. He's wearing shorts and no shirt and his hair looks like someone else's fingers have been running through it all night. Probably hooked up with one of those hippie chicks from the Grateful Ten. Rah-rah. Good for him.

"Hey," I mutter.

"Hey," he replies, voice throaty and tired.

There's a brief moment when we don't know what to do. Then we silently agree to say nothing more and move on, me further down the hall on the second floor, him down to the first floor or wherever he's going this early in the morning without a shirt.

As I step toward room number six, the floorboards creak wildly. At the end of the hall, a door clicks open and I freeze. A head pokes out and looks right at me.

It's Robert.

He's wrapped in a blanket, his bare dark shoulders peeking out over the edges. A panicked look wafts over his face and he stands more rigid than usual. I half nod and he returns the casual greeting. Then he steps back into his room and clicks his door shut.

And only now do I piece it together. Robert totally hooked up with his beefy roommate! Whoa! I had no idea that dude was *gay*. Robert for sure. He told me he was gay within like two minutes of meeting him at HOBY. But that *other* guy does *not* strike me as being homosexual. Not even *bi*sexual.

But I have no time to dwell on this major bit of gossip. I've got to tell Rani what kind of epic plan Farmer Ted and his evil sister have concocted so we can come up with something better by 8 a.m. It can be done. It *must* be done… Jesus, there's no *way* it can be done.

I tap on our door as quietly as possible and whisper Rani's name. I don't remember where I put my key—or even *getting* a key. Pressing my ear to the door, I hear nothing on the other side. I try the latch. Miraculously, it opens. Then it hits me—I have no key because there are no *locks* on the doors. Richard Gains even made a slightly vulgar comment about it at the party last night: *"It's an old house with no locks. But we're all friends here, right? Nothing to steal but each other's innocence."* Man, that guy is creepy.

I tiptoe inside, quietly latching the door behind me. "Rani," I whisper toward the lump under the covers. "*Rani*. Get your bony ass out of bed."

Rani darts back the covers, revealing just her face. "What?!"

"The twins? Those farmer twins? Their plan completely *crushes* our 'Empty Rooms, Full Hearts' plan. It's, like, straight out of scripture. Like the hand of Yahweh writing the Ten Commandments."

"It can't be *that* great," Rani says with the hint of a smile.

"I'm not kidding." Then I whisper, "I think they talk to God."

"How do you know what their plan is?" she asks, eyes darting around the room, blanket tucked all the way to her chin. If I weren't so intent on beating the twins, I'd ask her why she's acting so weird. But I let it go and focus on the matter at hand.

"Oh-ho-ho, you are not going to be*lieve* the night I had. The *morn*ing I had. This place is crazier than an episode of *Gossip Girl*." Out of the corner of my eye, I notice a tray of food. That seems unlike Rani, to wake up early and get breakfast? "Hey, where'd you get this stuff?" I ask grabbing some pineapple from the fruit salad.

The bed covers suddenly fly back. "*I* brought it."

Startled, I spit the pineapple onto the floor. It's that boy Rani's been flirting with all weekend. The one she ditched me for last night.

"What the hell?" I manage to say.

"I figured Rani was famished. We sure worked up an appetite last night." And he gives me the cheesiest wink and smile I've ever seen in my life. "How'd *you* do, Harvard? 'Dja get lucky?"

Rani just stares at her recent hook-up, jaw slack. I'm equally speechless. So I turn to go. But as I open the front door and peek into the hall, I see the Amish Boy Wonder making *his* way up the stairs, so

I quickly duck back inside and turn to Rani and her boy-toy.

"Seriously, Rani? This is the biggest day of our lives and you're…" I gesture at the dude in bed with her. He smiles and winks at me—again! I feel like I might throw up. I shake my head in disgust and fling open the closet door. I grab my overnight bag off the floor and rip my 'power outfit' off the wooden hanger. "To be continued," I add. Then I turn to go again, but stop first to take the bagel off Rani's tray (as a sort of punishment and also because I'm starving). Then I slam the door and leave.

I storm down to the powder room on the first floor and look at myself in the small oval mirror.

Upon seeing what I look like for the first time all morning—mascara smeared down my right cheek, lipstick on my chin, dirt on my forehead, grass *in my hair!*—I open my mouth, take in a huge breath, and scream. As loud as I've ever screamed in my life.

RANI

I wake to soft hands caressing me. Fingertips gently tracing random patterns around my arms and legs. Goosebumps making my whole body tingle.

When I open my eyes, though, I'm alone in bed, exactly the way I started the night, the edges of my dream slowly slipping away for good. I rub a sleepy hand across my eyes and look at the sun streaking though the window. Last night seems so close and so far away at the same time.

Minutes after Emily and I arrived at the party, Tyler found me and basically never left my side (much to the chagrin of Emily). Tyler and I even won the "couples limbo contest." But at the end of the night, after he walked me to my room, and we talked and talked by the door, he finally leaned in and kissed me goodnight, a soft perfect kiss. Then he looked at me with those puppy-dog eyes (so open and nonjudgmental that it was almost disarming), twisted a piece of my hair between his fingers and said, "Well…" But I totally chickened out and said, "Okay, see ya in the morning," and closed the door on his face. I'm sure he hates me. But it's fine. I need to focus on the presentations. Besides, girls like me never end up with the guy anyway.

There's a soft knock on my door and I call out, "Come in," assuming it's Emily raring to go. But it's Tyler. With a tray full of food!

"*Buon giorno, bella,*" he says, his voice hoarse and sexy.

"Hi," I say, smiling dumbly from bed, wondering how awful I must look right now.

"You look even more amazing in the morning," he says, as if he knows what I'm thinking. I blush, self-consciously touching my face and hair. While he sets down the tray he adds, "Hope this is okay. I broke into the kitchen early. Brought us up some fresh fruit and bagels. I wasn't sure if you were an OJ or coffee girl, so I got both."

Oh my God, is this guy *too* perfect? Maybe. But I also think I'm genuinely falling for him. I know he's an actor and all, but no one is *this* good. He can't be faking this. Not now. Not the next morning. Especially since I put the brakes on and all we did was kiss goodnight. He's totally into me, too, I can feel it.

"Wow," I manage to say. "You got breakfast? What time is it?"

"Um…"

As he strains to get a look at the clock on the nightstand, purposely leaning over me on the bed, pressing his chest into my face, I can't help but giggle. It's so forward and charming and cool and sexy and oh Jesus I'm falling for every move he throws at me. Dammit, Rani, pull it together. He's just a *guy*! How did I fall for him so fast? But maybe it's okay. I've read about love at first sight and people meeting their husbands and just *instantly* knowing they were their "one and only." Maybe that's happening to me. Right now. Maybe he's my one and only. Maybe I met the man of my dreams because of a hurricane. No. How can that be? I'm only seventeen! I've never had a serious boyfriend. Less than twelve hours ago, my best friend thought I was a lesbian! I went to the ninth and tenth grade dances with the same dorky guy who I only kissed twice and it was terrible both times! (He led with his oversized teeth.) So, no, my first serious boyfriend can't be "the one." Besides, Tyler's not even my *boy*friend. He probably doesn't even like me that much!

This all passes through my mind in the two seconds that Tyler is leaning across me to see the clock. When he tells me what time it is, I snap back to reality.

"6:57?" I repeat. And I'm instantly in school mode: If I get up right this second, I can be showered and ready to go by 7:02. By then Emily should be back from wherever she ended up last night, and by 7:05 she and I can be out the door and on our way to the library for our final prep before the presentations at 8. We can do this. Wait. *Can* we do this? Oh, God, we are *so* not prepared.

"Hey," Tyler says. "Don't worry."

"Worry about what?"

"About anything."

Whoa. He *can* totally read my mind! Regroup, Ran. Say something casual. "Why would you think I'm worried?"

"Your face. Got all scrunched up and anxious. I could tell you were thinking about something that was worrisome."

"I'm not worried," I lie.

"Good," he says. "Because this is a great moment. We should cherish it. And the best way to do that is…"

He leans in to kiss me. Just as I start to lean in, too, I hear footsteps in the hall and a tapping at the door.

"Did you hear that?" I whisper fiercely.

"Hear what?" Tyler asks, still ready to kiss.

"Shhhhh!" I say, violently pushing him under the covers to hide him as the latch clicks and the door opens. I close my eyes and duck under the blanket with Tyler, praying that whoever is coming in will realize they're in the wrong room and go away. Stupid Richard Gains and his old house with no locks on the doors!

"Rani," a voice whispers from the door.

Perfect. *Now* Emily shows up. She couldn't have come two minutes ago, *before* Tyler? Forget it. Ignore her. Pretend to be asleep and she'll go away.

"*Rani*," she whispers louder. "Get your bony ass out of bed."

I hate it when she calls my ass bony. I make a fierce *Shh* gesture to Tyler, and dart back the covers, revealing just my face. "What?!"

Oh my God. Emily looks *awful*. Make-up smeared all over her face, dirt on her knees. And is that *grass* in her hair?

"The twins?" she says, before I can remark about her appearance. "Those farmer twins? Their plan completely *crushes* our 'Empty Rooms, Full Hearts' plan. It's, like, straight out of scripture. Like the hand of Yahweh writing the Ten Commandments."

Yahweh? When did she become a rabbi?

"It can't be *that* great," I say, trying to remain motionless as Tyler tickles my feet under the covers.

"I'm not kidding." Then she whispers, "I think they talk to God."

This is the *last* thing in the world I need right now, but for some reason I engage her. "How do you know what their plan is?" I look around the room. Maybe there's a way to distract Emily while Tyler makes a quick getaway. Instinctively, I tuck the blanket up around my neck even tighter.

"Oh-ho-ho, you are not going to be*lieve* the night I had. The *morn*ing I had. This place is crazier than an episode of *Gossip Girl*. Hey, where'd you get this stuff?" She grabs a piece of fruit salad and stuffs in in her mouth.

Before I know what's happening, Tyler pulls down the blanket, pokes his head out and says, "*I* brought it."

Emily spits out the fruit and stares at Tyler. "What the hell?" she says. I look at her pleadingly, but before I can speak Tyler takes over.

"I figured Rani might be famished. We sure worked up an appetite last night." And he ever so slightly pinches my side under the covers. I try not to squirm, squeal, or smile. "How'd *you* do, Harvard? 'Dja get lucky?"

I stare at Tyler. Mostly because I'm afraid to look at Emily. No one talks to her like that. Ever. She might go nuclear on him right here in this tiny room. But luckily, she says nothing. Just opens the door. Maybe she'll leave without further incident. She peeks into the hall and I angrily mouth to Tyler, *What is wrong with you?* He just smiles, amused. Emily turns back toward us and I plaster on a fake smile.

"Seriously, Rani? This is the biggest day of our lives and you're…" She points vaguely at Tyler, too disgusted to complete the gesture. And it's worse than if she'd gone nuclear. My best friend is disappointed in me. I feel like I might throw up. Emily opens the closet and grabs all her stuff. She points a long finger at me and ominously pronounces, "To be continued."

She hesitates by the door, snags a bagel off the tray, and then she's gone. I lay back and breathe for the first time since she walked in.

"Well. *That* got her to leave," Tyler announces, triumphantly leaning back on one arm, slightly above me. The sunlight cascades through the open curtains, casting his hair and muscular arms in golden light. His carefree smile and total ease are so foreign to me, so unlike anyone I've ever known. It's more than refreshing. It's intoxicating.

"Who *are* you?" I say with awe and wonder.

"Oh. I'm Tyler Voss—we met at the train station the day before yesterday—"

I playfully hit him on the shoulder. "Stop. You know what I mean. You're like… Okay: everyone here is *after* something. And you don't seem to care about *any* of it: what you say or what other people think of you. You're just digging the atmosphere and enjoying the ride and…"

"Living life?"

"Yes!"

"So… What's your question exactly?"

"…Can you teach *me* how to do it?"

He smiles and leans in for that kiss.

This feels right. Scary and weird and right. Maybe I should just live life, like he said. Not worry so much. Enjoy the moment.

As I kiss him deeply, squeezing my arms around him, a horrifying scream reverberates throughout the entire B&B. Tyler jumps back, startled. I bet everyone in the hotel was startled. Everyone except me. Because I know that scream. I've heard it many times and I'd recognize the combination of frustration, resentment, fear and loathing anywhere.

"What was that?" asks Tyler breathlessly.

"That," I say, "was Emily's war cry."

ROBERT

The sun peeks through my second-floor window and gently rouses me from my slumber. I open my eyes and see the sky is not as dark or ominous as I would have imagined it would be hours before a hurricane hits. But there's still a feeling in the air—a "morning after" vibe. Things were done last night that cannot be undone.

And I feel a sense of relaxation I haven't felt in years. I'm kind of grateful for it, actually. Before all the stress of senior year and grades and college and achievement, I'm simply here. Lying in this plush bed at The Tao of Peace. Not a care in the world. But then Mac's arm stirs beneath my back and my heart starts beating faster and my palms begin to sweat. So: last night actually happened. Mac kissed me. We were sharing a bottle of wine and laughing about the most absurd hilarious thing I've ever seen.

"Oh. M'god," I'd said dramatically, coming back from the bathroom.
Mac smiled without knowing what was funny. "What?"
"Emily Kim. Is totally macking on that farmer dude."
"Nuh-unh!"
"I kid you not. Check it out." I pointed across the lawn, near the pool, sort of directing Mac's gaze with an arm from behind him, enjoying the close proximity.
"…Huh," Mac said finally. "Good for them."
"Seriously?" I said, disappointed by his lack of astonishment.
Shrugging, Mac poured me a glass of wine. "Yeah. I mean… supposed to be the time of our lives, right? Fifty years from now, I'm not gonna be thinking back with regret on all the people I made out with. I'm gonna be regretting the ones I didn't. Enjoying life is never a regret." He punctuated his statement with a long pull directly from the bottle.
"I don't think you've been with enough losers to understand regretting it," I told him. "All your hookups are super hot."
"Maybe," Mac smiled. "But humans are meant to enjoy each other's company. The Romans had it right. No rules. Just unadulterated pleasure."
"I'm thinking the Romans are not really a high bar in terms of how to model a society."
"No?" Mac laughed.

"Slaves and gladiators and murdering emperors? Not my kinda thing." Then we both started laughing.

"What about this?" Mac asked. "Is this your kinda thing?"

And he kissed me. Just leaned right in and planted one on me. I was so stunned—here it was, the sudden realization of my three-year fantasy—that it was almost too much to process. I broke away and gave a hysterical laugh.

"Wh—why. What... Why did you... do that?" I stammered.

"Wanted to see what it was like," Mac said matter-of-factly. "Thought it might be fun. And nice."

I touched my face and mouth self-consciously. "Oh... Um. Was it?"

"Was it what?" Mac asked mischievously.

"...Nice?"

Mac nodded and we moved slowly toward each other.

"When in Rome..." I said.

We kissed for a while and then he looked around (a bit sheepishly) and asked if maybe we should go upstairs. I thought we'd maybe do more inside, but we just made out some more and fell asleep in each other's arms. It was kind of wonderful.

But now, in the light of day, with Mac snoring softly under my left arm, the doubts creep in. What if it was a mistake; what if he was just drunk and confused; maybe he's *after* something—my money or connections? Not that I'd mind. I'd totally let him hook up with me the rest of the year in exchange for helping him get into a good school or land a great job or help pay for his living expenses at college or whatever. It's just. Well. I want him to like me for *me*. But I guess that was always a long shot. I mean, look at him there. His long eyelashes practically sweeping his cheeks while he sleeps. The faintest bit of stubble on his rugged chin. No way a guy like him would ever fall for someone like me.

His shoulders, strong and supple, flex and stretch as he begins to wake. He opens his eyes and looks at me sleepily.

I don't know what comes over me, but before I can stop myself, I tell Mac everything I've been feeling since we met—a speech I've rehearsed many times in my head, praying, like a young actor who dreams of an Oscar, that one day I'll actually be called on stage to deliver it. Now I'm here. And it all tumbles out in rapid succession.

"I've had a crush on you for three years. Ever since I came into our room that first day freshman year and saw you hanging a poster of The Who sleeping under the British flag—*The Kids Are Alright*—and I used to dream about *us* sleeping under that British flag, leaning on each other like Roger Daltry and Pete Townsend, wondering, hoping, praying you felt the same way, thinking you *must* see through my lame attempts to spend time together, looking at the tags on your shirts—*while* you were wearing them—using it as another pathetic excuse to be close to you—and then watching sadly as you started going out on Friday and Saturday nights, your countless dates with countless girls, telling myself you weren't interested in me, would never *be* interested, trying to get over you, resigning myself to four years of torture because *not* living with you would be an even *worse* kind of torture, and, and, and, and—I don't know why I'm telling you this now. I just... I wanted you to know."

Silence. My words lay there like a fresh turd. I wish I could take them back. Take them all back. Rewind the last minute and start over.

Mac blinks and says, "I knew that."

"...Which part?"

"All of it."

"Right—of course you did." I turn away, smiling nervously, holding back tears. "I'm an idiot. Forget I said anything."

"You're not an idiot." He rolls on his back, stretching his arms over his head, turning out his ankles and curving at his hips. "It was fun. Ya know. We got... caught up in the moment. But now we have work to do... Right?" And he looks at me with total sincerity. Without an ounce of regret or embarrassment. Maybe he *does* like me. Sure, it's back to business now, as it should be. But the door seems open with endless possibilities.

"Right," I say, hardly able to contain my smile. "Absolutely. Back to work."

"Great. Maybe you can... draft a little speech. For the presentation to the governor?"

"Sure," I say. "We can work on it together."

"Actually," he says, grabbing some socks and running shorts from his duffle, "I'm gonna go for a run. Sweat out some of this booze, ya know?"

"Okay…?"

"And, uh… best to keep *this*," he gestures to us both with a nervous puff of laughter, "on the DL. No need for people to be whispering about us today, right?"

And there it is. The shame. The embarrassment. I knew it was there. But it hits me like a punch to the heart anyway.

"Right," I say, trying to hide my disappointment. "Don't want that."

"No, just. It's better if people aren't talking about us in that way. Better they talk about our *idea*, our *presentation*. 'Don't let your personal life distract from your professional one.' Bill Clinton."

"I don't think Clinton ever said that."

"Well, he should have. I'll be back in thirty and we can walk over together?"

A glimmer of hope, perhaps, offering to walk over together? But no. He's not even looking at me. He's stretching his quads and tossing a T-shirt over his shoulder. Not even taking the time to put on his *shirt*. God, he really can't get out of here fast enough.

"In a hurry?" I say, full of hurt.

He sort of laughs and bounces on his toes. "Early bird gets the worm."

And he's gone. Out the door. Out of my life. Well, not really. I'll see him in like thirty minutes, but still. It feels pretty final. He doesn't like me at all, I know it. He was using me. Or he's confused and curious. Sowing his oats. Scratching two things off his list at once: black *and* gay. Now he can say he tried that. I can see it now: Mac laughing about me at some fraternity party next year, using me as an anecdote in a twisted drinking game: *"I once hooked up with a black GUY—top that, bitches!"*

Screw him. And his easy charm and perfect body. I don't need Mac. I'm gonna tank this stupid presentation. That'll show him.

I hear the floorboards creak outside my door. He's coming back! He feels bad about what he said! Why did I ever doubt him?

I wrap the blanket around myself, shuffle to the door, and open it to welcome him inside. But it's not Mac.

It's Emily Kim.

Standing in the middle of the hall, staring at me, is Emily freakin' Kim. She's wearing her little cocktail dress from the party last night;

she's barefoot, hair a mess, eye makeup smeared, lipstick nonexistent. And is that *grass* in her hair? Well, well. Looks like someone *else* got lucky last night.

She half-nods at me. I return the casual greeting, and then step back into my room, clicking the door gently behind me.

What the what!? There must be something in the water here. Or in the air. Could it be the low barometric pressure from the impending hurricane? More like the hurricane *punch*. Whatever it is, this B&B is like a "love shack, baby, a little old place where we can get together." And she got together with that sexy farmer kid! Jedediah or Ebenezer…? Elijah! That's it. Elijah the farmer and Little Miss Perfect. Oh, this is priceless!

I almost forget about Mac completely, my mind is racing so fast, swirling with ideas for our presentation. I can't tank it now. Emily was my biggest competition and there's no *way* she's going to be prepared. She still looked *wasted*. I've got to get ready. I toss off the blanket and head for the shower.

In the bathroom, I look at my reflection with a renewed sense of purpose. So what if Mac doesn't like me or was using me or was—what did he say?—*"Caught up in the moment?"* (Translation: regrettable hook-up, let's pretend it never happened.)

I'm over it. Over him. Maybe forever. And I think it was a good thing, us hooking up. Got him out of my system. Saw who he really is, *what* he really is. He's not made of gold, not some perfect specimen (although his body *is* amazing—that's gotta be genetics; working out alone can't give you that body). But it doesn't matter. Because I realize that Mac is just a guy. Another person. Lost and confused. And, deep down, kind of a dick. I don't need him. I'm gonna make the presentation by myself. I'll leave *before* Mac comes back from his stupid jog to "head over together." He's nothing without me. Look out, Cawdor, there's a new sheriff in town. (Okay, that was a bit much.)

As I turn to hop in the shower, a god-awful scream comes wailing from the first floor. I clutch the doorframe and stare at the bathroom vent. After the initial shock wears off, it dawns on me exactly who is screaming. I lean my hands on the sink and sigh.

Because I know: Emily Kim is not going down without a fight.

A.J.

There's something about being alone in a library that's equally calming and sad. I've been in this reference room since 7 a.m., trying to show initiative, and hoping to get a chance to talk to Governor Watson alone. To tell him about the party and about some of my concerns from the email I never sent. (Since I woke up, I've been going over what I want to say, hoping to come off less preachy in person.) While I was waiting, I slid three massive tables together and dragged in chairs and benches from all over to make the room more presentable.

When Governor Watson arrives at 7:45 wearing a rumpled polo shirt and jeans, I beeline to him, ignoring Teddy's attempt to intercept me.

"Governor Watson. Good morning."

"Alexis," he says without looking at me, his eyes on a series of index cards he keeps flipping through.

"I was going to send you an email last night, sir, but thought it was better to speak in person."

"About?"

His unusually curt demeanor throws me and makes me completely forget my "prepared remarks." I decide to wing it.

"Well, sir, for starters. The party at Richard Gains' hotel got a little out of hand last night."

"I don't care about the party. We've got bigger fish to fry. What else?"

"Okay. Well, um…" *Is it getting warmer in here? Why are the lights so bright?* "I was also a little… concerned. About how we left things last night. I thought we were all going to sit down and figure out the best plan of attack for today. If we want to make a strong impression on the young voters, it would behoove us to be tweeting about the contest, the storm's path and progress, information about how to help and donate money. There's a lot I could be doing on that front."

"Thanks, sweetie, but again… bigger fish."

He pats me on the shoulder and moves away. Teddy gives me a

sheepish look and follows the governor to the head of the table.

I try not to read too much into it, try to act like a team player. It's his job to be tough, to not play favorites, to treat everyone equally. But it's hard to believe that when the governor and his staff commandeer one end of the room and leave me in the cheap seats, stuck between a fire exit and a shelf of large books about ocean life.

What's happening here? Wasn't I the girl he started the slow clap for after I essentially *created* this entire contest? Has the governor become a manifestation of the Janet Jackson song "What Have You Done For Me Lately?" I get a knot in my stomach and feel light-headed. This was not how I expected the morning to go.

At exactly 8:00 a.m., Governor Watson pours himself a tall glass of water, looks out at the hundred of us crammed into this makeshift conference room, and says, "Okay. Let's get right to it. Who's up first?"

As the governor sips his water, he sits and looks to Teddy to take over. Teddy smiles winningly and stands to make a few opening remarks. He informs the twenty-three teams that they'll have two minutes each for their presentations, and that Governor Watson will be making an immediate decision about the winner since we all need to be finished by 9 a.m. Those evacuating must be on the buses and trains departing Cawdor by 9:30. Those staying are required to ride out the storm in the elementary school auditorium. Apparently it's the largest windowless room in town and the building is, according to Teddy, "more solid than an Egyptian pyramid!"

"First up," Teddy says proudly, "the girl who's kind of responsible for *all* of this—Miss Emily Kim. And partner."

I click my pen and jot Emily's name and the number "1" on my legal. I want to be ready to talk intelligently about the presentations should Governor Watson ask for my input. Though after our awkward tête-à-tête and my current seating assignment, I'm not so sure he'll ask. But I want to be ready anyway, *need* to be ready. This is the job I want, the new career path I've chosen. If I need to put up with a little taste of the boy's club mentality to get a seat at the adult table, so be it. Better women before me have had to suffer much worse. I shouldn't complain, right?

There's a smattering of tepid applause as a surprisingly un-sharp-looking Emily Kim moves to the front of the room. Her partner, Morgan's sister, doesn't seem to be here. Perhaps she bailed early, fearing the impending destruction from Calliope.

"Good morning," Emily begins. "My partner Rani Caldwell was unavoidably detained, so I'll be proceeding without her. Our idea is simple. As recent storms like Katrina, Irene, and Sandy have devastated towns along the Gulf Coast and closer to home in New York and New Jersey, we've learned all too well how heartbreaking the destruction can be. Those of us here today, for the most part, are among the privileged class. And as these hurricanes wreak havoc, we sit back in our homes, with electricity and heat and water, watching the coverage on TV, saying to ourselves, 'What can *we* do to help?' Maybe we volunteer our time. Maybe we give money. But do we really know that money is getting into the hands of those who need it most? And what do these people really need? They don't want a handout. They don't want to feel 'less than' us. They want to get back on their feet. They want to be able to take care of themselves. To feel *normal* again. They just need a little help.

"Now, FEMA and the Red Cross and organizations such as these do fine work, but they can take days or even *weeks* to mobilize and actually get the much-needed supplies and funds into the hands of those affected by the disaster. Our plan takes away the middleman. If you're sitting at home and have a spare room, an open guesthouse, blankets, clothes, food, you name it... you can download our free app, enter your information, and within *seconds* find a needy family in your area and connect with them directly. It's called 'Empty Rooms, Full Hearts.' And we think... *I* think... it's going to change the way communities connect. And get those affected by this storm, and those affected by *future* natural disasters, back on their feet faster, more efficiently, and with more dignity. Thank you."

Jesus! That was incredible! But the other teams don't seem to care, silently agreeing not to clap after any of the presentations, I guess. Maybe they don't want to sway the governor's decision. Either that or they're more competitive than *I* was in high school.

Emily sits as Teddy calls the next set of names on his list. Standing and moving to the front is a group of six boys who are very overweight or very skinny (nothing in between), and they're all wearing different *Star Wars*-themed shirts. (My favorite is the one of Luke Skywalker made to look like the Obama "Hope" poster.) The tallest boy, who appears to be the leader, is the exception. His shirt has the Milky Way Galaxy on it with a small arrow pointing to a dot that says: "You Are Here." I like these guys already.

But as I try to focus on their presentation—a promising idea about solar-powered water pumps—my mind keeps going back to what the governor said not ten minutes ago: *"Thanks, sweetie, but again… bigger fish."*

Governor Watson's kind of an asshole, isn't he? And I threw away a good job, a nice boyfriend, and a solid life in government for the chance to work for this guy. And then he treats me like *that*? I haphazardly tossed away everything I had to be on his team, to score a chance at a front row seat on the road to the White House. All so he can call me "sweetie" and dismiss me like some third-rate intern.

Okay, maybe I'm overreacting. Congresswoman Clark warned me about responding emotionally on the job. I'm tired. A little hungry. And perhaps a little scared that I might actually be close to getting what I want—the old cliché of being afraid of success. Plus, doesn't everyone have to take a little abuse on the way up the ladder?

Forcing myself to refocus on the presentations, I suddenly feel guilty. Other than Emily Kim, I've barely heard a word anyone has said. I look up at the front of the room and see two boys mid-presentation: a puppy-dog-looking white kid and his black friend, who's clearly in love with him. The black kid is doing all the talking. The white one seems embarrassed or apologetic somehow. Like he doesn't want to be standing up there. Or like he and his partner had a fight earlier. I don't know. They seem like good kids, so I listen as intently as I can.

"Our idea is not revolutionary," the black kid says. "But sometimes the best ideas are ones that have worked in the past. So we've designed a line of low-income sustainable green housing. Sort of piggy backing on what Brad Pitt did in NOLA. Made entirely from recycled wood and metals recovered from the devastated neighborhoods, with added rooftop solar panels and energy efficient appliances, these are not only stronger, longer-lasting structures that can weather the next hurricane, but homes that will have a smaller impact on the environment and give their owners a sense of pride. With heating and cooling costs up to forty percent less than that of traditional structures, and by not requiring as many repairs, the homes will pay for themselves over the next two decades. Our goal was to make something that is not only practical, but also an architectural breakthrough. And I think we've achieved that here. Of the many nicknames for our state, like 'The Constitution State' or 'The Nutmeg State,' my favorite is 'The Land of Steady Habits.' Which is why our green-housing design is called 'Steady *Habitats.*' Homes for now, homes for the future. Thank you."

Another solid idea. I have no idea how Governor Watson will decide. By the look of it, neither does he. He keeps running his hands through his hair and scratching the back of his head like a twitch. I can't tell if he's nervous or bored.

The two-minute time limit is being adhered to vehemently, and toward the end, the proposals fly by in a blur.

"We'll use hot air balloons for post-flood evacuations."

"Replace the levees completely with a wall... like The Great Wall? Of China?"

"Rain coats and waders for everyone in the flood zones."

"A really, really... really big sponge. To, you know... soak up the water?"

"It's called Relief Jam. And it'll make the 12.12.12 concert look Lame. Lame. Lame."

At five minutes to nine, Teddy stands, looking a little worse for wear. He glances over his list, ticks off a box, and then smiles. "And... last but not least," he announces, "Prayer and Elijah Jones."

The brother-sister duo make their way to the front of the room to a round of uniformly hostile looks. I guess "plays well with others" isn't on their homeschool report cards.

"Hello," the boy says timidly. "Our plan is actually quite simple. One of the, uh, major threats of course with a storm like Calliope is flooding, something we've unfortunately become all too familiar with on our farm in the last decade. In fact, after Hurricane Irene in 2011, we decided to prepare ourselves better by constructing a device that would protect us from future floods. Last year during Sandy, our idea was put to the ultimate test and it passed with, uh, flying colors. So what we've done for the past thirty-six hours—with some amazing help from dozens and dozens of our church members, and of course through the steady, guiding hand of Our Lord Almighty—is we have taken apart, transported, and reassembled that same device—a, uh, massive wooden lever, if you will, that acts like a dam. There's a valve we can crank open or shut that essentially diverts the rising river water—in this case, to the west into smaller estuaries, away from town. What's more," Elijah continues, clearing his throat; he's a decidedly nervous public speaker, "the re-routed waters can also be directed to the Angus reservoir. That water can be siphoned off to local farms north and west of town that, as we *also* know all too well from personal experience, have suffered greatly during this summer's drought. The entire thing is controlled via computer and, uh, as the storm rolls in, we can monitor the water levels, opening and closing the valve. As needed."

Holy shit! And I mean "holy" literally. That is the most mindboggling, biblically epic thing I've heard since Noah and the goddamn ark! If their idea even *half* works, that has to be the winning proposal.

For a few seconds, there's complete silence. No one moves, coughs, breathes… nothing.

Then, as if on cue, all eyes (including mine) instantly, anxiously move to the governor.

"Well," he says, after a beat. "One thing's for sure. Our nation's in good hands for the next few decades with *this* generation waiting to take the helm."

There are some laughs and nods. I see the governor is hesitant, but like all great leaders, in an instant his face fills with resolve and it's clear he's made his decision. It's time to rip off the Band-Aid. (Guess he won't be needing *my* input.)

"But," he continues, "there's no use beating around the bush. I know it's fast. I know there's a lot on the line. But I gotta go with my gut. And that's with the, uh… The Jones twins."

The twins instantly join hands and shut their eyes in prayer. The rest of the room sits in shock. Including Teddy. But he regroups quickly, clapping his hands.

"Okay! Let's all congratulate Prayer and Elijah Jones for their winning proposal!" Again some tepid applause, but mostly anger, jealously, and hurt. Upset teenagers sulking like six year olds who wanted the last cookie, even though they knew they didn't deserve it.

"And I want to thank you *all*," Teddy continues, trying to keep things light, "not only for your time and brilliant ideas, but for your hard work and generosity over the last two days. Connecticut will forever be in your debt. Now let's get you to some safer quarters!"

Everyone slowly rises. There is very little conversation, just the harsh sound of wooden chair legs scraping against linoleum. Only Emily Kim remains seated. Refusing to believe it's over. Maybe thinking it's all a bad dream and surely she'll wake up any second. I press my lips into a thin apologetic smile and give her as appreciative a nod as a lame nod from thirty feet away can be. She just stares at me, incredulous.

As I make my way toward the governor to follow him out, Emily Kim stomps across the room, blocking the exit.

"Oh. Miss Kim," Governor Watson says. "Excuse me."

"Excuse *me*."

He blinks a few times, quickly gauging her temperature like a true politician. "I, um. I want to thank you again for making all of this happen," he says diplomatically. "You won't be forgotten."

"Damn straight," Emily says. "Because I'm not leaving until you change your mind."

"…I'm sorry?"

I make eye contact with Teddy across the room. He senses that the governor is in trouble and tries to hustle over, but there's a crush of people around Teddy peppering him with questions, sucking up one last time, attempting to lock down internships and recommendation letters.

I turn back to the standoff between Emily and the governor. She repeats, slightly louder, "I said. I'm not leaving. Until you change your mind."

"Hey," I suggest, "maybe we can discuss this outside?"

"Because there is no WAY their stupid Bible plan can work in time," Emily shouts. "If it even works at *all!*"

Elijah Jones overhears this outburst and turns, looking more hurt than angry. His sister attempts to usher him out, but he shrugs her off and steps closer to hear what else Emily has to say about his winning proposal. I'm frozen, wondering if I should start escorting people out like a TV cop ("Move along, people, nothing to see here"), or if that's overstepping my bounds. By default (and slight cowardice) I stand and do nothing.

"Well," the governor says to Emily, keeping his voice low, a small, curious crowd now lingering by the exit. "I can understand your doubts, but there were a lot of factors going into my decision…"

"Such as?"

"Well, for starters: economy, timing, practicality, feasibility…"

"Feasibility?!" Emily cackles. "Their plan is to divert the water with an enormous wooden *dyke!* That Little Boy Blue crap is less feasible than *any* of the other plans!"

Teddy has made it halfway across the room, but gets caught up by the Relief Jam crowd. I can just make out what they're saying, how they understand the governor's choice but still think their concert idea should be investigated further to "raise money for the state—*and* future disaster awareness." Um… *what?*

Just as it looks like Emily is about to launch into another tirade, Prayer Jones steps in.

"Excuse me, Miss Kim, but you had your shot." Her words are measured and even. "Governor Watson did not pick your plan. He picked ours. And I can assure you, and everyone else in this room, that our plan works—and will continue to work. The Cawdor system is already in place and will do exactly as we say it will—diverting potential floodwaters to neighboring farms suffering from drought. It's a win-win, a nearly flawless plan."

"Oh, bite my ass, 'flawless plan,'" Emily mocks, but Prayer presses on, undeterred.

"Now, I'm sorry if your feelings were hurt because things didn't go your way, but you can't blame everyone else for your disappointments, and you can't bully your way through life. Just because you really, really want something doesn't mean you get it. We can't always win. Someone has to come in second and third. And last. That's life."

Oh, man. It's the thing I hate most: girls turning on each other. I would've stepped in and said something, but after yesterday and this morning, I'm a little gun shy about speaking my mind in front of the governor. Though I'm not sure why *he* didn't put a stop to the girls' bickering.

Nothing left to say, Emily exits with as much dignity as she can muster, but she appears emotionally tattered by the exchange. Elijah watches her leave with a look resembling pity. His sister sees this and steps over to him, leveling her brother with a cool, withering gaze. "You can do better, Elijah. I won't tell Mom and Dad about her. But I'm very disappointed in you."

Prayer pivots on her heels, looks right past me, and says, "Governor, thank you for your faith in us. Shall we move to the shelter so my brother and I can get the device ready with our remote?" Prayer flips her blond hair and saunters away, leaving us in her wake.

The excitement over, the lingering kids make their way out, finally clearing a path for Teddy, who says, "What the hell was *that*?"

The governor stands up straighter, takes a breath, and says, "Damned if I know. But I don't want this turning into some big thing." He turns to me. "Alexis, maybe you can go talk to Miss Kim, cool her jets a little. You ought to be able to speak her language, a young girl like you."

And he winks at me before making a hasty exit. Teddy doesn't even look at me, just follows the governor out. And I'm suddenly in an empty room, not sure what I'm supposed to do. Or what I *want* to do. It feels like a crossroads. But I have no idea where either road is headed. I'm happy the governor enlisted me to help out, but the task seems kind of demeaning. And the more I get to know the governor, the less likable he becomes. But you don't have to *like* your boss, do you? You just have to respect them. And I do still respect Governor Watson and what he stands for.

I look at the clock on the wall that reads 9:05 a.m.

It's gonna be a long day.

RANI

Tyler and I arrive late and see the crowd fanning out of the library in two distinct groups, one going east, the other going west.

"Aw, shucks," he says with a wry smile. "Looks like we missed the fun."

After Emily's war cry reverberated around the walls of the B&B, Tyler leaned back in to pick up where he left off, but I wasn't into it and he could tell pretty quickly.

"You're still worrying," he said in a sing-song way.

"I'm sorry," I said. "It's just…"

"What?"

"We came all this way, Emily and I. And I feel like I'm ditching her at the eleventh hour."

"You're not ditching her. We'll get to the library in plenty of time. Trust me."

"Why are you here?"

"Um, because I like you," he said as if it was the most obvious thing in the world.

"No, I mean… here. In Cawdor. You're not on any of the teams, you aren't vying for the scholarship. Why are you here?"

"I don't know," he said with a smile. "Beats riding out the storm with my family. And when I met you at the train station, and you said you were going to stick around, I thought… what an even better reason to stay. To get to know you."

My heart melted a little and for an instant—a crazed, hormonal, irrational instant—I wanted to give in and go all the way with Tyler. He was cuter than any boy who had ever paid attention to me.

But something about that worried me. Like deep down I knew I wasn't good enough for him, so he must be up to something. I've never been lusted after or pursued—and now that it's happening I don't trust my pursuer's motives to be completely pure. How screwed up is that?

But I took a risk anyway and kissed him. It was like an out-of-body experience this time. I wasn't "Rani" anymore. And I thought about going further. Thought about taking off his shirt, letting him take mine off, as well... But I couldn't do it. I kept stopping and asking if he really liked me, and he continually assured me that he did, so I asked what was going to happen after the hurricane, don't worry about it, he said, but you live so far away, I've got a car and the train is super cheap, but what about next year and college, don't think about that it's so far away, and you really like me? yes yes yes I really like you I think you're amazing, then if you really like me it's okay if we stop—for now?

So we stopped. And he said all the right things. But I could see he was disappointed. We held each other in bed for a few more minutes, him calculating when he could make another move, me trying to get up gracefully without hurting his feelings. By the time I finally got dressed and ready, we were already late for the presentations.

So here we are, watching the kids file out of the library. We seem to have missed everything. Not that I mind. It's just that I know how maniacal Emily can get. And considering the state of mind she was in *before* the presentations, I can only imagine how she's feeling now. I'm convinced she'll find a way to blame me if we didn't win. And some gut instinct tells me we didn't. But I need to know for sure.

I stop the first kid I see, a little Duck Dynasty protégé with a mesh trucker hat and cutoff camouflage shorts. "Hey—is it over?"

"The presentations?" he says, sliding his hat back on his head a few inches. "Yeah. Watson picked the farmer twins. Some flood-diverting lever they constructed 'with the Lord's help.'" The kid sort of sneers a laugh and then adds, "Seems crazy to me. But if that Jesus device works... it'll be pretty epic."

Damn. We lost. I bet Emily is cornering the governor right now to demand a recount.

While I'm lost in thought, Tyler asks the kid where everyone is headed.

"Train station mostly—fastest way outta here. Few others are taking buses and cars, I guess. And a small group is ridin' out the storm at the school. Me? I ain't no hero. I did my bit, didn't win squat... now I want me some dry land and cable TV."

The kid trots off to catch up with his friends. I look at Tyler and raise my eyebrows as if to say, train station or school? Before he can answer, my cell phones rings.

"It's my parents," I say, looking at it.

"Don't answer," Tyler says casually.

I laugh at the outrageous idea. "I have to answer. They'd kill me."

"Whatever you say." Tyler sort of looks around at the passing crowd, giving me a bit of privacy.

Maybe I'm paranoid, but Tyler seems to be cooling to me by the second. No time to dwell though. I press the "answer" button and say, "Hey, I was just going to call you."

"How'd it go?" my mom asks. "Did you win?"

"Uh, no. He picked another plan. But we did okay, I think. Made a good impression."

"Did you talk to Teddy?" my dad calls out.

"Uh… yeah," I lie. "It was nice. He's a… a nice guy."

"Oh good!" my mom gushes. "See? It wasn't weird was it?"

"Nope. You were right."

"You can tell us all about it when you get home. Are you driving back with Emily or are you taking the train?"

"I think, actually… I'm gonna stay. Here."

Tyler turns, pleasantly surprised. I scrunch my shoulders up and grit my teeth in a silent, excited gesture.

"What do you mean, 'stay'?" my mom asks.

"I wanna, you know… stay here in Cawdor. A lot of kids are riding out the storm. There's a safe shelter—a school nearby? Then we can all be on the ground right away to help during the aftermath."

There's a brief silence. As I wonder if my cell phone cut out, I realize my mother is just trying to collect herself.

"Rani Lakshmi Caldwell," she says sternly. "I am all for you giving your time or money or whatever you *can* to help those in need. But you do *not* risk your *life* for something like this. Nothing is more important than your safety."

"Mom—I'll be fine."

"We're coming to get you… Daddy can be there in an hour. Doug!"

"Gotta go. Love you!"

"Rani—!"

I hang up. My hands are shaking. I've never hung up on my parents before. Tyler looks at me, impressed. Any lustful feelings that had cooled seem to be heating up again. He looks like he wants to kiss me right here in front of everyone.

But before we can do anything, my phone rings again, somehow sounding louder and shriller. I look down at the screen, which reads 'Mom & Dad.' The little green 'Answer' button and the little red 'Decline' button on the bottom taunt me. The phone rings a second time. And I push 'Decline.'

Silence.

Everything stops. The noise around me. The sound of the wind in the trees. The voices in my head. My heartbeat...

I breathe in. It's shaky and unsteady. But once I exhale, the noises come back. I hear the crowd milling around behind us. I hear cars starting and pulling out of the parking lot. I hear Tyler, his voice fading in like when a coma victim wakes up in a movie.

"Hey... hey! You okay? You all right?" He touches my arm, looking me in the eye.

"Yeah..."

"You sure?"

"...I'm good."

My phone rings again. I deftly flick the little ringer button down to silence it once and for all and then stuff the phone in my back pocket. My hands are still shaking, but my breathing is returning to normal. I look around, irrationally afraid that my parents will barrel up at any minute, even though they're a hundred miles away. After a few seconds go by with no Lexus, I sigh heavily and turn to Tyler.

"I, uh... I told you what my name means, right?"

"Uh, yeah," he replies, unsure where this is going. "Princess, or... queen or something?"

"Mm... I ever tell you what my *middle* name means?"

"I don't even *know* your middle name."

"It's Lakshmi," I say. "And it means a lot of things. Goddess of wealth, good fortune. But the one my parents always stressed was... ambition."

"Ambition... Huh."

We look at the few people still coming out the library, a few going east toward the school, most heading west to evacuate.

"So," I say, taking a few steps toward the east, "we've come this far. Might as well see this bitch to the end."

§

Tyler and I clutch hands in the back seat, more out of fear for our lives than as any sort of romantic gesture. We're in a smelly van with Rory, Josh, and two other members of the Grateful Ten (I guess the other six bailed after they didn't win). On the bench seat in front of us is a total hippie chick who looks like Janice from "The Muppets" and a cute, crunchy girl with dreadlocks who seems to regret staying behind. Janice, on the other hand, appears to have "waked and baked" and doesn't care *where* she is. Her gaze drifts out the window, but she's not really taking in the passing scenery.

Rory drives aggressively, swerving across the dotted yellow line, speeding up to pass slow moving cars, braking and swerving back in when it's clear he won't make it. After changing lanes for the seventh time and still not being able to pass anyone on the two-lane highway, Josh finally says something about it being cool, bra, Relief Jam can still be a reality.

"Duh—I know. Quit trying to placate me, okay? I'm fine."

"Well, your driving is kind of wigging everyone out."

"They can freakin' walk then. It's my freakin' van!"

We ride another minute in total silence and then Janice suddenly says, "You guys remember *That 70's Show*? With Ashton Kutcher? Why'd they ever cancel that—it was a really great show."

Josh does a perfect slow burn to Janice, who's already forgotten what she said and is back to not-really-gazing out the window.

Finally arriving in one piece, we pull into the mostly empty parking lot. Rory follows a string of cars which proceeds like a funeral procession, each one peeling off simultaneously into a spot on the left. The elementary school in front of us hangs under the darkening morning sky, the ashen clouds now almost the exact same color as the school: battleship grey. The low squatting building with bars on the windows looks more like an inner city public school than something you'd expect to see in a small coastal town.

We pile out of the van and I'm not sure if I should hold Tyler's hand or not. It sort of seems like a moment when I should—hustling into an evacuation area, an impending storm, looming danger—but it also feels totally weird and out of place. So I opt to just stand super close to him like "we're together but not dating" as we follow the other groups into Millard Fillmore Elementary.

"Millard Fillmore?" Josh says enthusiastically. "It's a sign, dude. We should do Relief Jam at the Fillmore. In San Francisco!"

Rory gives Josh a contemptuous look that sucks away all of his optimism. But then I see Rory's wheels turning, as if the Fillmore West *wasn't* such a bad idea. Maybe Rory will steal it and make it his own. Dump the Grateful Ten and go solo. The Rory Garcia Band.

Making our way into the auditorium, it's exactly like every public school auditorium I've ever seen: bland cement walls, no windows, a sad stage with red asbestos curtains, and energy-sapping fluorescent bulbs in wire cages forty feet above it all. The few dozen people who have decided to ride out the storm in Cawdor are scattered throughout, the dark wooden chairs creaking and moaning under them with every slight movement.

On stage, Elijah Jones and his sister are perched by a long table with a few computers on it. A chubby techie is frantically running cables and wires from the computers to some other complicated-looking equipment on and off stage. An instant later, Elijah's laptop display is projected onto the auditorium's ancient pull down screen. (Presumably so we in "the audience" can follow what Elijah is doing?) Since we missed the presentations, I'm not sure why this would be necessary, but Tyler and I settle into some seats near the middle left aisle, away from the Grateful *Four*, offering a decent view of the screen and an even better opportunity for a hasty exit.

Governor Watson and Teddy Hutchins are standing off to the side of the stage near a podium, looking up at the screen, arms folded, faces serious, like baseball coaches watching an important playoff game unfold; expressionless on the outside, jangles of nerves just below the surface. The girl who was Morgan's RA (I think she said her name was A.J.?) stands a few feet away from the men, making no attempt whatsoever to hide her nerves, peeling the label off a water bottle, readjusting her shirt collar, rolling out her wrists.

I spot Emily in that space between the front row and the raised stage, pacing like a tiger waiting to be fed, like she's trying to intimidate Elijah or even the governor. For a split second I consider saying hi. But I decide to slump further into my chair and watch anonymously.

There's a crackle over the speakers, some high-pitched feedback, and then the words "testing, test—one, two—sibilance, sibilance. All right, Elijah, you're good to go." Now I recognize the chubby techie as the guy who kept launching himself into the pool last night, naked. (I think he was the one who soaked Elijah after an especially robust cannonball; I guess they've made nice since then.) The techie hands Elijah a headset microphone and scurries off backstage, hiking up his pants, which desperately want to fall to his knees.

"What the hell are we watching?" I ask Tyler.

"I don't know," he replies. "But it's hypnotic."

"Okay, um. Hello. Can everyone hear me?" Elijah says over the loudspeakers, his voice less sure than I remember it being during our brief encounter yesterday. There are a few affirmative murmurs from the sparse crowd. Elijah takes that as an okay to press on. "So what you're seeing now," he says, vaguely indicating the screen overhead, "are four live shots from cameras we set up near the top of the existing levee where the, uh, Lennox River crosses the Cawdor town limits. Clockwise from upper left, we have the north, east, south and west-facing cameras..."

As he explains in detail how the entire thing will work, I give Tyler an impressed raise-of-the-eyebrows.

"Epic, indeed," Tyler whispers.

I glance toward Emily, who's still pacing down front, biting her thumbnail down to a nub. Unannounced, Mac slides into a seat behind Tyler and me, while Robert stands, his hands leaning on the back of the chair next to Tyler's.

"If we start rationing food," Robert proclaims, "I call the veggie ramen. Since I'm vegan and all."

"I call shrimp," Tyler retorts.

"Joke's on you. It's shrimp *flavored*," Robert teases.

"Probably safer that way. I don't wanna get salmonella, puke all over the bunker room."

The two boys chuckle. I look over my shoulder at Robert and smile weakly in lieu of an actual laugh. He smiles down at me, looking oddly refreshed and chipper under the circumstances: an insanely physical day yesterday, a long night partying and drinking, and then rising early for the presentations. Mac, however, looks nervous, like an aerophobe anxiously waiting for a plane to finally taxi to the safety of the gate. He catches me studying him and sits up higher in his seat, presses his lips into a tight smile reserved for passing the lone stranger on a sidewalk at 6 a.m. He glances at Robert and then at me before looking up at the screens, a neutral zone. I look at Robert again and see a satisfied glow in his cheeks.

Holy crap. They totally hooked up last night!

Not that I care. I'm sure Emily would make a huge thing out of it. But it's not that big of a deal, I guess, not *that* crazy or out of left field. Boarding school roommates, lots of late nights alone in one small room… It's bound to happen once in a while. I look at Mac one last time, hoping to catch his eye again, and offer some level of understanding, but his gaze remains steadfast, as if the unchanging camera angles on the Lennox River are endlessly fascinating.

Robert finally sits behind us and emits a long, weary sigh. "I guess it *is* a pretty good plan. And it actually addresses immediate problems the storm may cause, rather than just cleaning up after the mess, blah blah blah… But I really wanted that scholarship."

"Yeah," I say vaguely, not intending anything more than general commiseration. But as the words escape from my lips, I realize that I *did* want that scholarship. I wanted to win. Not just for Emily. Or for my parents. But for me. I wanted to win for me.

I was just afraid to *want* it. Afraid to care and be disappointed.

Sitting there, watching the Jones twins tap at their laptops while the multiscreen display broadcasts bland shots of the river like a traffic camera blandly broadcasting an intersection at rush hour, I realize that my aloofness the past couple years has been an act, something to prevent me from being disappointed with life. If I don't have any expectations, if I don't *care* about anything, nothing will let me down. It was a sound strategy and one that I could have coasted on for the rest of my life. But it failed to protect me here. I still feel slighted. Hurt. Angry. For Emily. For my parents. For me.

The trip wasn't a total bust. I met Tyler—that was a nice surprise. But I didn't win. Didn't even cross the finish line. And I realize that *"not crossing the finish line"* is what upsets me most. Skipping the presentations with Tyler was fun, but it was the easy way out, the passive-aggressive technique. Don't engage. No skin in the game. If you lose, so what? You didn't try that hard anyway. And if you win, bonus.

But that's a coward's life. And I don't want that. I don't want to sit on the sidelines anymore and fail to contribute. With a sudden jolt, I stand up, knowing what I have to do.

"Excuse me one sec," I say to Tyler and, by proximity, Robert and Mac, too.

I step quickly down the raked aisle to the front area by the stage, and tap Emily on the shoulder, not exactly sure what I'm going to say.

"Hey."

"Hey," she says softly. We both kind of stare at our feet, then vaguely look toward the multiscreen display hanging a few feet above our heads.

"Crazy night, hunh?"

"To say the least," Emily says cryptically.

I shuffle my feet some more and then ask, "How'd the presentations go?"

"Peachy."

"Did they at least seem to *like* our idea?" I ask hopefully.

"Who cares? We lost."

"I know but—"

"I don't want to talk about it."

"…Sorry."

She scoffs. "No you're not."

"Yes, I am," I insist.

"You never cared about *any* of this."

"No, really. I'm sorry."

"About what exactly?" she says facing me.

"About *that* and… about *every*thing." And it all comes out. "Ditching you for Tyler last night. Not being there for you this morning. Not really *being* here for you, period. It was a good idea,

Em. A *great* idea. And maybe we could have won if I'd been a little more present—"

"Doesn't matter," she says flatly. "We had no chance."

"What do you mean?"

"There are two of us. Some teams have four, six, the Grateful *Ten*...? But those farmer geeks had like *fifty* people helping them. It was never a fair fight."

I watch Emily as she stares vacantly at the stage. "Do you wanna, like, protest or something?"

"No," Emily says, letting out a sigh. "I'm over it. I know I say that a lot, but... I mean it this time."

"Over what?"

"All of it. This hurricane, the scholarship, the rat race. I'm 17 years old and I've never had *fun*." She hangs her head and begins to cry. Just her shoulders quivering at first, then her whole back, and then she's sniffling and hiding her face behind her sleek black hair. It's the first time I've seen her cry. Ever. Not even when she broke her wrist in third grade PE.

I place a hand on her back and rub in small, soothing circles. "What are you talking about? We have fun all the time."

"It's smoke and mirrors, it's not real," she says, her voice cracking, her face wet with tears. "I laugh and *act* confident, kick butt in school, crack jokes dripping with sarcasm. But deep down I'm petrified. *All* the time. My mother's voice in my head on a constant loop: *How going to movie get you better GPA? How dancing in bar get you to Harvard?*"

I puff out a laugh at her spot-on imitation of Mrs. Kim. Through her tears, Emily finally cracks a smile.

"I never enjoyed any of it," she admits. "So I'm done." She wipes her eyes and sniffs back her runny nose. "Done racing, done striving... done *achieving*. My grades are fine. I'll get into a good school. Maybe even Harvard. But if not—so what? I'm gonna *enjoy* college, wherever I go."

"Wow," I say, genuinely stunned. "Did you... decide all of this now?"

"I don't know. Losing the scholarship didn't help. But I was kind of feeling this way last night. It's why I..." She pauses to look over both shoulders like a drug dealer and then whispers, "I kissed Elijah Jones."

"*What?*" I'm smiling and flabbergasted at the same time. This is literally the most unbelievable thing I've ever heard.

Emily shrugs and smiles too. "We just *kissed*. I think. Whatever, it was seriously stupid. But also kind of awesome. Like, for the first time in a while... I totally let go. I mean... I've never done anything like that in my *life*. Got hammered, made out with a random dude, and crashed outside? Kind of wackadoo."

"Wait. You slept out*side* last night?"

She nods. "Not my proudest moment. But," she leans in to whisper, "Eli's kinda *hot*."

"...Really?" I ask, looking toward Elijah on stage, trying to glean some heretofore-unseen hotness.

"Oh, working on a farm has kept him in *prime* shape."

"Sounds like you're smitten."

"I'm not *smitten*," she says, elbowing me. "He's just... different."

"So are you going to start chicken-whispering now?"

"Hey, if it'll get me into Harvard, I'll have *sex* with a chicken."

This time I can't hold back my laughter. It literally explodes out of me, the way milk squirts out of a kid's nose, which of course makes Emily laugh, too. And now people are staring at us. Emily waves a hand in apology to no one in particular, both of us giggling and leaning on each other like kids in church, like we used to in the back of our middle school French class. (Say, *"My seal is on the roof."* *"Mon phoque est sur le toit."* Endless entertainment.)

"Oh and guess what?" Emily whispers excitedly. "That guy Robert...?"

"Totally hooked up with his roommate," I blurt out, finishing her sentence.

"*How* did you know?!"

"How did *you?*"

We laugh even louder this time and some adults in the front finally shush us and ask us to please find a seat. We apologize, still giggling, and make our way up the other aisle, grabbing some new seats on the right side of the auditorium.

We sit down. Wordless. Model citizens.

Then, unprompted, we bust out laughing at exactly the same time. The entire room turns to us but we don't quiet down. Don't care about anyone else. And for a minute it's just the two of us again. The same little girls who met on a playground what feels like a lifetime ago. And it's nice. My best friend is back.

ACT IV

THE STORM IS UP

A.J.

Calliope is on her way.

That's what everyone is saying. The local news. National news. The Weather Channel. FEMA. Our internal guys.

Everyone but this pesky kid, this skinny little hipster in a Billionaire Boys Club jacket who's been chirping in my ear all morning.

"Don't trust those reports, little lady. I'm gettin' tons o' hits on Twitter sayin' this baby isn't following *any* of the models. Hashtag: MuchAdoAboutNuthin."

I guess since I'm the youngest member of the governor's team, this kid feels like *I'm* the one he should speak to. Lucky me.

Teddy keeps trying to usher the boy, whose name is Duncan Rodriguez, away. I only know his name is Duncan Rodriguez because he re-introduces himself every time he breezes through, saying something obnoxious and attention-grabbing. Then when you look at him like he's nuts, he thrusts a hand out for you to shake, announcing, "Duncan Rodriguez—amateur weather enthusiast and Twitter sensation." Teddy always shakes the kid's hand and politely asks him to step off the stage. But ten minutes later Duncan's back with a new Twitter report. "My boy in Southampton says no dice on Calliope. Nada, nil, zippo. Looks like another correct prediction for the D-man! What-*whaaat!*"

Finally Teddy doesn't even bother to get rid of the kid. He just stares at me, eyes wide, silently asking, "Could it be? Could the storm pass us completely?"

I look at the governor on the other side of the stage. He seems remarkably calm. (He silently moved away from Teddy and the rest of us a few minutes ago, our collective nervous energy probably hitting maximum annoyance levels.) He isn't pacing. He isn't fidgeting. Just leaning against the stage right proscenium, arms folded, eyes glued to the Jones twins at their computers. He remains fixed on them even when they stand and leave the stage. (Presumably for a bathroom break; do twins generally get the urge to pee at the same time?)

I wipe my sweaty palms on the back of my jeans for the hundredth time, grab another eight-ounce Poland Spring and down it in one gulp. And it dawns on me that I'm not nervous because I'm worried about the hurricane or how the twin's device will handle the gathering flood waters or how thousands of lives might be in danger or how my *own* life might be in danger. I'm nervous because it's almost 11 a.m. and it's not even *raining* yet. I'm nervous because... what if that annoying hipster is right? What if there's no hurricane? No clean up, no Chris Christie moment for the governor (who was already planning what he'd wear to the press conference, something vaguely patriotic, with hints of red, white and blue, and a patch of the Connecticut flag on one arm: Presidential-Casual). And if he doesn't have his big moment and isn't thrust into the spotlight and the national conversation, where does that leave me and my hopes of landing a job in the White House before I'm thirty?

Just then the governor steps by us, absently handing his still full bottle of water to Teddy, who grabs him by the shoulder. "You all right, Chucky?"

"Yeah. Just need some air." Governor Watson smiles at us both reassuringly and slips out an exit at the back of the stage.

"Glad *he's* okay," I mumble, "because I'm about to throw up."

"Don't sweat it," Teddy says. "No matter what, this is a win. Storm hits and he's an instant legend. Storm passes and, well... we were lucky, but wasn't that governor prepared? And wouldn't he be great leading us on the *national* level? Got it?"

Teddy sounds like he's trying to convince himself as much as me.

"Yeah," I agree. "It's just..." I trail off, sort of laughing, and then scratch my arm, my neck, and my head. The itch seems to be traveling all over my body, constantly *just* out of reach. Teddy stares at me as one would stare at a crazy homeless person on the subway.

"You all right, A.J.?"

"Ah, you know. Just anxious. The whole thing—it's nerve-wracking."

"Better get used to it," Teddy says, patting me on the shoulder. "Like Tiger on the seventy-second hole. Learn to love the pressure. *Thrive* on it."

Before I can respond, Teddy's phone beeps. Then the entire

team's. Then mine.

We all look down at our BlackBerrys and read the text from the National Weather Service. Oh my God.

Still glued to his screen, Teddy says, "A.J.… Find the governor. Tell him he's needed right away."

I nod and make my way briskly toward the stage door. My head is swimming and my steps echo as I move from the bright lights on stage to the darkened wings, feeling my way through black curtains and finding the fire exit push bar covered in glow tape. I lean into it and step outside.

Daylight. Patches of sun. Not a breath of wind. A dumpster thirty feet away smells typically rancid. I hold one hand up to my forehead like a visor and squint around the alley behind the elementary school. But the governor isn't here. I thought for sure he went this way to get some air.

Just as I'm about to slip back inside to alert Teddy, I hear soft groaning *behind* the dumpster. Maybe the governor is nervous and throwing up?

I step around the corner of the dumpster and for a split second I see it: Prayer Jones is leaning against the brick wall, her right leg dangling in the air, while Governor Watson crouches on the ground and sucks the heel of her right foot.

I'm going to repeat that because I needed to look at it twice myself. The governor of Connecticut. Is crouching behind a dumpster. Sucking the heel. Of a teenage girl's foot.

I literally gasp and they quickly break it up, the governor slipping out from under Prayer's leg and stepping away in one smooth motion.

"Alexis," he says, trying to maintain some sense of decorum. "What can I do for you?"

Oh, no. No no no no no no no no no no no no. This did not just happen. There's an instant pit in my stomach. The sky spins. My legs wobble. I brace myself with one hand on the side of the dumpster and try to breathe quietly through my nose.

"Uh…" I stammer, my mind reeling, unsure what to say first, wisely choosing to ignore the elephants in the alley doing weird stuff to each other. "They… need you inside."

"Has it started? The hurricane made landfall?"

"Um..." I glance at Prayer Jones, her cheeks flushed as she discreetly slips on her right sandal. "I think Mr. Hutchins wanted to tell you himself—"

"*Just tell me*," he barks. "Where's Calliope?"

"...Not coming."

Governor Watson blinks at me and then sprints back inside the auditorium. Prayer and I are left gaping at the exit door, which slowly drifts shut. After five paralyzed seconds, we also sprint back inside.

And everything slows down. I can hear my heartbeat. I can hear Prayer's steps behind me, crunching the pebbles in the asphalt.

It all makes sense. Why the governor was behaving so strangely last night. Why he wanted to keep me at bay. Why he didn't want to strategize about this morning. He has some bizarre fetish and wanted to scratch his itch. With a teenage farm girl! I feel like I'm going to be sick.

When I arrive on stage, time goes back to normal. I spot Teddy talking to the governor alone. I walk right over and join them, like it's my job to be there. I want to confront the governor. Force an explanation out of him. Grab him by the shoulders and scream into his face, *"Are you insane? Sucking on some girl's FOOT? What is that? Is she even 18? Not cool, asshole!"* But I say nothing. I'm speechless. Dazed. Eyes darting, thoughts cascading. Teddy and the governor barely register that I'm standing there. Too busy "frying bigger fish."

"I'm telling you, Chuck, they're *all* calling it. Even the guys at FEMA."

"How is this even possible?" the governor asks.

"They're saying the storm is following the Clipper model—one of the less sophisticated models developed back in the '80s. No one really pays it much attention these days. I mean, it had like a point-zero-zero-*three* percent chance. But it's tracking along that line like white on rice, pushing dead into the Atlantic. Calliope's gonna be a no show."

Over my shoulder I can feel the auditorium go silent, the acoustics making Teddy's private conversation more of a public declaration. I see Elijah standing by his computer, bewildered. He looks pleadingly at his sister, standing in the wings. She looks like someone just punched her in the gut, a devastating blow that's more grief than pain. I turn to face the crowd, half-expecting to see smiles, cheers, waves of relief: *Disaster averted! There will be no flooding, no downed power lines or rooftop rescues. Calliope is no more!*

Instead all I see is confusion, anger, betrayal. And I instantly recognize their disappointment because it's partly mine as well. These kids are missing that sad, sick moment of *excitement* that comes during a disaster. That rush of being alive. That sense of purpose. The promise of recognition for a valiant job well done.

This storm was supposed to be my ticket to 1600 Pennsylvania Avenue. But it was supposed to be *their* ticket, too. Their ticket to a better college, a better life. These students left their homes and families to volunteer for forty-eight hours. They built levees, stacked sandbags, delivered fresh drinking water, evacuated the elderly, rescued stranded pets, spent their other waking hours creating presentations for the best disaster relief effort, collectively held their breath as the storm approached… And it didn't come. And now they feel abandoned and betrayed. As if none of them were volunteering to actually help people. They were volunteering to help *themselves*.

In stunned silence they sit, staring blankly at the pull-down screen, watching the four static angles on the same patch of river meeting land, waiting in vain for the images to change, for rain to cascade down, for wind to rip the trees from their roots. But it's simply a breezy, cloudy day. If I didn't know better, I'd think it was a nice break from the hot, hazy summer we've been having, a brief respite from the norm. But the decent weather is not a welcome relief to these ambitious students, these rising seniors looking forward to standing out from the crowd, standing out from the throngs of ordinary college applicants. To these kids, it's a harbinger of failure.

Just then, the doors at the back of the auditorium burst open with a bang.

"Whoo-hoo!" the skinny Latino hipster yells from the doorway. "Sayonara, Calliope! *Oh* yeah! Duncan: One. Rest of the stupid media: a big-fat-*nada*!"

At least *someone* around here is happy about the way things turned out: Duncan Rodriguez. I make a mental note to remember that name. I have a feeling he'll be part of the media sooner rather than later. (Always good to have a friend in the press. And he could help sway the Latino youth vote, too!)

While Duncan makes his way down the aisle, high fiving anyone who'll let him, the governor steps off the stage to shake Duncan's hand, forcing a smile as if he's thrilled Duncan was right.

"Well done, Duncan," he says, giving his best Bill Clinton. "We *all* won today."

"Some of us more than others," Duncan quips, giving the governor's shoulder a patronizing pat. And then he's off again, collecting accolades from the crowd.

And while I'm sure everyone (somewhere deep down) is happy that the crisis was averted, it's also clear (particularly as I watch Rani and Emily reluctantly high five Duncan) that part of them, a large part of them, *wanted* to be called to action—*wanted* to test their mettle and gain some real world experience that would make them feel alive and worthy, and, oh, yeah, by the way, also look amazing in a college essay. Their generation—and my own to some extent—seems destined to lack any real hardship. So we cling and rush to controversy, sometimes stirring it up unnecessarily. We need a Vietnam or an Occupy Wall Street or a massive hurricane to throw our collective energy behind. We need something to focus on other than ourselves. Otherwise our wheels are just spinning and it all seems so pointless: fighting to get into college for what exactly? So we can land a great job and make lots of money so our kids can go to college and land a great job and make lots of money so *their* kids can go to college... Where does it all end?

I don't know. These kids don't know, either. Our parents just taught us to fight. (That felt sort of like a campaign speech. Maybe I should jot that down.)

Duncan finishes his mini-gloating tour, exiting the way he came in, and the auditorium instantly feels like the loser's headquarters at 11:30 on Election Night. Some students begin to trickle out; some hang around, not wanting to believe it's over. But as the morning turns into early afternoon and the techies pack up their computer gear, the elementary school remains eerily quiet. There's no driving rain on the roof, no high winds pounding at the doors and windows, no falling limbs outside. Calliope has taken a hard right turn off the eastern tip of Long Island. Montauk gets a passing shower. The storm wreaks havoc in the northern Atlantic, giving a few fish a bumpy night's sleep. And that is all.

Not with a bang but with a whimper it ends. The goodbyes are brief and full of false promise. Appropriately, the governor shakes my hand without a word, just a sad, sheepish expression.

And I find myself at a loss for words, as well. My immediate shock at the governor's actions turned quickly to anger, but that anger has already fizzled into disappointment. Not just because I saw Governor Watson in a rather uncompromising position. (*Heel-sucking!* I mean seriously, is that really a *thing?*) But because, quite simply, the governor abused his power. And he should know better.

And I'm also disappointed because the man I believed in, the man I thought was so different, turned out to be no better than the rest of the politicians out there using their authority to fulfill their fetishes and fantasies. (It's like the Roman freakin' Empire!) I thought politics was about helping people and getting things done. I thought it was about results, and character had nothing to do with it. But now I see that you can't separate the man from the job. How you are in life is how you are at work. And it's clear that what Governor Watson cares about the most isn't the people of Connecticut. It's himself. Because in the end, aside from being weird and sort of gross and recklessly inappropriate, what he did was extremely selfish. And when he officially gets caught (and he *will* get caught—maybe not this time, for *this* bizarre indiscretion, but he'll screw up again and the world will discover who he really is—though I'm not going to be the one to rat him out), he'll disappear for a while, but then he'll bounce back. They all bounce back (see Spitzer, Weiner, Sanford). Yet his *staff* will be the ones who are outcast and unemployed. *They* will pay the price for *his* pathetic behavior. And screw you, Governor Watson, for almost putting me in that position and making me part of "your team."

But I can't muster the courage to say any of that. I just look dumbly at my feet while the governor circles the stage, thanking the rest of "the troops." By the time he's shaken a dozen hands, it looks like he's forgotten I'm even here. A year from now, I doubt he'll remember my name.

Teddy swings by and pats me on the back. "Coulda been, A.J.

What coulda been."

I nod and wonder if he has any idea about the governor's strange sexual preferences or recent tryst with Prayer Jones, wonder if Teddy knew all along, wonder if that's why he sent *me* out there looking for the governor: to open my eyes, so I could get out while the gettin's good.

And though I could leave right now, say nothing more and just go, I feel like I have to say something, *must* say something, just to make sure I'm not crazy, not imaging things.

"I, uh... I saw the governor in the alley... with Prayer Jones."

Teddy looks at me, his face slack. I have his full attention.

"Oh yeah?"

"He was, uh... sucking on the heel of her foot?"

Teddy hangs his head and closes his eyes. For about three seconds, he's silent. Then he mutters, "Goddammit, not again."

He exhales loudly, looks up at me with pathetic eyes, gives a slight shrug, and heads back to the stage. No goodbye, no apology, no thank you. Just shuffles over to trail the governor, shaking more hands. Just another day in the life. Politics as usual. Return to the status quo. Unbelievable.

I look out at the mostly empty seats, the auditorium almost restored to the neutral state in which we found it. A state that will remain undisturbed for less than three weeks before hundreds of five- to ten-year-olds clamor through these halls again, fighting for a seat next to their best friends during a Welcome Back assembly, climbing on the stage for a back-to-school presentation, unwittingly enjoying this time before the competition sets in.

A time when kids can be kids.

Suddenly the smell of the auditorium hits me (old wood and stale milk) and I'm back in fifth grade in my elementary school auditorium. We're "graduating" to middle school and my parents are hugging me on the stage and telling my younger sisters to smile as they put their arms around me, posing for pictures, and my mom tells me how proud they all are and my dad jokes that I need to stop growing up so fast, because it's making him feel old.

And I get the sudden urge to go home. Not back to my stupid apartment, but to my parent's house. Just for the weekend. It's been a while. And if I leave soon, I'll be there in time for dinner. I missed Shabbat yesterday, but still. It'll be nice to see my family.

While Teddy orders the crew around the stage, I trudge up the aisle and make an anonymous exit, contemplating my next career move. Maybe the state senator will bring me back as a policy advisor. Or I heard Congresswoman Clark is looking for a new deputy chief of staff… It's not the White House, but maybe that's okay.

I step into the quiet, empty hallway where several glass cases of crude clay sculptures and kids' paintings line the walls. By a sad, mostly empty trophy case, I spot Prayer and Elijah Jones, their matching sturdy suitcases and gear by their feet. I still can't get the image of Prayer and the governor out of my head and find myself staring at her, wondering what series of bad decisions took place that led to a middle-aged man sucking a teenage girl's foot by a dumpster in the alley. Before the silence gets too awkward, I call out, "Nice work, you two. This is only the beginning."

Not sure what I even mean by that but Elijah nods, seemingly bolstered by my platitudes. He grabs his suitcase, tucks the gear under his arm, and scuffles down the hall.

Prayer watches her brother walk out the front door, then turns to me and says, "I'm not what you think I am."

"I don't think you're anything," I say, actually meaning it.

"Well…" she sighs. "I'm not the bad guy."

"I know."

We shrug a goodbye and I watch her leave.

I feel sorry for her (and her *foot*, I can't imagine that felt good). But I also wonder: even though she *isn't* the bad guy, and even if she had no ulterior motive and just got carried away or manipulated or taken advantage of… how much longer before Prayer Jones realizes that letting the governor of Connecticut suck her foot didn't get her what she wanted, didn't get her *where* she wanted, so she decides to get back at him and tells someone about his indiscretion and his foot fetish and turns it into a book deal and appearances on Fox and CNN and all of the daytime talk shows and eventually a third-place finish on *Dancing With The Stars*?

I give her three months tops. Because that's what this country has come to. Kids don't want to be the next Steve Jobs or Condoleezza

Rice. They want to be the next Bachelor or Kim Kardashian.

Maybe I'm just being cynical. Or maybe I'm pissed off (and I'm *really* pissed off) because Governor Watson wasn't the great hope he promised to be. And how long will it be before we realize this isn't the way forward? What the Democratic Party needs isn't another JFK or Bill Clinton. What we need is another *Hillary* Clinton. A *woman* who has her head on straight and can resist the urge to use her power for sexual gain and knows what's it's like to be the underdog and...

Wait a minute. Screw being a policy advisor or a deputy chief of staff. I'm gonna hire my *own* staff. Because *I'm* gonna run for office.

Alexis J. Gould for... I don't know yet. But I'm definitely dumping the A.J. and going back to Alexis. I could be a councilwoman. Or a state senator. Maybe a congresswoman? No, wait. I've got it...

Alexis J. Gould for governor.

Sounds good. Besides... I've got a feeling there's going to be an opening for that position very soon.

EMILY

"Hey… Eli!"

Elijah and Prayer are leaving the elementary school. Most of the crowd has dispersed but a few lost souls remain, wandering out front, still in shock that nothing happened, that we didn't have to rescue any flood victims or bring clean water and batteries to the elderly. Elijah gestures to his sister to give us a minute. She looks at me, wanting to be angry or cruel, but it's as if she's too tired or upset about something else to waste the energy. I give her an apologetic look and she gives a little nod and meanders toward the parking lot.

And then it's just me and Eli.

"I liked your plan," I say to him, the afternoon sun hiding behind the clouds over his shoulder.

"Thanks," he says. He seems wounded, like a kid who just learned that Santa isn't real, that the people he trusted most have been lying to him his whole life. He also looks especially cute, the patchy skies and soft light giving him a natural movie star sheen. What can I say? I'm a sucker for wounded, vulnerable hotties.

"Sorry I kind of freaked out on you," I say. "Last night at the party. And this morning by the pool. Then later after the presentations. I just… I wanted it so badly, I didn't know who I was any—"

"It's okay," he says, cutting me off. "I get it. I used to be the same way."

"Really?"

"It's why our parents pulled us out of school. My sister and I were *hyper*-competitive. And stressed like Japanese businessmen. They were afraid we were going to be the first teenage *karōshi* victims ever."

"Excellent use of the word *karōshi* in a sentence," I say, touching his shoe with mine affectionately.

"Thanks," he says with a hint of sarcasm. "One of the many useless bits of information I know because I'm homeschooled."

We laugh lightly, kick at some pebbles on the pavement. We're kids again. Awkward, hormonal, shy, and anxious kids.

"Can I… call you sometime?" he says.

"*Call?* Not text or Skype or instant message?"

"We're pretty old-school on the farm. Just got the one land line."

"Ouch."

"I know. Pretty sad."

I giggle again and say, "Um. Yeah, sure. You can call me. Anytime."

His hands are full so he leans his head toward me, offering the pen behind his ear. I take it and write my cell phone number on the inside of his left forearm, which is bulging with well-defined veins and ever-so-sexy.

"Cool," he says when I finish. "And who knows? Maybe we'll end up at the same college next year. Where are you applying?"

"Um. My parents want me to go to Harvard?"

"Oh," he says disappointed. "Well, maybe the same city, then? I hear Boston has some other decent schools, right?"

"A few," I deadpan.

He nods, offering a goofy, amazingly toothy grin. He looks like he wants to say more, but he simply hangs his head and shuffles off toward his sister.

"Wait!" I call out.

He stops. I walk to him slowly and tuck his pen back behind his right ear. Electricity. Chemistry. Thunderbolts. Wow.

"Thanks," he says. He takes a few steps backwards, as if he doesn't want to stop looking at me, but eventually he rights himself and walks off toward his sister. With a quick turn over his shoulder, he calls back to me, "Good luck."

I'm not sure if he means about Harvard or high school next year or life in general. And though I'm usually of the Holden Caulfield school of thought (I hate it when people wish me luck for no reason!), I don't let on. I just smile and say, "You too, Eli."

He stops again. "Ya know… No one calls me Eli."

"Oh. Really?"

"But I like it when you do."

He smiles his rugged-farmer smile again, a matinee idol who doesn't even know it. Then he puts his bag and all of his gear into the back of a station wagon. I look at him, surprised that he actually has a *car*. He sort of shrugs at me with his hands open wide and climbs behind the wheel. A small nod and a wave and he's off.

I turn toward the main road, ready to walk the half-mile or so back to the B&B, happy not to have a ride, knowing I wouldn't take one even if offered. I look up to the sky. Ominous grey clouds have given way to patches of sun; the afternoon is full of hope and fear, promise and heartbreak.

Maybe Calliope wasn't such a bust after all.

ROBERT

"See ya back at school," he says.

"Yeah," I say.

Mac and I are standing on the curb outside the B&B front gate. He's ready to walk the nine or ten blocks to the train station, his backpack on, his duffle at his feet. I offered him a ride in my mother's car (which is still parked on Church Street), but he politely declined. Normally I'd have tried to convince him to come with me or make up a pathetic excuse about why I should leave the car here and take the train with him. But it didn't seem right. I can already feel that our relationship will never be the same. My infatuation sated, the allure no longer mystical, Mac is (I hope) just another cute boy on a long list of cute boys that I will fall in and out of love with, enjoying a luscious hook-up between the lust and the disappointment. Mac was never going to be "the one." I see that now.

He will most likely chalk this up as his "one gay experience." A secret he'll share with no one. Not his wife or three strapping kids. Not his work buddies, drinking buddies, fraternity buddies.

I'll see him at the Choate reunion—the twentieth, most likely. We'll all be nearing forty and will have settled into our future selves and future lives. He'll introduce me to his wife, Melissa, an attractive but forgettable blonde with freckles on her nose and one of those figures that doesn't look pregnant except for the volleyball-sized bump in her belly. He'll be nervous and fumbling, unsure what to call me: his friend from high school? His roommate? His one and only homosexual fling? I'll be cool and demure. Shaking Melissa's hand as she's being pulled on by little Hamish MacKenzie—a six-year-old with the devil in his eyes, a mini-Mac that will no doubt break many hearts when he grows up, both male *and* female, a chip off the old block. Melissa will excuse herself ("Hamish, get back here; don't go under that nice lady's dress!") and Mac and I will be alone. We'll talk about our jobs and families. I'll point out my current boyfriend across the dance floor, a savagely tan Nuyorican who looks like a cross between Ricky Martin and Bobby Cannavale: buff, tough, and romantic. Mac will blush, paranoid that someone will make the connection between me being Mac's former roommate and our having hooked up one drunken summer night during the false, furtive hurricane that was never meant to be. He'll politely make chit-chat (where do you live, did you see so-and-so), desperately waiting for an escape which I'll graciously provide, saying I need to say hello to some other friends by the dessert station. Relief will waft over him and he'll become the charming and dashing Mac that I knew, one last time. He'll offer a manly hand, and we'll shake firmly. When he lets go, he'll pat my upper arm and shoulder casually, but I'll know he's secretly feeling my toned muscles and fondly remembering that sweaty summer evening together, a memory he'll never fully forget, one that will come to him at inopportune times, like when he's making love to his wife after she's had their third child, and he'll question his sexuality for the briefest of moments and it will make me happy, in my loft in Tribeca, to know that I will never be forgotten by Mac, that I will always be a small part of his life.

"See ya in a couple weeks," I tell Mac, standing on the sidewalk outside The Tao of Peace.

I wish I could say more. I wish I could tell him what he means to me, all these thoughts I have about us and what our future holds, that's it's okay, it's going to be awkward for a little while, but it doesn't have to be, and just acknowledging that it's awkward will by definition alleviate the awkwardness.

But I don't. We soldier on. Do what boys do. Say nothing. Refuse to discuss our feelings. Allow our friendship to be forever-strained and altered and damaged. And ruined. It was so much better before, when I coveted him secretly (or not-so-secretly, as it turned out, but at least I *thought* no one knew). I was ignorantly blissful and miserable at the same time. And we danced the dance and played the game and it was wonderful and awful. But now we've crossed the line, named the unnamable, and our friendship is over. I'm sure we'll be cordial to each other in class and at the cafeteria and walking by one another on the quad. But the late nights studying and talking and flirting are gone. Swept away by Calliope and her fickle trade winds.

Mac slings his duffle over his shoulder and heads down the street.

I watch after him, hoping he'll turn around, say one last poetic thing, offer one last romantic gesture. The romantic-comedy version of my life would surely include a final ray of hope at this moment, when it seems like things are at their worst. But this isn't a rom-com. This isn't even a bad afterschool special. It's life. My life. And nothing spectacular or romantic will happen to me. Not while I'm living in this God-awful state, surrounded by these God-awful people. My lot in life is to suffer through this torture. It will make my spring awakening in Europe so much more meaningful.

Soon after Mac disappears around the corner, my phone rings ("Parents Just Don't Understand") and I answer with a ready apology.

"I'm fine, Dad. Everything is fine. The storm missed us and I'm coming home now."

"…Good," my father says. "Your mother and I were worried about you."

"*You* were worried?"

He clears his throat. "What time do you think you'll get home?" he asks, ignoring my little dig.

"Uh. I don't know. Couple hours?"

"Okay. We'll be here."

"You mean you're there? In Westport?"

"Mm. Got in this morning."

"So you *did* evacuate the Vineyard?"

"Yeah… you know how your mother worries."

"Uh-hunh."

"Summer was almost over anyway. Time to get back home."

There's a silence that he doesn't seem eager to fill, so I finally say, "Okay. See you soon then. Love you guys."

"Right… We love you, too." And he hangs up very quickly.

I stare at the phone, stunned. He said it. He actually said it. For the first time in my adult life, the first time I can *remember*, my father said he loved me. Technically he said 'we,' lumping him and my mom together, but it still counts. On a technicality, my father told me he loved me. It may be the last time I ever hear him say it until he's on his deathbed or something, so I look around, trying to make sure I remember this exact moment, standing on the sidewalk outside The Tao of Peace in Cawdor, Connecticut, a few hours after

Hurricane Calliope passed everyone by.

I soak it in. Every detail. The paint chipping off the white picket fence. The American flag lying limp against the porch post. A few seagulls overhead, breaking an otherwise pin-drop quiet afternoon.

And I realize that as I was saying goodbye to my dad, saying goodbye to Mac, the B&B, and the town of Cawdor, I'm also saying goodbye to Connecticut, to my life here, my life as a teenager. Twelve months from now, I tell myself, I will be in Paris—on the road I'm supposed to be on. This day, this trip, this year, is but a blip, a tiny blip on the journey that is my life.

I pop in my earbuds, find the song on my iPhone that I want ("Stronger" by Kelly Clarkson), and walk off toward my mom's car.

Au revoir, Connecticut. *Bonjour*, my new life.

RANI

"Huh," Tyler says nonchalantly, studying the skies. "I thought it was supposed to rain or something today."

I nod and sort of laugh. He shuffles from foot to foot. I can't tell if he's anxious to leave or nervous about saying goodbye. My overnight bag rests on the rocking chair on The Tao of Peace's front porch. The streets are quiet. The misty, almost fall-like morning has slowly given way to a classic hazy, hot and humid August afternoon. The sun is struggling, but finding more and more moments to peek out from behind Calliope's ever-shifting cloud formation, any hint of the threatened hurricane fading with each minute.

At the end of the road, Robert is just leaving. He passes Rory and the three remaining Grateful Ten members, who are packing up their van. Robert stops, taking out one of his earbuds to say a few words. There are some hugs, handshakes, and even an insanely awkward "bro hug" from Josh. Then Robert is on his way again. The Grateful *Four* pile into their van, trying to stuff a final bag into the back that clearly isn't going to fit. Tyler and I watch with detached curiosity.

These strangers were a big part of our lives the last thirty-six hours. Now they're about to drive off, and most likely we'll never see them again. (Unless they track me down on Facebook—I don't have the guts to "ignore" a friend request from someone I actually know, even if I don't know them well or don't particularly "like" them. So I usually accept the friend request and then choose to hide them from my newsfeed. Passive-aggressive Facebooking!) But for all intents and purposes, when Rory and company drive off down Birnam Road, they will no longer exist. At least not in my life. Almost like they were part of a dream.

Rory finally gives up trying to make the last bag fit (a black garbage bag that appears to be full of clothes) and shoves it into Josh's hands, telling him to "just hold it on your lap, for Christ's sake!" The two friends climb into the van and slowly drive out of sight.

I absently watch the spot where their van used to be, the streets quiet save for a lone lost seagull circling above.

Tyler squints up toward the hazy sun, admiring the wayward bird, and says, "You know, it's funny. Even after the most catastrophic, life-altering events, we don't really change that much. The needle only moves so far. Look at Rory. Kind of a dick when we met him. Still kind of a dick now. Despite the enormity of everything that happened—to him, to his friends—he's still the same guy he was three days ago, the same guy he'll basically be for the rest of his life. Our DNA is carved out and determined long before we take our first breath. And two days protecting a town from a Category 3 Hurricane that ultimately amounted to nothing doesn't change you. It doesn't make you a better person... or even a different person. We are who we are."

I nod like I understand, but I don't really see the connection. (I'm not even sure what he said makes *sense*.) And why is he saying all of this stuff *now*? Telling me about how people don't really change just as he and I are about to say goodbye?

And then I get it.

"Is that an eloquent way of saying you're not going to call me?"

Tyler shrugs, kisses his hand in the most douchebag manner possible and slinks off, down the porch steps and out the front gate.

O. M. F'ing. G. I was just used. Tyler Voss just used me as a "girlfriend" for two days. What a complete and total jerk! Thank God all we did was kiss! Seriously dodged a bullet. But I'm still floored by his cavalier "break up." All that crap about how people don't change? What horseshit! He seemed genuinely into me! God, was *any* of it real? Was I just his little experiment with "diversity?" Make out with an Indian girl...? Check. *It was definitely fun,* he'll tell his buddies back home, *exotic and all that, but not really for me. I need a girl I can bring home to mom!*

Damn. I guess he *is* a good actor.

Before I can dwell on it more, I hear a car door slam and turn to see the governor's chief of staff, Teddy Hutchins, standing next to a town car down the road. He's about to get into the back seat when an odd, panicked confidence comes over me and I hear myself call out, "Mr. Hutchins!"

He looks up, squinting across the road at me on the porch. "Yes?"

Before I can think too much, I grab my bag and walk/jog down the path and across the tiny street to the black town car. He bends down and says into the car, "Gimme a minute," and closes the door.

"Sorry to bother you," I say, dropping my bag at my feet, "I just. Um. I'm not sure if you remember me from one of the photos with the governor the other day? But my name is Rani. Rani Caldwell, and… my father is *Doug* Caldwell…?"

"Okay…" he says blankly.

Wow. I thought he'd respond more to that. All right, pressing on. "And anyway—he wanted me to say hi. Since you two went to school together…?"

"Oh, right! Dougie Caldwell. Of course. Yeah… great. Um, say hello to him for me, would ya? Thanks. I gotta go." As he ducks into the back right seat, I can see Governor Watson leaning against the rear left window with his eyes closed. The car pulls out before the door even shuts all the way.

I watch the tinted back window as the car drives away and stare at the few leaves tumbling across the road, early signs of fall. So much for using your connections, Dad.

"Rani?" a voice says from behind me.

I turn to see Morgan's RA wheeling her overnight bag out of a small B&B across from The Tao of Peace.

"Yeah," I say. "A.J., right?"

"Actually, it's Alexis now. I'm going old school."

"Right," I say, not really understanding.

Before we can say anything more, Emily rounds the corner where the governor's car just disappeared. She's walking toward The Tao of Peace, hands in her pockets, a peculiar smile on her face, a little bounce in her step. I wave to her over Alexis's shoulder and she waves back, surprised but happy to see me. Then her face turns curious with a little "what have we here" look.

Alexis sees me waving and turns around. "Hey—Emily," she says with a winning smile, almost like a politician but more sincere. "Alexis Gould. We met at the photo op the other day."

"Right. Good to see you again," Emily says rather demurely—for her.

"You guys were partners, right?" Alexis says and we nod. Then she turns to me and asks, "So… how come you weren't at the presentations?"

"Oh," I say, embarrassed. "I kind of… overslept?"

"Is that code for hooked up or hung over?" she asks. Emily and I share a knowing smile, but Alexis doesn't seem to be joking. "I, uh, I actually swung by the party last night and saw you both. Oversleeping."

"Oh my god," I say. And then like a reflex, I add, "Don't tell my sister."

Alexis laughs. "Don't worry, I won't. But come on! You're smart girls. You don't need to be like the rest of these jokers. Drinking and hooking up and being obnoxious assholes. It's cool *now*. But you know what's *really* cool? Being a huge success in ten years."

Emily and I hang our heads. I feel ashamed and inspired at the same time.

"But it's totally fine!" Alexis says. "I was the same way in high school. I just wish someone had told me early on that I didn't need to waste my time trying to be like everyone else… Anyway. Lecture over. What I really wanted to talk to you about is that social media idea of yours."

"Empty Rooms, Full Hearts?" Emily offers.

"Yeah. Great name, by the way."

"That was all Rani," Emily adds, nudging me with her elbow, making me blush.

"Well, I love it. It's an excellent idea."

"Really?" Emily and I say at the same time.

"Absolutely. There's something there. You shouldn't throw it away completely."

"Well," Emily says, "not sure what we'd *do* with it exactly…"

"You're smart girls. You'll figure it out," Alexis says. "And if either of you want an internship or something next summer…"

"Oh," Emily says, perking up. "In Governor Watson's office?"

"Well…" Alexis sort of laughs. "Not sure *anyone's* going to be working for Governor Watson in the near future. But you should look me up. Both of you." She reaches into her bag and hands us each a business card. It's off-white with raised navy lettering that simply reads:

```
┌─────────────────────────────────────┐
│                                     │
│                                     │
│          Alexis J. Gould            │
│        ajgould59@gmail.com          │
│                                     │
│                                     │
└─────────────────────────────────────┘
```

"What's the 59 for?" Emily asks.

"Ugh, my golf days," she says dismissively. "I need to change it. But seriously, next summer, or definitely once you graduate in four years, drop me a line. Happy to help out however I can."

"Oh, thanks," I say, "but we don't want to impose or…"

"Please," Alexis says. "It's not imposing. It's using who you know. Plus, us smart chicks need to stick together, right?"

"Amen to that," Emily says, looking longingly at Alexis's card.

"You two especially," Alexis tells us. "You make a good team. I could see you running a company together some day, or a nonprofit, or even… finding your way to The White House." Emily and I sort of laugh and shuffle our feet. "It's true," Alexis insists. "Nine times out of ten the chief of staff or communications director isn't some smarty-pants politico… just one of the president's most trusted friends."

"Seriously?" Emily asks.

"I've worked in enough offices to see that no matter how smart someone is or how experienced or qualified, at the end of the day, you're spending seventy, eighty, ninety hours a *week* with this person. They don't care how much you *know*. They need to *like* you. And, more importantly, they need to *trust* you. As my dad would say, that beats experience seven days a week and twice on Sundays. You may not see it now, but a good friend and partner is the hardest thing to find. And when you do… the world is your oyster."

A black town car pulls up, clearly for her, and Alexis gives us a smile and a nod as she opens the car door. "Give my best to Morgan."

"I will. And thank you!" I say, holding up her business card.

With a final wave, Alexis closes the door and the car pulls away.

"Wow," Emily says. "*She's* awesome."

"I know."

We watch the town car disappear around the corner, and then we sort of stare at the empty road ahead of us, silent save the calls of the lonely seagull still circling overhead. After a few moments, Emily says, without turning to me, "Ready to get outta here?"

I take one last look at The Tao of Peace, and realize that I feel at peace myself. I'm not bitter about Tyler or losing the contest. I'm grateful for everything I learned here. It was better than any high school lecture, college course, or self-help book. And I know it's a cliché, but it was forty-eight hours in the School of Life. And I think I came out on top. I grab my bag, look at the road ahead, and say, "Yeah, let's go."

The two of us walk toward Emily's car, parked a few blocks away, not speaking, but not needing to, our minds filled with possibility and hope. Then, at exactly the same time, we turn to each other and say, "I get to be president!"

Emily laughs her throaty laugh. I just smile and shake my head.

"Why do *you* get to be president?" she says.

"Because I'm nicer than you."

"Nicer?" she says, still laughing. "Who wants a nice president? I want someone that can kick some ass."

"Also," I add, "no one would ever vote for a Korean president."

She laughs even harder and counters with, "Korean-*American*. And you think they'd vote for *your* brown ass?"

"Hell-ooo? They just re-elected the first brown president. Who happens to be half-white. Like yours truly."

"Oh you're gonna play the half-white card, now?"

"Listen, the country can only handle one thing at a time. First it was a half-white man. Obama. Next will be a white *woman*."

"Hillary," Emily says.

"Right. Then a *Jewish* woman. Alexis Gould."

"And clearly we'll be working in her administration," Emily says, holding up Alexis' business card.

"Clearly," I say. "Then the next step will be a *half*-white woman… me. And then *you* can be the first completely non-white woman. Baby steps."

"I'm glad you've given this so much thought."

"Hey, 2032 will be here sooner than you think."

"Is that when you're gonna run?"

"*We're* gonna run. You'll be my chief of staff. It's better than VP. And yes. It'll be the first election year we're eligible. Have to be at least thirty-five years old."

"Nice math skills."

"See? Nicer *and* smarter."

Emily pushes me affectionately. We walk a little ways, still giggling to ourselves but not saying anything more. After a while I say, "Thanks for dragging my bony ass up here for this."

"My pleasure," she says. "Thanks for being my friend."

We keep our eyes straight ahead, walking down the road, not willing to look at each other for fear of getting weepy or sentimental. I try to say something back, something along the lines of "thanks for being *my* friend," but the lump in my throat won't let me.

It's okay though. I'm sure she knows what I'm thinking. After all, she's my best friend.

ACT V

AFTER EVERY TEMPEST
COME SUCH CALMS

PERSONAL STATEMENT

"A Funny Thing Happened on the Way to the Hurricane"

I've wanted to go to Harvard my entire life. That is to say, I have no memories that do not include my desire to attend the oldest institution of higher learning in the United States. My crib was crimson and white. Pennants with the Latin motto "veritas" were strewn about my nursery.

And I was raised to maintain this singular focus. It was behind every decision I made, and my parents made sure that focus never waned, never wavered. My college visits last spring made me fall in love with the city surrounding the university as well, and I was nothing if not *more* convinced that Harvard was the place for me.

Three months ago, when Hurricane Calliope threatened the shores of my home state of Connecticut, I saw an opportunity. An opportunity to help out my fellow Nutmeggers, sure, but more importantly to me at the time, I saw an opportunity to round out my resume and add yet another volunteering notch to my belt, one that would further separate my application from the rest and make *this* Emily Kim stand out from the other Emily Kims (there are a *lot* of us out there, as you probably know).

But a funny thing happened on the way to the hurricane. Nothing went right. Nothing went my way. I got exactly zero lucky breaks while others around me seemed to wallow in them. And when I felt the most adrift, the most lost and untethered, I realized that the only thing making me feel that way, making me angry, frightened, and upset, was dreading how it would affect my chances with Harvard. How everything that happened during those two days in Cawdor seemed to be *hurting* the probability of getting an acceptance letter from the school I'd dreamed about since infancy.

With the clarity of someone who struggles to see the hidden image in a Magic Eye poster, then suddenly *gets* it and cannot *un*-see it, cannot understand how they ever missed it, I realized *Harvard* was making me miserable. Pinning my hopes on one school as if *that* was going to be the key to my future success, my future happiness, my future life. I thought

I needed the front-line, in-the-trenches experience to separate me from the pack and get me where I wanted to go. But in fact, I needed that experience to *save* me from where I wanted to go.

So it is with great humility, sincerity and hope that I submit *this* application—to Tufts University. Because I still love the city of Boston. It's tough, wise, and full of heart—like me (and like a good friend or two who might also find themselves enrolled at a nearby college).

Harvard was the dream of a little girl. A smaller girl. One who was fulfilling her *parents'* dream, not her own. Now that I've realized that you can't live someone else's life, you can't please anyone but yourself, you only get one life, one shot, one voice, one chance to make your mark, make your stand, make your life worth living… I'm doing things differently. I'm not out to win at all costs. I don't think everyone is my competition. I'm breathing easier. I want to study for the joy of learning. Enjoy the city's sights, sounds, smells, and tastes. I'm gonna root, root, root for the home team (even though the Sox are awful); I'm going to ride the T, eat chowder, get drunk with townies, run the Charles, do everything I love about your fair city. But I'm *not* going to live the life my mother wants. And I need Tufts University to help me continue on this journey, this journey of self-discovery.

And isn't *that* what college is about? Finding yourself, finding your way in the world? Besides, those Ivy League kids can be pretty uptight. (Most of them are assholes; I know *I* was.)

Please help me become less of an asshole.

-Emily Kim,
October 17, 2013

<u>BALDWIN FELLOWSHIP ESSAY</u>

"Je Ne Regrette Rien"

There are so many wonderful words and turns of phrase from the French that we've adopted in America because there's simply no better way to say it. *Joie de vivre. Je ne sais quoi.* I think there should also be one for: "get me the hell out of this place, I don't belong here."

I've never felt at home. Not in my own family, my own house, my own room. I know who I *am*—I've never had self-worth issues or an identity crisis. It's just that who I am does not belong here. In Connecticut. Or in America, for that matter.

When I was thirteen, I was fortunate enough to travel to France with my ninth-grade French class. And it was like a homecoming. Walking out of the airport, smelling the French air… I had found where I belonged. For years I tried to make my life in America more like that fantastical trip to *l'Hexagone,* to fill my life with adventure, magic, whimsy, and excitement, as if I were living in my own personal Godard film and I was the young car thief (or a film by Michel Gondry, or Jean-Pierre Jeunet and I'm Amélie). But alas, to no avail.

This summer was the kicker. I thrust myself headfirst into a deed I thought would be good for me and for my fellow man. I was volunteering for the Calliope relief effort; one that amounted to, as someone aptly put it, #MuchAdoAboutNothing. I won't go into the sordid details, but by the end of my time there, it was clear that my place was not here in America among the feeble-minded and weak-of-character. I gave it a good shot, but just as some believe they were born in the wrong era, I believe that I was born in the wrong country. And *also* the wrong era; I'd have been better off in the 1980s—or better still, the 1920s! But I digress.

My family likes to brag "the Clintons have been free men since the mid-eighteenth century." Well, I would like to take that freedom to a country where being black and gay would not *define* who I am.

It would simply be a part of it.

I am applying for the James Baldwin Fellowship at la Sorbonne not just because I feel that I perfectly embody Mr. Baldwin's spirit and his passion for the written word, but because I believe the first rate-education I will receive (not to mention the first-rate *life* experience) will help shape me into the person I am destined to become: the new expatriate voice of my generation.

Vive la France!

-Robert Clinton III, October 21, 2013

FAIRWICH POST

Oct. 24, 2013

FAIRWICH—Political newcomer Alexis J. Gould has announced her candidacy for state representative in Connecticut's 132nd District. Gould will be opposed for the Democratic nomination in that district by Richard Gains, the former actor and longtime star of *John Proctor, Homicide.*

A Fairfield resident all her life, Gould graduated Phi Beta Kappa from Princeton University with a degree in US History and Political Science. Her experience on Capitol Hill in the office of Congresswoman Fiona Clark (D-CT) and later as the deputy legislative council for Connecticut State Senator Iva Ellison Eisinger have given this relative novice a wealth of high-level government experience that she plans to bring to play at the local level.

"I understand the dichotomy between how the system currently works and how the citizens of Connecticut *expect* it to work," Gould told the press yesterday where she also unveiled her new website, electalexisjgould.com. "And I believe my youth is an advantage. I will work tirelessly to ensure that the people of this state are represented fairly and to guarantee that the local government works with full transparency and efficiency."

Her campaign said Gould will "focus on jobs and education," including a progressive pilot program for 18- to 20-year-olds that will offer scholarships to high school graduates who defer college for one to two years in exchange for full-time government-sponsored volunteer work.

She has been endorsed by her former employers Congresswoman Clark and State Senator Eisinger, as well as Governor Charles Watson's former chief of staff, Theodore Hutchins, who described Ms. Gould as a "smart, capable woman, and someone to watch out for in the future." Gould was briefly a part of Gov. Watson's staff during the Hurricane Calliope scare in August of this year.

A former Div. I All-State golfer, Gould is the oldest of four girls and "proudly single," remarking that "nowhere in the Constitution does it say a woman needs to be married with kids to serve her state or her country." When the elections take place next fall, Gould will be 27. Should she win, she will be the youngest person ever elected to Connecticut's General Assembly.

PERSONAL STATEMENT

"The Storm That Never Was"

Calliope never made landfall. But she changed me all the same.

I'd been coasting. Getting by on a dry sense of humor and a knack for test-taking. But I'd also been getting lazy. So when my best friend insisted that we drive to Cawdor, Connecticut to help potential hurricane victims, I went along simply because saying "no" would have taken more effort.

So I did my time. I stacked sandbags, reinforced levees, passed out clean water. I even fell in love for the first time. It didn't work out, but that's okay because it all led to an epiphany: I'd been living for myself. But a life should be bigger than that.

And I have to thank my best friend for dragging me to seaside Connecticut. Because volunteering for "the storm that never was" renewed my sense of purpose. And it allowed me to rediscover my passion and my desire to make a difference. A desire that had been buried for too long.

It reawakened my ambition as well. Which I used to think was a dirty word. (And it happens to literally be my middle name; Lakshmi is a Hindi name meaning ambition.) But now I realize that ambition can be used for good, too. And my ambition is to help other people.

Eleanor Roosevelt once said, "When you cease to make a contribution, you begin to die." Well, I think the reverse is also true. When you begin to make a contribution, you start to live.

My life is just beginning.

I hope to continue it with you—at Harvard University.

~ Rani Lakshmi Caldwell,
November 1, 2013

Acknowledgments

I would like to give a big thank you to:

The enormously talented, generous, and guiding minds of Carey Albertine and Saira Rao who came to me with this brilliant idea and these beautiful characters, characters that I felt privileged to write. It was an absolute joy to be a part of this creation. All writer-publisher relationships should be this fun, easy, creative, and inspiring. Wahoowa!

Genevieve Gagne-Hawes for her insightful and brilliant edits and notes, including one suggestion that led to the creation of an entirely new character; now I can't imagine the book any other way.

Tim Schmidt for being such a champion of my work.

Desi Duncker for being a benefactor.

My entire family (especially my mom, dad, and sister Corie, Doug, Chuck, Mariellen, Ian, Dan, Kaitlin, Patrick, Erin, Aunt Pat, Stacey, Amy, Jamie, Alec, Jane, Auntie Dell, Gene, Chris, Douglas, William and Caroline) for always supporting me and telling me that I'm brilliant even when I'm not.

My amazing wife, Charlotte, who inspires me daily, encourages me, gives me notes and ideas, and allows me to have the time and space I need to work even when I should be doing chores around the house or helping with our daughter.

And lastly, to our little girl, Imogen, who makes me want to be a better person and teach her about all of the scary wonderful awesome things in the world to help her grow up and make it a better place.

Together Book Club Questions

1) All of the characters are quick to state that they hate something, whether it be golf, Martha's Vineyard, or Emily Kim. Except Rani, who says "I don't really hate anything. But I don't love much of anything, either." Do you think Rani's apathy makes her a more or less sympathetic character?

2) Do you think Emily Kim feels more pressure from her parents or from herself?

3) How do you perceive Mac's decision to hook up with Robert? As a drunken social experiment or a true questioning of his sexuality?

4) Do you feel the stress involved with today's college application process has gotten out of control? Why or why not? How could the process be changed?

5) When it becomes clear that the storm Calliope will not hit, A.J. thinks to herself, "Their generation – and my own to some extent – seems destined to lack any real hardship. So we cling and rush to controversy, sometimes stirring it up unnecessarily." What do you think about this statement?

6) A.J. decides not to tell the press about the governor's involvement with a teenage girl. Do you believe she did the right thing? Why or why not?

7) Which character do you believe changed the most throughout the novel?

8) Do you think Duncan Rodriguez's claim that the college education will become meaningless with the digitalization of higher education is legitimate?

9) Did you feel that race was an important theme of *Personal Statement?* Why or why not?

10) Did you love or hate Emily Kim? Did you view her character as satirical or were there parts of her that were realistic?

Facts About College

- In 2013, Harvard's acceptance rate dropped to 5.79%, its lowest rate ever.

- At over $59,000 per year, Sarah Lawrence College in Bronxville, NY is the most expensive school in the United States.

- About two-thirds of the college grads in the Class of 2013 will graduate with some student loan debt.

- Students in the class of 2013 graduated with an average debt load of $30,000, according to an analysis by Mark Kantrowitz, publisher of FinAidorg.

- The rate of unemployment in 2012 for college grads – defined as 20-24 years old- was 6.3 percent.

- The average student uses 400 sheets of paper during the college application process.

- "Demonstrated interest" in a school now ranks higher in importance than teacher or counselor recommendations.

- 1 in 10 people aged 16 to 34 have been turned down for a job because of something they have posted on a social media website.

- 1 out of 4 teenagers submitted seven or more college applications in 2010!

About
Jason Odell Williams

Jason is an Emmy-nominated writer and producer of National Geographic's hit television series "Brain Games," as well as an award-winning playwright. He lives in New York City with his actress-singer-director-producer wife, Charlotte Cohn, and their daughter, Imogen, who is working on her hyphenates as we speak. *Personal Statement* is his first novel.

Connect with Jason Odell Williams:

www.jasonodellwilliams.com
http://on.fb.me/16iUr1n
Twitter: @JOWinNYC
Tumblr: in500wordsorless.tumblr.com
Goodreads:
www.goodreads.com/book/show/17337123-personal-statement

Other books by In This Together Media:

Playing Nice by Rebekah Crane
Soccer Sisters: Lily Out of Bounds by Andrea Montalbano
Soccer Sisters: Vee Caught Offside by Andrea Montalbano
Mrs. Claus and The School of Christmas Spirit by Rebecca Munsterer

Connect with In This Together Media:

www.inthistogethermedia.com
www.facebook.com/InThisTogetherMedia
Twitter: @intogethermedia

33178113R20123

Made in the USA
Charleston, SC
06 September 2014